MW01129587

THEM DAYS

Glenn P. Booth

Them Days
Copyright © 2022 by Glenn P. Booth

Front cover photo:
Beatrice and Helen Lesko in their
maids' uniforms (circa 1918).

Tellwell Talent
www.tellwell.ca

ISBN
978-0-2288-7844-5 (Hardcover)
978-0-2288-7843-8 (Paperback)
978-0-2288-7845-2 (eBook)

Dedicated

To
The Memory of
My Grandmother

Helen Gillis
neé Helen Lesko
(adapted from Lyszko)

BOOK ONE

GROWING UP
ON
THE HOMESTEAD

Chapter 1

THEM DAYS

"In them days, we wuz poor but happy."

You're probably laughing at how trite this is. But I've heard my sister Helen, and several other members of my family, speak those exact words more times than I care to remember. And it's exactly how they remember "Them Days."

For us, Them Days goes back to growing up north of Winnipeg on marginal farmland at the turn of the 20th century. Like tens of thousands of Ukrainian and other Eastern European immigrants, my family had come searching for a better life in Canada, lured by the promise of free land.

For the most part, the promises were kept, although, as it would turn out, a few "extras" were thrown into the deal. Unfortunately for my family, like many Ukrainians, they had requested land with wood on it. Back in the old country, they had often frozen through long winters on the Steppes because of a lack of wood for building fires. The Canadian government's land agent obliged, and they were given some scratchy stony ground near Gimli,

Manitoba, where the fertile prairie gives way to swampy Boreal forest. But it had wood!

With this endowment, it was bound to be a hard life. But my sister still remembers it as a time of happiness.

Memories—how they play tricks on us—and how they vary from person to person. It never ceases to amaze me how my family members remember the same events so differently.

It was a warm June day in 1982, the last time the seven of us who had survived to late adulthood had gotten together for an informal family reunion. We were sitting in my youngest sister's trailer, which was parked on the old family homestead. None of us were regular drinkers, but the occasion had inspired my brothers to have a little whiskey, and my sisters and I were sipping some white wine.

Sure enough, whether it was the heat, the alcohol, or just our age and the occasion, my siblings waxed maudlin. And it didn't take long before Helen spoke those familiar words, "In them days…," and my brothers nodded in agreement. Soon, happy stories of Them Days came pouring out like a prairie river spilling over its banks in the spring.

I wanted to shout at them, "That's not the way it was!"

But what would be the point? After all, each of us has spent a lifetime telling and retelling our stories to ourselves so they fit our narratives of who we are and where we've come from. Would my brother John change his mind after a lifetime of shaping his personal narrative just because his 78-year-old sister says he's wrong about something? Hah!

But listening to their interpretations of our shared family history, I was inspired to put some of it down in my words. So these are my stories based on my memories of Them Days.

Take them for what you think they are worth. I have tried faithfully to put them down as they happened, but of course they are shaped by the stories I have told myself over and over again as I've tried to make some sense of my life.

And whatever the "truth," they are my reality.

By the way, my name is Sofiya, which means wisdom, but of course I've been known as Sophie most of my life. I'll let you decide whether I live even partway up to my name.

Chapter 2

TROUBLE FOLLOWS THAT GIRL

"Frank, get off your rear end and get a coupla buckets of water for me," Mama barked.

"Yeah, yeah, don't get yourself all hot and bothered, woman," my half-brother muttered.

"What did ya say?!" Mama cuffed him on the head. "Get the water now."

Frank reluctantly raised himself off the rough wooden bench at the kitchen table and shuffled to the door. I sat eating my oatmeal with my older sister, Beatrice, and my younger sister and brother, Helen and Mikey. It was cozy in the warm kitchen as Mama kneaded the bread dough, and I nestled between my siblings.

Frank opened the door, and a blast of cold air came in, accompanied by a blinding shaft of sunlight. It was late March 1909, and the winter snows still covered the farmyard, but we were getting more sun every day. He trundled outside, grumbling all the way, while we girls stretched our necks to get a glimpse of him walking across the yard to the well.

"Stop gawking and eat your breakfast," Mama told us.

We did as we were told and, when I had finished, I got up to put my bowl in the washbasin. There was no sink and no running water, and the tin washbasin just sat on a long wooden work counter. As I put my bowl into the basin, I looked into the eyes of baby John, who was snuggled in a sling wrapped around Mama's chest. He stared at me with big eyes, drool running down his cheek, and I smiled at him.

I heard Frank approaching the outside door, and, thinking to be helpful, I ran and pushed it open.

"What? Jesus!" Frank yelled as the opening door caught him by surprise.

He tried to stop, but his feet slipped out from under him. The day before, the sun had melted a lot of the snow and it had refrozen overnight, creating a treacherous ice slick just outside the door. The buckets of water flew into the air, and Frank fell hard on his back.

"Aaah!" I screamed as I was doused in ice water.

"What the…!" Mama yelled, waddled over, and grabbed me roughly under my arm.

"I swear trouble follows you like your shadow!" she said as she yanked me away from the door.

Frank was lying on his back in the snow, yelling, "My arm, my arm. I think it's broken."

Mama had hurt me when she pulled on my arm, and I started crying.

"I was just trying to help," I bawled.

I looked at baby John, and he immediately started wailing too.

"God Almighty, you kids are going to be the death of me!" Mama moaned as she went to help Frank get up.

Beatrice came over and put her arms around me.

"Come here," she said. "We'll dry you off."

She pulled me into the far corner of the kitchen and grabbed a towel usually reserved for our rare baths. She quickly undid the top buttons of my frock and vigorously rubbed me down.

"You better take it right off. We'll need to let it dry."

Meanwhile, Mama was helping Frank get up.

"Careful of my arm, I think it's broken," Frank was still groaning.

Mama put her arms under Frank's shoulders, got him up, and he staggered into the house.

"You'd better go lie down on the bed in the front room," Mama said.

We sisters all looked at each other. Normally, no one was allowed to lie on that bed unless we had an important visitor, like Didus (Grandpa).

When Frank was lying down, Mama examined his arm and saw that his right elbow was swelling rapidly.

"Bea, get a big pan and fill it with snow—quickly," she ordered. "And don't fall on the ice!"

Beatrice went outside and did as she was told. When she returned, she hesitantly took it to Mama. We weren't usually allowed to go in the front room, so this was a bit of a special occasion. Helen and I stood by the curtain partitioning off the kitchen and watched as Mama put Frank's elbow into the pan with the snow.

"Hold it there as long as you can stand it. The cold will keep the swelling down."

Bea hung my frock on a line near the kitchen stove so that it would dry, and, standing in my underwear, I continued to gawk at Frank.

He was clearly suffering, and when he caught my eye, I sniffled and said, "I'm sorry, Frank. I didn't mean to hurt you."

"That's alright Sophie." He winked at me. "It was just an accident, and I'll be okay."

"What am I going to do with you?" Mama asked as she looked at me. "Bea, go get your good frock, and we'll put it on Sofiya."

I only had one frock of my own, and that was a hand-me-down from Bea. But, as a six-year-old girl, I didn't really care. Growing up on the homestead, I had no idea that little girls should be pretty.

"Mama, where's Papa?" I asked.

"He went into Gimli to get some supplies before the snow melts and the track gets too muddy. He'll be back late this afternoon."

It was pretty close to an all-day trip by horse and sleigh to Gimli and back, and Papa would have left in the middle of the night. There were no proper roads in them days, and as it was 1909, no one out there had a car yet. To us children, Gimli was an exotic, distant place to which we had only been to get vaccinated at the hospital.

Later in the morning, Mama sent us girls outside to play, cautioning us not to get too dirty, while Mikey and John stayed with her. It was a sunny day and the snow was getting soft, so we could make little snowmen.

"Hey, Bea," I said. "Let's make a snow woman."

"I don't know about that. Don't we just make snowmen?"

"Why is that?" I asked.

"I don't know. It's just the way things are."

I started on my little snow woman and built her with a stout base, just like Mama. Then I added a couple of large breasts, also just like Mama. I put her head on and then looked around for some twigs for her hair. While I was doing that, Mama came out.

"God in heaven, child. What are you making now?"

"It's a snow woman, Mama, like you," I said, smiling.

"Where you get these shameless ideas from, I don't know," she said, striding over. "Do you have the devil in you?"

Mama knocked over my snow woman and gave me a cuff on the head. "Don't let me catch you doing that again!"

I started to cry, partly from the cuff, but more because Mama said I had the devil in me, and my snow woman had been wrecked.

We spent the rest of the afternoon playing in the snow, anxiously waiting for Papa to return. Who knew what treasures he might bring back from Gimli?

Finally, as the sun was sinking near the tree line, and we were blinded by the bright white light, we heard the whinny of a horse. As we squinted into the sun with our hands shading our eyes, we saw the horse and sleigh come out of the trees. We squealed in delight and ran to Papa.

The horse trotted into the yard, vapour steaming out of its nostrils.

"Hallo, my little jewels," said Papa. "How are you all?"

Beatrice and I jumped at his legs, each vying to be picked up. But he looked past us and waited until Helen came toddling up and scooped her into his arms.

"She's lighter than you two big girls." He laughed.

He took my hand and we walked across the yard, excitedly babbling to him about Frank's fall and the snow woman I had built. I also told him that Mama had wrecked her.

"Papa, why can we make snowmen, but not snow women?"

"Hmm, I suppose people just think that some things are proper and some things aren't."

"But why? Why isn't making a snow woman 'proper'?"

Papa laughed. "Sofiya, you always ask such profound questions."

As we approached the house, Mama came out. Papa stepped up to her and gave her a kiss on the cheek. "And how is my lovely wife?" he asked.

Mama smiled briefly, swept along by the irresistible current of Papa's charm. But her face soon turned to a scowl as she recounted what had happened to Frank.

Papa said to wait while he hitched the horse up and got it some feed.

Mama called us in and told us to line up at the kitchen basin. She dabbed a cloth into the basin and wiped down our faces and hands in turn.

"Girls should be neat and clean and shouldn't be rolling in the dirt like pigs," she said.

"Oow, oow, oow!" Frank wailed from the front room. We all looked over, wondering what was happening to him.

When Papa came in, we jumped up, asking, "What did you bring us, Papa? What did you bring us?"

"Oh, I got some cough medicine and some dry oatmeal." He smiled.

Helen's face fell, but I said, "Don't tease us, Papa. What did you really bring?"

"All in good time, precious ones. All in good time. I need to see how Frank is doing first."

When Papa came out of the front room a few minutes later, he said, "It doesn't look as if the arm is broken. I could move it around okay. But he may have chipped his elbow joint, and that's really painful. So you did the best thing by icing it down."

I later learned that Papa had a lot of experience with injuries from his time in the Austrian-Hungarian army in the old country, so he had an idea of what to do.

Papa finally went out and brought in his purchases. Mainly it was sacks of flour, but he had some pickles, a piece of salted pork, kubasa, and some salted pickerel.

Lastly, after first pretending that was it, he put a little bag on the kitchen table and told us to open it up. Bea and I quickly scrambled for it and dumped the contents out.

Our eyes popped as we saw bright jelly beans, some red licorice, various hard candies, some cough drops, and, I blush to say it now, some "N…" babies. These were little black licorices in the shape of babies with bright red lips. Of course, in them days, we had no idea what an "N…" referred to and had never seen or even heard of a black person. We kids just thought it was a type of candy, like a jujube.

* * *

That evening, we had a bit of a special supper. It included some roast pork, potato dumplings, and, as always, sauerkraut.

Father said grace as usual and told us that Didus was not feeling well.

"I ran into Wasyl on the way back and he said that Didus was in bed, coughing and having trouble breathing. I better go visit him tomorrow."

I didn't know our grandpa that well, but he was kind to us every time we saw him. He lived with Papa's younger brother, Wasyl, mainly because there was more space in their house.

By the time supper was finished, it was dark out, and the room was lit by two kerosene lamps. We all sat around the kitchen table while Mama washed the dishes. It was just about bedtime for us girls, but we were allowed to stay up for a few minutes longer as we ate our ration of jelly beans and licorice. Frank had gone to lie down in the front room to ice his elbow some more, and Mama went with him to make sure he was comfortable.

We were alone with Papa for a moment.

"Papa, Mama says trouble follows me like my shadow!" I sniffled. "Is that true?"

Papa suppressed a smile and said, "No, that's not true, Sofiya. You are a very active girl, and it's true that the more you do, the more likely you are to get into trouble. But that's better than sitting and doing nothing."

That made me feel a little better.

"Papa, Mama also says I have a devil inside me! Is that true? Am I a bad girl?"

Papa looked at me seriously and said, "No, of course not, malenka kit[1]. Mama just means that you have a strong spirit, and maybe sometimes you have to control your spirit a bit."

"What's your spirit, Papa?" I asked.

"It's what's inside you that makes you into the person you are."

1. Early Ukrainian homestead near Gimli, built by Wasyl Ewanchuk, 1904

I thought about that for a minute while Papa returned to his whittling, making yet another clever tool. He seemed able to carve anything out of wood, and the entire kitchen wall was covered with wonderful implements he had made. There were various ladles, mortars, cutting boards, large knives, bowls, an egg beater, and much more.

---

[1]   My 'little kitten'.

As he whittled, he hummed softly in Ukrainian—of course, that was all we spoke at home. Papa spoke a little English, and Bea was starting to pick up some words since starting school. Being the oldest and having gone to school for a few years now, Frank was the most fluent.

Papa stopped whittling and picked up his fiddle. He had bought it second-hand but was currently working on making his own, carefully copying as he went. He began to play a song.

"Do you have to play now?" asked Mama, returning to the kitchen. "Baby John is falling asleep and the girls need to go to bed."

"Just one or two songs, Mama, please?" I asked.

"I'll play a soft one," said Papa.

He began to draw the bow across the strings, and some sad, slow notes floated up from the instrument. His face, half in shadow, half in light, disappeared into another world as the light from the lamp flickered, and the music filled the room.

The song evoked a sadness, a longing for some faraway place. The music may have been coming from our little house on the edge of the Canadian frontier, but the song came from another land, another time.

We all sat enraptured, not making a sound, not wishing to break a sacred moment.

Papa played another song, after which he abruptly stopped, looking pensive.

There was silence for a moment, and Mama started to say, "Time for bed..." when she was interrupted by a flickering of the lamps.

It was the strangest thing—a gust of warm wind rushed through the room, and all the implements on the wall started to move with the breeze. The ladles clattered against the wall, and the eggbeater whirred. They suddenly stopped, and there was a moment of eerie silence, followed by one clear note coming from the violin resting on the table. Papa started and turned his head, and then complete silence engulfed the room.

Mama crossed herself. "Holy Mary, mother of Jesus, what was that?!"

Papa serenely responded, "It was the spirit of Didus saying good-bye. I felt his hand on my shoulder… as if he were telling me to take good care of you all."

I accepted Papa's words as the simple truth, and to this day I have never doubted them.

Sure enough, the next day, we found out that Grandpa had passed away shortly after the supper hour.

Chapter 3

EARLY LIFE LESSONS

A few days after Didus passed away, we were all seated around the kitchen table, eating our usual breakfast of oatmeal, getting ready for the funeral service.

"It's going to be a warm day," Papa said. "Tough to know whether to take the sleigh or the cart."

We had a sleigh for winter travel and a cart with wheels for summer travel. Trouble was that it was late March and the snow was melting fast.

"I think I'll take the cart," he said. "The snow's going to be turning into water by this afternoon, but we should get going."

Soon we were all bundled into the cart. Even though we were going to a funeral, it was a big outing and an exciting day for us younger kids.

Papa had hitched up two horses for the trip because the whole family was in the cart, and the pulling was likely going to be tough. We had no troubles on the trip to the church because the road was still reasonably firm, but it was warming up quickly by the time we arrived.

The service took place in the tiny hamlet of Berlo at Saints Peter and Paul Roman Catholic Church, which was probably the most stunning piece of architecture in the whole region. There was a high central tower, but rather than a flat façade, it was stepped back in a series of lesser columns, which, from a distance, gave the impression that you could walk up to the top along the side of the building. It was apparently constructed mainly from tamarack logs, fastened by wooden dowels.

The church was absolutely full, and we girls had to sit on the adults' laps. I don't know if everyone knew Didus, but I think there was a lot of support for one another in the community, and it was probably not only the kids who saw the funeral as a chance at a social outing.

2. Saints Peter and Paul Catholic Church
Berlo, Manitoba (circa 1920)

The service was an awesome mystical experience. The priest sang in a strange language which I later learned was Latin, and at the end he shook some exotically scented incense on me as he passed up the aisle. I didn't understand much of what was going on, but the whole affair had a spiritual air.

After the service, there was a reception in a nearby tiny community hall with great food, including kubasa, holobsti, and perohe.

The adults sat around and, like good Catholics, began to drink. It was boring for us kids, so we went outside and played in the melting snow. Some cousins were there, and we had a great time running around, throwing wet snowballs at each other, while slipping and falling in the slush. Soon my clothes were soaked, but I didn't care because we were having so much fun.

Joseph, one of my cousins, asked, "What are they doing with Didus's body?"

This question had never occurred to me, and I stopped dead in my tracks. Joseph's older brother, Tomas, said, "They're putting him into a storage room with other dead people from the winter."

"That can't be true!" I shouted.

"Yes, it is," Tomas said. "The ground is still frozen, so he can't be buried yet. The church waits for the ground to thaw, and then they bury all the stiffs from the winter."

"Don't call my grandpa a stiff!" I shouted again.

"Sorry, but I'm just telling you the facts."

"Where's the storage room, then?" I asked.

"There's a small building behind the church. Inside, the ground is dug out, and the bodies are put down there."

"I don't believe you!" I yelled and ran back into the hall.

I looked around to see Papa and spotted him with a group of men drinking whiskey. Most of the men drank a lot in them days, but we were lucky that Papa only took a little at a time.

I shyly approached him and took his hand.

"What is it, my little one?" he asked, looking down at me.

"Is it true that they're putting Didus into a storage room before they bury him?" I asked.

Papa excused himself from the other men and said, "Come here for a minute."

He took me to a small table and sat me on his knee.

"What's bothering you?" he asked.

"It just seems so horrible!" I said as I started crying. "They can't really be doing that."

"Malenka kit, do you remember last night when all the instruments were moving in our house?"

I nodded.

"That was the spirit of Didus passing through and saying good-bye to us. It was his way of letting us know that he loved us and that he was okay. There's no need to worry about him now."

"But it's awful to just stick him in a cellar with a bunch of other dead bodies."

"It will be done with respect, malenka kit. It will be done with respect. And you have to understand that your didus is no longer in the body. It is the spirit that is the true person, and when the spirit leaves, the body is no longer the person. Okay?"

"If the spirit is the true person, where did the spirit go?"

"Ah, no one knows for sure. But we believe that Didus has gone to a good place where he will be with all of his family whose spirits have also left the earth. Some people call this place heaven."

I don't know what I understood or believed, but I know I trusted my papa. I listened to him much more than to what the priests or nuns ever said. Papa always seemed to have good sense, and I knew I could rely on him.

"Now look at you. You're soaking wet! We need to get you and the other children home."

Papa went round and said good-bye to relatives and friends, and pried Mama away from a group of ladies. After they got Beatrice and Helen, we were soon all bundled into the cart again.

The day had grown warmer and warmer, and the snow was melting so fast that little lakes were forming. The horses were having a hard time pulling the cart through the mud, slush, and water that had been a nice firm road that morning.

Things were going alright until we came to a bend that the horses took too sharply. The cart rolled off the side of the road, and the wheels quickly sank into a quagmire of mud.

"Quick, everyone out on this side!" Papa ordered.

He didn't want us to be in the cart in case it rolled over on top of us. Although the cart tilted to the right, it fortunately didn't tip over.

"What have you done now?!" Mama yelled at Papa.

"Maybe with everyone out, the horses will be able to pull the cart out of the mud," Papa replied.

"If you hadn't been drinking, this wouldn't have happened," Mama said.

Papa ignored her and, while holding the reins, went around to the front and tried to cajole the horses forward. They were clearly trying to move, but the cart had sunk deeper and was mired in the mud. Although the wheels rocked a bit, the cart didn't budge.

"Hey-yah! Hey-yah!" Papa yelled and pulled on the reins. The horses strained, their great chest muscles bulged, but they just twitched again and again from side to side. Papa tried one more time, and the horses strained, raised up on their rear legs, and...went nowhere. Papa let up on them.

"Looks like we're stuck," Papa said.

We had our jackets, but Bea, Helen, and I were all shivering. The sun was dropping fast, as was the temperature. On top of that, a cold breeze had sprung up.

"The girls will catch their death of cold if we don't get them home quickly," Mama said.

"I know, I know, Mama. We'd better start walking."

Papa unhitched the horses and held the reins in one hand while picking up Mikey and holding him with the other arm. Mama carried baby John in her sling, and the rest of us started walking. The going was difficult as the road had turned to a slushy mush, and our feet sank in. After a few minutes, Helen cried that it was too difficult for her.

"Come here, little one," Papa said. "I'll carry you. Frank, you take Mikey."

Because of Frank's bad arm, Papa helped hoist Mikey onto Frank's back while Mama held the horses' reins.

"Now you hold on tight," Papa said. Mikey grinned, and our little caravan set off again.

"I guess we can't put any of the girls on the horses?" Mama asked.

"No, you know they're not trained to carry people, and it's possible the horse would bolt, so it'd be too dangerous."

There was a spectacular sunset, followed by the slow fading of the light as we trudged along, me hand-in-hand with Bea. Bea was always a trooper, and she pulled me ahead for a long time, talking softly now and then.

"Look! There's the evening star." She pointed to a brilliant star in the southwestern sky, off to our left.

I was shivering, but it was impressive.

"Papa, is that the star the three wise men followed to baby Jesus?" I asked.

"That child never stops asking questions," Mama said.

But Papa said, "It might well be, it might well be."

I don't know how far we walked as I fell into a dream-like trance, shivering and gaping in awe as the stars came out and lit up the night sky. Of course there were no street lights, and we were in the middle of the country. Although we were cold, we were walking through a magical world, a ghostly light coming from an infinity of stars. Papa's shadow from the starlight glided smoothly along in front of me, sliding effortlessly across the snow.

At some point, I stumbled and fell face down into the now-frozen slush. I must have cut my hands, and I started to cry.

Papa said, "Come here, and I'll carry you for a bit. Helen, you can walk for a little while, can't you?"

Helen nodded. Papa picked me up and I wrapped my arms around his neck. A little bit of warmth seeped into my frozen body.

We walked a little farther in dead silence when the stillness of the night was broken.

"Oooo-ooo-yooo!"

We all stopped dead in our tracks, goose bumps all over.

"Oooo-ooo-yooo!" An answering call came from another direction.

"Jesus, that's creepy." Frank shuddered.

"They're just some wolves in the distance," Papa said. "They won't do us any harm."

"I'll be happy when we're home," Mama said.

The wolves howled a few more times, but I must have drifted off at some point in Papa's arms.

I don't know when we got home, but I know that Papa made a roaring fire, and Mama put on the kettle. I think they were planning on washing us down with hot water, but Frank carried me upstairs and tucked me into the girls' bed. I heard Mama and Papa's raised voices for a minute, but I fell asleep as soon as Helen was laid beside me.

* * *

The next day, not surprisingly, Bea came down with a bad cold. She hadn't complained during the whole night march and had walked the entire distance on her own. She was tough, but she was still just a skinny little girl, and the cold must have got to her.

Apparently, Papa and Mama had been arguing about the cart stuck in the mud. Papa had wanted to go straight back out with our two oxen to pull the cart out before the mud froze overnight, but Mama had talked him out of it.

Fortunately, it was shaping up to be another warm day, so Papa figured that the snow and ice would melt again by noon, and he would be able to salvage the cart. I clamoured to go with them and, after some wheedling on my part, he chuckled and agreed.

He and Frank put the yokes on the oxen, and when they were ready, we headed out. The snow was melting fast again, but fortunately the road was still semi-solid and the oxen didn't have a cart to pull.

As we walked, Papa talked about how the fields around our farm would soon turn into mini-lakes.

"In some years," he said, "this whole Interlake region turns into one giant shallow lake, and farm families are stranded for days or even weeks before the waters subside. You could paddle a canoe from here to Gimli."

We trudged along at the sedate pace of the oxen, enjoying the warmth of the day. When we reached the cart, we could see that the mud around it looked all wet.

"If it's not completely thawed, the wheels will snap when the oxen try to pull it out," Papa said.

It was a real mess for sure, and I could see that Papa was concerned. We couldn't afford to be breaking carts and paying for new wheels. Farmers were the most hard-up in early spring because they hadn't had much of a source of income during the long winter. Like most farmers, Papa chopped wood and sold it as firewood, but people usually bought their wood early in the winter, so many months had passed since he'd had any money coming in.

Papa and Frank hitched the oxen up to the cart, and then Papa urged them slowly forward, immediately stopping them.

The cart hadn't moved and Papa was afraid that the wheels or axles would snap.

He moved in front with the reins and tried to get the oxen to back up, but they just stood stubbornly in one place.

"Hiya, hiya," Papa yelled in their faces while Frank pulled backwards on the yoke.

They didn't budge for several minutes, but finally they took a step back.

"Whew," Papa said. "Let's see if we can rock the cart."

He and Frank stepped partway into the mud, pushed hard and, eventually, the cart rocked back a bit.

"Good!" said Papa. "I think it's loose enough now. Let's try it again."

He returned to the oxen, snapped on the reins, and yelled, "Gee up."

The oxen slowly plodded forward and, as they stepped, the cart lurched and rolled through the thick mud.

I remembered the horses last night, twitching this way and that to no avail, and was amazed at how smoothly the oxen pulled the cart out of the mud. After a few minutes, the cart had rolled up and out of its sinkhole and stood upright in the road.

"Wow, Papa," I said. "Well done!"

"Thank the oxen, malenka kit," Papa said.

On the way home we were able to ride in the cart, soaking in the sunshine while the oxen plodded along.

"So, what did you learn from that?" Papa asked me.

I thought for a while, but all I could come up with was, "Oxen are really strong."

Papa chuckled. "You're right about that. But beyond that, I think it shows that patience is a virtue. I wanted to rush out last night, but Mama counselled me to wait until it was warm this afternoon. And she was right."

I smiled, snuggled up next to Papa, and enjoyed the ride home.

*   *   *

The next day was more of the same type of weather as the snow and slush froze at night and melted a lot during the daytime.

By now, Bea had a bad cold and was sniffling and coughing non-stop, which had everyone worried. Losing a child in them days was a common occurrence, and one never could tell when a sickness would take a sudden turn for the worst.

The few cows we had at that time had pretty much finished all the hay that had been set aside for them over the winter, so Papa let them out of their corral and onto our property to graze on the grass showing through the melted snow. The only problem was that the wolves we had heard the other night seemed to be hanging around, and Papa was worried that they might get one of our cows.

"A couple of the cows are pregnant and they might calve any day. I don't want them wolves killing a newborn," Papa said.

When it got to be later in the afternoon, Papa said he would set out to get some of the cows that hadn't come back yet. He told Frank to go south while he would go north. Like usual, I begged to come along.

"Lord, child, when are you going to stop being such a nuisance?!" Mama asked.

"Why is it a problem?"

"I have to walk pretty fast to cover the ground before it gets dark, and you might not be able to keep up," Papa said.

"I can walk fast." I put my hands on my hips.

Papa smiled. "It's true that she can walk pretty fast for such a little thing."

"And you'll get your frock all muddy," Mama said.

I looked down at myself and said, "It's already muddy."

Again Papa smiled. "That's true as well."

"Lord knows you're going to be the death of me, child, but I suppose you can wrap your silly father around your little finger, eh?"

I took that to mean it was okay for me to go with Papa, so I ran to put on my boots and jacket.

Frank had already put some of the cows into our small barn and headed off. So Papa and I set off in the other direction.

"Them cows like to go into the bushy areas because they're protected from the wind. And if one of the pregnant ones gives birth, they'll be in the trees for sure."

We walked at a fast pace for me, but I was happy to be with Papa, and it was exciting to be looking for cows in the bush—it was a treasure hunt!

There was a stand of fir and poplar all along our property's north boundary, and that's where Papa was headed. When we got into the bush, the snow was deeper, and it was a little harder for me to slog through it.

Papa made some strange sounds with his lips, which I guess imitated mooing. We tramped around for about ten minutes before, sure enough, we heard an answering "moo." We staggered through the bush in the direction of the "moo," and after a few more minutes, we came across a cow in a little clearing.

"Wow, Papa, look! She has a newborn calf with her."

As we approached, I could see that the mother was licking the side of the calf.

"Why is she doing that, Papa?" I asked.

"She's cleaning her baby. It helps the calf dry off and gets rid of the birth smell that could attract the wolves."

We stood and admired them for a few minutes.

"Best be going, malenka kit. The light's starting to fade."

Papa trudged up to the cow, grabbed her by the collar, and tried to start her walking toward the house. But she wouldn't budge.

"Bwaah, bwaah," she brayed like a goat.

"Come on, you silly beast," Papa cajoled her, but she still wouldn't budge and kept braying loudly.

This went on for several minutes, with Papa getting increasingly frustrated.

I don't know if I noticed the cow looking in a particular direction, but a little movement in the bush caught my eye. I turned and, although I didn't see anything at first, I spotted a branch moving. I stepped towards the movement, and then I noticed it.

"Papa, look! She has another calf in the bush!"

Papa let go of the cow and came over. "Well, I'll be. I should have known she had a good reason for not budging."

Papa went into the bush after the second calf and coaxed it back into the clearing, where it nuzzled up against her mother. Now when he took the cow by the collar, she happily complied, walking with us back towards the house with both calves in tow.

"That's what you call maternal instinct," Papa said. "The drive that every mother has to protect her young."

Running to keep up, I asked, "Does our Mama have a maternal instink, Papa?"

"Of course she does, malenka kit. Of course she does!"

"Sometimes, she can be pretty mean."

"Mama has a difficult life, and it can be hard for her. But what do you think she's doing with your sister Beatrice right now?"

I thought for a minute and said, "Taking care of her, keeping her warm."

"Yes, of course. And she's doing it partly because of her maternal instinct but mainly because she loves all of her children."

After that, we walked in silence for a while as I pondered what my father had said. It sure didn't always seem true when Mama was mad, but I realized that Mama always took care of us, and I decided that Papa was right.

*   *   *

When we got home, I was shivering and cold. Bea was worse though, as she was coughing and alternately freezing or running a fever.

After a simple supper of boiled cabbage and bread, I was tucked into bed upstairs with Helen. A curtain divider hung from the ceiling, and Frank and Mikey slept on the other side of it. Mikey had just been "promoted" to sleeping upstairs. Bea slept downstairs with Papa and Mama that night because she was sick.

The voices of our parents and Frank floated up from downstairs, always a comforting sound that helped us quickly drift off to dreamland. That night, the last thing I heard was Mama asking Papa to build up the fire because they needed to keep Bea warm.

The next thing I knew I was coughing, my eyes were stinging, and Frank was shaking me, yelling, "Get up, Sophie, get up!"

"What? What is it?" I coughed.

"There's a fire! I've got Mikey. Helen! Get up! Get downstairs!"

He roughly grabbed me with one arm and almost hurled me in the direction of the ladder and then did the same with Helen.

"Papa, Mama, get up!" Frank screamed.

Smoke poured into the upstairs bedroom, flames leapt around the chimney, and the curtain that divided the boys' area was ablaze. I could feel the heat and choked as I scrambled down the ladder. It was dark downstairs, but Papa was barking orders, "Mama, get baby John and Bea outside now!"

"I'll just grab my coat from the other room," I heard her say.

"NO! Get outside now!" he yelled.

Fortunately, there wasn't too much smoke on the main floor, but the flames were crackling upstairs. Frank had come down the stairs with Mikey and shouted that we were all downstairs.

"Good, get outside now!" Papa answered.

I grabbed Helen's hand and stumbled towards the door when Frank accidentally plowed into me and I fell. I don't know how he did it with his sore arm, but he reached down, set me up on my feet, and opened the door.

"Get out now!"

With Helen at my side, I staggered outside into the cold, and started crying when my feet got cut on the refrozen icy ground. Frank stumbled out with Mikey right after me.

"Get away from the house!" he yelled.

I forced myself to walk across the snow with Helen, both of us yelping from the pain.

The moon was up and giving off light, so when we turned, we could see the outline of the house. Flames shot out the roof, and smoke billowed up.

Mama crashed out of the door holding John in one arm and Bea in the other. I couldn't see well, but it looked as if they were wrapped up in blankets.

"Alex, come out now!" Mama screamed.

We all waited breathlessly as the fire gained strength. Sparks and burning embers were flying off the roof, and the fire was lighting up the night.

The door opened and, although we couldn't see anything but a silhouette, Papa threw out our coats. The fire roared now, perhaps fueled by extra oxygen that entered when Papa opened the door.

"Papa, come out," I wailed.

"Just a second." He coughed harshly, shut the door, and went back in.

"No, Alex, come out!" Mama yelled.

"Pa, it isn't worth it!" Frank joined in.

"Frank, go get him!" Mama screamed.

Frank had already put down Mikey and was on his way. I stood transfixed at the horror of it all.

Frank yanked the door open, but thankfully Papa stumbled out, holding some things in his arms.

He was coughing badly but managed to croak, "Just grab the boots."

Frank stepped into the doorway and threw out our boots, which were right next to the entrance.

Papa fell, crawled towards us, and sputtered, "Get away from the house. Move away."

Mama grabbed Helen and moved farther away, but the fire hypnotized me. Then, just as Frank stepped through the doorway, there was a huge crash, and flames shot out the door.

He screamed blue murder as his shirt caught on fire.

"Roll on the snow," Papa managed to croak loudly.

Frank fell down, screaming and rolling on the ground. It was awful to watch, but thankfully the flames went out quickly. Frank still wailed, though, and it looked as if he grabbed something from his neck and threw it off—a glowing ember arced through the night.

Papa kept coughing and urging us to move away from the house. Mama grabbed us kids and pulled us along, but then she said, "Wait here while I get the coats and boots."

Mama walked back towards the house, past the prone figures of Frank and Papa, who were still crawling in our direction, Frank cursing and Papa coughing.

Mama was silhouetted against the blazing house like some great demon commanding the fires of hell. But all she did was quickly gather up the boots and throw them in our direction before picking up the coats.

"Get away from the house," Papa croaked.

As she turned towards us, there was another huge crash, probably from the ceiling falling in, and another blast of flame shot out the door.

"No!" I cried as it looked as if Mama would be engulfed.

We all stared in shock, but Mama just walked up to us, flaming pieces of wood hurtling all around but somehow not touching her.

She passed out the coats, and we scrabbled around to get the boots. Then we inched farther away from the house until, forming a little semi-circle and spontaneously holding hands, we watched transfixed as our home went up in flames.

I don't remember being cold. I suppose because the fire sent out a wall of warmth. For a few strange moments, it was as if we were all just happily watching a giant bonfire.

The fire reached a climax, and then the roof caved in, sending out a giant shower of flames and sparks up into the sky in a weirdly beautiful fireworks display.

When the roof caved in, it signalled a finality that we hadn't felt up to that moment. Although it had been clear that everything was lost, any remaining hope that something could be salvaged was gone.

As the fire continued to rage, Papa told us to get down on our knees as we kept holding hands. He knelt before us, a slim shadowy figure, black against the flickering flames, and said a simple prayer of thanks for our deliverance.

I never felt closer to my family than I did in that moment.

Chapter 4

SCHOOL LESSONS

After our homestead burned down, we went to stay with some nearby cousins, who had children a similar age to us. It must have been difficult for our parents with everyone crowded into a small house, but I remember it as a great time for us kids. We always had someone to play games with, like hide and seek in the yard.

One day in late May, on a gorgeous evening with a good breeze that was keeping the bugs down, Papa and I were walking together around our cousins' garden.

"Are you happy here with your cousins?" he asked.

"Oh yes, Papa. It's so much fun playing with them."

He smiled. "Don't you miss our old house?"

I hesitated and thought. "I guess so," I said. "But I'm happy with all of us together here."

"So, what does that tell you?"

I thought some more and ventured, "Our family is important?"

He smiled again. "Yes, malenka kit, family is important. And wouldn't you agree that it tells us that people are more important than things?"

Papa said many wise things, but that one really stuck with me.

I suppose we were lucky in a way that our house burned down at the end of March because it meant we had lots of time to build a new one before the next winter set in. I don't remember the details, but I know that many cousins and neighbours pitched in, and we had a new house built by September of that year. The main floor was considerably larger than the first home. Papa and Mama were afraid of living in another place with the children sleeping upstairs—they knew we had narrowly escaped the fire, and the kids upstairs could have easily died.

I'm not sure where Papa got the money to finance the new house, but I do know that he had salvaged a small roll of money from the front room when he went back into the fire—it had been risky, but I'm sure he was happy he had done it. We were also fortunate that Bea recovered quickly from her cold, despite having made a trek to the neighbour's house in the middle of the night.

The next few years are kind of a blur in my memory, except for moving into the new house, which was a big event. It seems that my brain stores two types of memories: first, memories of events, such as the fire, and second, memories of feelings, such as how I felt about Mama and Papa and each of my siblings. Although the "feeling" memories tend to be vague in details, the attached emotions are powerfully clear.

I don't seem to have any sharp memories of the first type, until some events which took place in the fall a few years later when I was about eight years old.

*　　*　　*

At some point when I was a child, a small one-room schoolhouse was built in Berlo, where they'd held the funeral for Didus. Berlo was a small German-settled community not too far from our homestead, and the school was named Bismarck. It was within walking distance, just under three miles from our homestead, and it would have been much farther to go to any other one. Besides, the "Germans" were actually immigrants from the Ukraine who had previously moved from Germany, so they spoke Ukrainian and German.

Frank had left the farm by this time and worked in the city, which of course meant Winnipeg, and also meant that his schooling was over. Like most young men on the Gimli homesteads, they left the farms looking for jobs that could pay more than scrounging out an existence on marginal lands. Some of the young boys from better-off families went to high school, but the majority were like Frank. Unfortunately, many of the new immigrants didn't appreciate the value of higher education, especially when money was short and there were mouths to feed.

One fine autumn day, Bea, Helen, and I were walking to school together. The poplar and birch trees were turning golden, and the sky was a crisp brilliant blue that you only seem to get in the fall. After the first hard frost, most of the moisture comes out of the air, creating spectacular clarity.

We girls always had fun walking to and from school together and often held hands. When we arrived at the school that day, a few boys were standing around the "playground" outside.

"Dobroho dnya sestry," said one.

"Dobre rano," said another.

"Dobroho ranku brate," I responded, whereupon the third boy said, "Guten morgen."

That little exchange, which was nothing to us, illustrates what life was like in our community in them days. We had just said good morning to each other in Ukrainian, Czech, and German—what could be more normal?

3. Berlo/Bismarck School, circa 1915

In fact, the kids at the school spoke a mix of languages from Eastern Europe: Czech, Russian, Polish, and German, but mainly Ukrainian, which we called

Ruthenian in them days. We somehow managed to pick up a little of each language. I suppose it wasn't too hard because they're all Slavic languages, with the exception of German. Nonetheless, it seems like a minor miracle that we learned these languages on the playground and at lunch breaks, with no formal teaching.

We kids just accepted everyone around us as equals, and it didn't matter what your mother tongue was. And, to give them credit, the adults seemed to have the same attitude—they had all left the old country for a life in the new, and they wanted to leave behind the sectarian strife that had plagued their lives for centuries.

There was also one dominant bond linking us—we were all immigrants, and we weren't "English." When Papa and Mama talked about the English-speaking people in far-off Winnipeg, they always referred to them as the English. Growing up in the Ukraine, they saw England as the most powerful country in the world, and Canada was just a British colony run by the English.

We had a new teacher that year, and he was an "Englishman." In the first year of the school, the founders could only locate a local Ukrainian lad, and he had taught us in Ukrainian. That had been good from the point of view that we learned to read with the Cyrillic alphabet, but it was no good for becoming English.

There were about twenty of us in the school, evenly mixed between boys and girls, with the boys on one side of the room and the girls on the other side. We were also roughly arranged according to grade, with the youngest kids sitting up front and the oldest at the back.

The teacher, Mr. Bainbridge, wore a suit and was very formal and strict. He made it clear that we were there to learn and that there would be no fooling around. One of his rules was *"No Ukrainian in the classroom."*

That day, Mr. Bainbridge was teaching us simple words to copy in our notebooks, like bat, cat, fat, etc. The problem was that Helen hadn't found a seat in the front row, and Mr. Bainbridge was writing smaller because his blackboard was already full of material for the older kids. Helen had weak eyes from birth, and she was having trouble seeing what he was writing. She was afraid to ask him, so every time he wrote a new word on the blackboard, she'd ask me what it was while he had his back turned. And of course, she'd ask me in Ukrainian.

I'd whisper back to her "C," "A," "T." I hoped she'd pick up on the pattern, but she couldn't see any of it, and Mr. Bainbridge wasn't speaking the words out loud, just writing them down.

Sure enough, he spun around after writing "hat" and caught Helen leaning over, asking me what he had written, speaking in Ukrainian.

"Helen Lesko!" he barked.

Helen looked at him, already trembling. She managed a "Yes, sir," two of the first words we had learned.

"What did I tell you about speaking your foreign language in this class?!"

Helen didn't have much English vocabulary and was afraid, so she didn't say anything.

"I'm speaking to you!" Mr. Bainbridge raised his voice. "Get up here right now."

Helen may not have understood, or she may have just been terrified, but she didn't budge.

Mr. Bainbridge took a couple of quick steps, yanked Helen out of her chair, and dragged her to the front of the room.

"It looks as if you need a lesson, you stupid little girl."

He reached for his leather strap, which he kept handy on his desk. It always sat there, like a silent warning of what might happen to us at any moment.

As he lifted the strap, I blurted out, "But, sir, she can't see!"

"What?!" he turned to me, his rage seemingly out of control. "Did I ask you to speak?!"

"No sir, but Helen can't see the words."

He turned red and said, "Just wait your turn!"

With that, he brought his strap down hard on Helen's outstretched hand. She had been crying before he hit her, but now she screamed and started bawling.

"Maybe now you'll learn not to speak that language! Hold out your hand again."

Helen tentatively held out her hand partway, so Mr. Bainbridge grabbed it, pulled it up, and said, "hold it here!"

Helen was an incredibly pretty little girl, with a round sweet face and beautiful blonde curly hair. Mr. Bainbridge seemed huge to us because he was much taller than Papa.

Helen's hand was held high, but she looked tiny and vulnerable standing in front of the raging giant in his authoritarian suit.

"Whack!" came the strap once more, and Helen wailed louder.

"One more time for good measure," he said.

He went through the process again, all the students transfixed, not daring to make a sound. When he finished, he ordered Helen to go sit down.

"That should be a lesson to all of you! This is an English school and we only speak English here. Do you understand?"

Everyone nodded.

"Now you, Sophie Lesko, up here!"

I got up and walked slowly to the front of the class, dreading what was to come.

"Another rule is that you don't speak out of turn in class. You only speak when I speak to you or give you permission. Do you understand?"

I nodded. I wanted to say it was unfair, but I thought it best not to speak.

"Hold out your hand."

I was trembling, but I did what he demanded.

The strap came down, and it stung like hell. I must have gasped, but I didn't cry. I wasn't going to give him the satisfaction.

"Again," he demanded.

I held up my hand again, stretching it out as he had done with Helen.

"Whack!" came the strap again.

I'm sure tears welled up in my eyes, but I refused to cry.

He looked at me and our eyes locked. I'm not sure what he saw, but he tensed for a moment and then relaxed.

"Okay, go back to your seat," he said, without giving me a third strapping.

Later, on the playground, which was really just an open dirt space outside the school, a couple of the boys who had said good morning to us came over and told me they were impressed at how brave I was. There were a lot of older boys who cried when they got the strap, so they really thought I was something.

I suppose that, in some weird way, I learned that people respect you when you show that you're strong.

On the way home, we agreed not to tell Mama about the strapping because she would probably blame us and get angry. Unfortunately, Helen couldn't keep her silence. When Mama asked us how our day had gone, Helen started to cry.

"What's the matter, child? Why are you crying?" asked Mama.

Helen showed Mama her bruised and purple hand.

"What happened to you?!"

For a second, we were all quiet, although Helen sniffled. Then it dawned on Mama that Helen had got the strap.

"Acting up in school, were you?! How many times have I told you that you have to listen to your teacher?"

"But Mama, Helen can't see well enough to read the board," I exclaimed.

She turned on me and cuffed me on the head. "Don't give me any backtalk! If Helen got the strap, she must have been acting up. I don't want to hear any excuses. Now go do your chores and get some vegetables from the garden."

This reaction was typical of our parents and probably most of the Ukrainian settlers. They respected teachers as representatives of the state, as authority figures, and they had to be obeyed. They weren't interested in the fairness of the teachers' actions.

All I know is that it certainly didn't seem fair to me—what gave the teacher the right to hit a little girl anyway?

After he strapped Helen, Mr. Bainbridge started using the strap more judiciously, and he didn't strap very young girls anymore. Perhaps he had made his point, and there was no need for further strappings of little girls to establish the discipline he was looking for.

While he may have established discipline, the whole thing just left me with a distrust of authority.

*   *   *

The establishment of the little hamlet of Berlo was a blessing for our family in another way—a small store opened up there about 1912, which meant we didn't have to travel to either Camp Morton or Gimli for basic supplies. It was also the first time we could go to a store owned by one of us, i.e., a Ukrainian immigrant.

Apparently, when the first settlers came to the area, the Canadian government didn't let Ukrainians purchase land in and immediately around Gimli. The purpose of "importing" us was to settle and develop the land, not to be merchants and run businesses. That was why we were allowed to come to Canada, and being farmers was our defined role.

Previously, we had to shop in the stores in Gimli and Camp Morton, which was much smaller. These stores were run by the Icelandic immigrants who had come much earlier, in the 1870s, and had given Gimli its unique placename. To my knowledge, the two groups got along well. The Eastern Europeans provided a good market for the Icelandic storeowners who even learned some Ukrainian to better deal with their new clientele.

I'm not sure why the Icelanders, as we called them, never got into farming, but I suppose it hadn't been their traditional way of life. They mainly lived along the shores of Lake Winnipeg, fished, had small gardens, and raised a couple of cows and chickens for milk and eggs.

One time in early winter, when I was still eight years old, I went to the store in Camp Morton with Papa. When we arrived, some First Nations people, who we called Indians in them days, were sitting outside. I think it was the first time I had ever seen them, and I was probably staring.

One man was tall and very impressive looking, with piercing black eyes and chiseled cheekbones. I made eye contact with him and shivered a little as he seemingly appraised me with his fathomless eyes.

Inside the store, I asked Papa, "Who are those people?"

"They're Indians," said Papa. "They live farther up north and come down here to trade some goods."

"Like what?" I asked.

"I think they come with some furs, fish, and moccasins."

When Papa told me that, I noticed that the lady in the store, who was certainly Icelandic, was wearing moccasins.

"Like those, Papa?" I asked.

"Yes," he said. "You have very sharp eyes, malenka kit. I hadn't noticed that myself."

When we came out of the store, I turned to look at the "Indians" again. I was fascinated, but they didn't seem very friendly, and Papa tugged on my hand to go with him.

I noticed that they were wearing different clothes, which Papa later told me were deerskins. When we were in the cart again and heading home, sliding over the snow, I asked Papa a few more questions.

"Who are they?" I asked again. "Where do they come from?"

"They're the native people to this land. They lived here for a long time before we came from the old country."

"They seem quiet, almost angry."

"That's just their way. Best to stay away from them."

"Why? Are they dangerous?"

"I don't think so, but it's best to be careful. They might get dangerous when they drink."

"What do you mean?"

"When they get money for their goods, they buy booze and get drunk. Then they could be dangerous."

Needless to say, I don't remember the details of this conversation or any subsequent conversation about First Nations people. But I do remember the general things we were told about them, and they weren't very nice.

We were pretty much told all the stereotypes you might imagine, such as:

"They're lazy. They don't work."

"All they do is drink."

It was only much much later that I started to learn some of the truth about Canada's relationship with First Nations peoples. I'm not sure what more to say about our relationship with them because they weren't a large factor in our lives. They existed at the margins of our homesteads, physically and ethereally, and didn't form part of the central fabric of our existence.

I know from later discussions that all the Ukrainian settlers were told to come to Canada, where there was "empty free land" just waiting for the taking. The settlers, like my mama and papa, believed what the federal land agents told them and just accepted it as a fact that they were coming to take up empty lands.

Children are born into this world as innocents and only acquire the knowledge presented to them and what they see with their own eyes. Unfortunately, our parents didn't know the truth of Canada's history with the First Nations, and they could not communicate that to us. They only knew what they saw and, too often, that would have been the wreckage of First Nations' families that had been displaced and humiliated by the actions of the Canadian government. We children just accepted what our parents told us as the truth.

Perhaps I'm apologizing for our attitudes towards First Nations people, but the first step towards a better understanding has to be knowledge and sharing of the truth of our collective history. The sad truth is that in them days the Ukrainian settlers were completely ignorant of Western Canada's real history.

Chapter 5

EASY COME, EASY GO

Mama was basically a baby factory, and, like most of the women on the farms in them days, she churned out children at the rate of close to one a year. By the time I was ten, we had two more siblings, Paulie and Annie. Paulie was about two and a half years old, and Annie was a little over one at the time. I remember that because we had had a little party when Annie turned one. That was very common in them days because so many children died before their first birthday, and making it to that milestone was a cause for celebration. After that, there usually wasn't much in the way of parties to mark birthdays.

One other incident from the fall of 2013 stands out in my memory.

I remember our garden with great fondness. It was at its peak in the fall, full of potatoes, cauliflowers, carrots, sunflowers, and daisies and cornflowers that Mama planted to attract bees and keep away insect pests.

When the harvest arrived, we had a sudden abundance of food, and all the homesteaders were busy reaping their produce, preserving what they could, and trying to sell the surplus. The trouble was that with all the cabbages, cauliflowers, carrots, and other root vegetables ripening simultaneously, the prices for all this produce fell sharply.

Farmers would often send their sons and daughters to trek around the countryside, trying to sell what they didn't need for themselves.

One fall day, Bea, Helen, and I were out in the yard near our garden when two young women entered our property, towing wagons behind them.

They were both pretty big, although one of them was particularly large.

Bea ran in to get Mama, and the two of them quickly emerged from the house.

As the two women approached, I heard one of them saying something that sounded like, "Hatcha Mama, hatcha Mama."

Then she started saying, "Cauliflower missus? Cauliflower missus?"

Out of curiosity, Helen and I drifted nearer.

The smaller woman said, "Dobroho dnya," to Mama, who responded in kind. But the other lady just kept saying, "Cauliflower missus? Cauliflower missus?" Then she would twitch and blurt out, "Hatcha Mama, hatcha Mama!"

I realized that there was something not quite right with this woman, but I smiled when she looked at me. She stopped going through her routine for a moment. Mama asked the price, and she bargained with the younger woman for a bit, after which Mama said she would buy two cauliflowers. I think she did it out of pity because we didn't need them ourselves.

Mama turned to go inside for some money when we heard a big commotion.

A tremendous squawking and screaming rose up from the direction of our little pond. We all looked there at the same time, and, to our horror, one of our geese was attacking little Paulie with its wings, beating at him repeatedly. The goose knocked him down and pecked at the poor little guy.

We all bolted towards him, but Bea was the fastest. As she came running up, shouting "scram!" the goose relented and backed off, still spitting and hissing.

I don't know what provoked the attack because the goose didn't have a nest at that time of year, but Paulie must have got too close to her, and she felt threatened in some way.

Mama scooped up Paulie, who was bawling and shaking, clearly terrified out of his mind.

"It's okay, it's okay," Mama repeated over and over and carried him up to the house.

We all followed and, while comforting Paulie, Mama swore and said she must have left the door loose when she came to see the two women. Paulie must have toddled out after her, unnoticed by any of us.

Inside, she gave me some money to give to the two women in exchange for the cauliflowers while she sat with Paulie. I went outside, and when I approached them, the slighter one said she was sorry for what had happened, and that she hoped our little brother would be okay. The larger one just kept twitching, saying, "Hatcha Mama, hatcha Mama."

Later, when Papa came home, I asked him about the "Hatcha Mama" woman.

"Malenka kit, sometimes when people are born, they are not formed perfectly. We are lucky that you and your brothers and sisters are all perfect. But that poor young woman was born with something not quite right. It isn't her fault—it's just the way it is."

"That doesn't seem fair!" I said.

"Life often isn't fair," Papa responded, while Mama said, "Amen to that!"

I looked at him, perhaps hoping for more.

"God works in mysterious ways, my little one, and we can't always understand his purposes."

That was perhaps the first time I heard that in my life, but it certainly wasn't the last. When I went to bed that night, I thought about it for a while, but nothing seemed mysterious to me—it just didn't seem fair, and that was that.

Everything was alright for a couple of days, but then Paulie started having seizures. It was frightening to see. One moment he would be sitting on the bench at our table, and then he'd fall off, and his whole body would shake uncontrollably.

This went on for a few days when Mama and Papa decided to take Paulie to the hospital in Gimli the next day and arranged for a neighbour to stay with us younger kids.

We all got up extra early because Mama and Papa would be setting out before sunrise. Mama asked Bea and me to go feed the chickens and get some eggs. When we got back, and I opened the door, Paulie was on the ground, convulsing and letting out a horrible wail.

Mama picked Paulie up, but he continued convulsing and started gagging.

"Get Papa!" Mama screamed.

Papa had gone to the outhouse, so I ran out to get him.

"Papa, Papa, come quick!" I yelled. "Paulie's having a bad seizure."

Poor Papa must have had his pants down, but he came charging out after a few seconds, and we ran back to the house.

When we burst through the door, Mama handed Paulie to Papa, "Do something, please! He's not breathing!"

Paulie had stopped convulsing and was lying limp.

Papa quickly turned him over in his arms and banged him on his back a couple of times, but that didn't seem to do anything. He laid Paulie on the kitchen table, rubbed his chest, and then tried to blow some air into his mouth.

But Paulie just kind of sagged, and before I knew it, Mama was wailing, and Papa was crying.

"He's gone," Papa whispered.

That night, as I lay in bed, I wondered if Paulie's death was another of the "mysterious" ways of God. What was the sense in a young child, who had been perfectly healthy a couple of days ago, suddenly dying?

*   *   *

So, those are some of the events of my childhood that stand out most in my memory. As I said earlier, I seem to have two types of memories: memories of events and memories of feelings.

I have to say that, despite all the awful events, when I look back at them days on the homestead, my feeling memories are ones of warmth, love, and togetherness.

BOOK TWO

COMING OF AGE
IN
THE CITY

Chapter 6

MOVING TO WINNIPEG

The most significant change in my life came when I left the homestead and moved to Winnipeg to work as a servant in an English "great house."

Not surprisingly, it came shortly after my monthly cycle started, and I was considered a woman. I had completed grade six and, according to the norms of the time, that was more than enough education for a woman. Like almost every young woman of my age on the farms, the intent was to ship me off to the city to earn some money to help support the family.

I remember once raising the issue of possibly continuing to high school.

"Papa, I heard that Josef Lukowicz is going to high school in Gimli. Can't girls go on to high school as well?"

"Don't be silly, girl," Mama interrupted. "Why would a woman need more schooling to learn to raise children?"

"Josef says he's going to become a teacher. Maybe I could be a teacher too?"

"Malenka kit, that may be alright for some richer families, but we can't afford that," Papa said.

"And, it's time that you were earning your way instead of eating us out of house and home."

I did have a big appetite, but this was a little harsh, even for Mama.

The reality was that at that age I didn't have any great dreams or aspirations. My life had been shaped by what I saw and experienced on the homestead, and I was incapable of imagining a much larger life for myself. But, at the same time, I sensed there was a bigger world out there, and I wanted to get out and see it, so moving to the City seemed to be the best route to take.

Besides, the bottom line was that I had an obligation to fulfill to my family, and I never questioned that obligation.

It was late August 1916 when the great day came. I was thirteen years old and I remember it as if it were yesterday.

"Do you have to go?" sobbed my younger sister Annie, hugging me tightly.

"Don't worry, Annie," I said. "I'll be back as often as I can. And one day, you can come visit me."

"Lucky you," said John. "You get to ride on the train and see the big city!"

"Yeah, it'll be amazing," echoed Mike, who was now too big to be called Mikey.

Papa came in. "Okay, it's time to go."

I kissed the new baby Nicholas and hugged Annie, who started crying.

"Please don't go, Sophie," she said.

I hugged her tighter and told her I would be back soon, not knowing if it were true or not. I hugged the boys quickly and gave Annie one more big squeeze. Lastly, Mama embraced me and told me to take care of myself. Surprisingly, her voice choked.

I tore myself away and ran outside where Papa was now waiting. I climbed onto the cart, Papa snapped the reins, and we were off.

It was a glorious morning, the sun rising above the tree line, with light puffy clouds in a clear blue sky. I glanced at the garden as we rode by. The air was rich with the scent of raspberry bushes, and the beans, carrots, and cabbage were all growing big and green out of their rows.

We rode in silence for a while, Papa leaving me to my thoughts. I watched the countryside slowly drifting by, blackbirds congregating in the fields, and swallows swooping here and there.

After some time, he asked me if I was alright.

"Yes, Papa, I'm fine. It's time for me to move to the city."

"Malenka kit, you will learn a lot in your new life."

Papa knew I loved learning, and, as always, what he said showed that he knew me well.

Since the trip took the better part of a day, we had arranged to stay at a cousin's place much closer to Gimli. We stayed there for the night, which proved to be a very pleasant interlude.

We left bright and early the next morning and arrived at the train station in Gimli a little before noon. Beatrice had ridden in on the train in the morning, and she was waiting for us at the station. She had come to accompany me on my first trip to the big city.

We had some time, so we ate lunch in a small café close to the lakefront. This was a special treat, as Papa would rarely splurge like that.

He noticed my concern. "Don't worry, soon you will be sending us so much money that we'll be eating in cafés every week."

I knew this wasn't true but just smiled. It would have been ungrateful to protest and take away his pleasure in doing a small thing for me.

When we finished lunch, we walked to the lakeshore. The water was shimmering light blue, and it was impossible to see where the lake ended and the sky began. Lake Winnipeg was truly an inland sea, and the immensity of it was a little scary. Nevertheless, it smelled delicious, and I took in several deep lungfuls.

Soon it was time to go, and we returned to the station. The steam train was huffing and puffing as if it were anxious to get on its way. Papa carried my suitcase on for me, we found two seats, and hugged one last time. Papa hung on, and soon he was shaking gently.

"It'll be alright, Papa," I whispered in his ear. "I'll be fine."

He let go and looked at me, his eyes shining with tears. "I know you will be, malenka kit. I know you will be."

The conductor came on board and, after one last squeeze of my hand, Papa stepped off.

"Now, remember what I told you," Bea whispered.

"Yes, I haven't forgotten."

The conductor reached us. "Tickets, please."

Bea handed him her ticket and said, "My sister is only twelve."

It was free to ride the train until you were twelve, so I had to be twelve at least until we got to Winnipeg.

"Twelve, eh? You look older than that, lassie."

"You know how it is these days, sir," said Beatrice. "Young girls grow up fast."

"Hmph," he said as he looked around. "And what would a twelve-year-old girl be taking a full suitcase to the city for?"

"The suitcase is mine, sir," said Beatrice.

"Why is she going to the city?" he asked.

"I'm just taking her in to show her where I live and to show her the sights."

"I've never been to the city, sir." I smiled at him.

He hesitated and then smiled back. "Enjoy your visit then, lassie."

A few minutes later, the steam engine belched steam, and the train lurched to a slow start. I looked out the window and made eye contact with Papa. As we pulled away and I looked at him standing there, the reality that I was moving on to a new life hit me like a blow in the stomach. A horrible panic rose in my chest, and I pressed my face to the window and looked back at Papa for one last second. Then Beatrice's hand closed on mine, and I sank back into my seat, closing my eyes and taking deep breaths.

I sat quietly for a few minutes, trying to process what was happening to me. It wasn't long, though, before I was enraptured by the scenes passing before my eyes. Neat green fields were soon flying by—I couldn't believe how fast we were travelling, and it was disorienting.

"It's marvelous, Bea!" I said. "Everything is such a blur close to the train, but you can see the landscape so well."

"Yes, dear. You'll experience a lot of new things in the next couple of days, and you'll soon get used to them."

The rest of the trip to the city was dreamlike but, before I knew it, we were pulling into the outskirts of Winnipeg. I couldn't believe how quickly we had arrived. We had gone sixty miles in less than two hours, a trip that would have taken at least a couple of full days by horse and buggy.

As we hit the city's northern edge, we encountered large buildings and smokestacks everywhere, shooting black and white smoke into the air. There were several scattered shacks around these buildings, and I saw a man come out of one and relieve himself.

"That's not very pretty," I said.

"The north end is where the poorer people live, Sophie," Bea said. "And there's also a lot of factories. The wealthier people live in the south where you'll be working, and it's a lot nicer there."

Soon we were pulling into the CPR station on Main Street.

We disembarked onto the platform and entered the building. There seemed to be hundreds of people—far more than I had ever seen in my life—milling and rushing about.

"Wow!" I said. "Is it always like this?"

"It's pretty busy when trains come in, so this is normal."

I could see that I was going to have to get used to a new "normal." Back on the farm, it was an event to see a neighbour, and we knew almost everyone we came in contact with. This was not going to be possible here.

Stepping out the front door was like stepping into a fairy tale—magical.

There were cars running back and forth on Main Street. Although they had been described to me, you have to understand that I had never seen a car before that day. There were also a couple of horse-drawn carts and a streetcar. The streetcar was especially magical because there was no obvious engine compartment, it being powered by overhead electric trolley lines.

And of course, there were the buildings—great squat monsters blocking out the sky that formed an unbroken wall along the south side of Main Street.

"My goodness, Bea, how many people live in those buildings?"

"Don't be silly, Sophie. Those are businesses where people work. That big one is called the Grain Exchange."

"What kind of work do they do? Are they building things inside?"

"Stop asking so many questions. It's time to get going."

She took my hand and guided me across the street while she kindly lugged my suitcase in her other arm. To my delight, it appeared that we were going to take a streetcar.

"Is this how you get around the city?" I asked.

"I usually walk most everywhere, but if you have a heavy load like your suitcase, the streetcars are best."

We waited for a few minutes, me looking wide-eyed at everything. I soon noticed a rough-looking one-legged man walking towards us on crutches.

4. CPR Rail Station Main & Higgins, 1912

I must have been gawking because Bea grabbed my arm and said, "It's not polite to stare."

I looked at her questioningly.

"There are a lot of returned men with injuries," she whispered. "You'll get used to it soon enough."

It was 1916 and the war was still on, but I hadn't seen any actual evidence of the conflict until now.

The trolley soon arrived, and we got on, managing the suitcase between the two of us. The trolley lurched when it started, but then it rolled silently and smoothly along the tracks, heading south on Main.

I continued to stare at everything. So many people hurrying here and there! At the next stop, another ragged man got on—this one with an eye patch over one eye. He sat down across from us, then rolled and lit a cigarette. This didn't surprise me because most of the men I had known were smokers.

I tried not to stare, but he must have caught me looking at him because he said, "Whatcha goggling at, girlie?"

"Sorry, sir. Nothing, sir," I mumbled.

He scowled at me but didn't say anything more.

I wasn't sure I would get used to the "returned men" so quickly.

The trolley rolled past Portage Avenue and stopped across from the CN train station. It was an even more impressive building than the CPR station.

"Wow, are there two train companies in Winnipeg?" I asked.

"No, dear. There are three companies, CPR, CNR, and the Grand Trunk Pacific Railway."

At the time, Winnipeg was the fastest growing city in Canada, was the hub of the west, and was even larger than Vancouver.

The trolley turned west onto Broadway, a beautiful tree-lined street, and stopped across from the Fort Garry Hotel. It was the most impressive man-made construction I had yet seen.

"It's a castle, Bea!"

"It's a hotel built by Grand Trunk. It's where all the big shots stay when they come to Winnipeg."

The trolley continued down to Osborne Street, where it turned south again, and passed by some grounds where a truly enormous building was under construction.

"That will be the new provincial legislative building when it's finished," Bea said.

The scale of the building was beyond anything I had imagined, but I was quickly getting used to each new sight exceeding the previous one.

The trolley crossed the Assiniboine River, and when we got to the second stop, Bea told me it was time to get off. We disembarked at Stradbrook Avenue and headed west.

Bea had to pronounce all the names of the streets for me.

"They all have strange English names," I said.

"Yes, Sophie, Winnipeg is an English city run by the English."

Bea had previously prepped me about the family I was going to work for, but she went over it again.

"The family's name is Reynolds. Mr. Reynolds is an important businessman in the city, and he's very wealthy."

"Yes, Bea, you told me that already."

"Mrs. Reynolds is effectively the head of the household, but the chief housekeeper is Miss Harriet Wilson. She'll be your boss, and you have to treat her with respect."

"Yes Bea."

"When she addresses you, you answer with 'Yes ma'am, or no ma'am,' and you bow your head in her direction. If Mrs. Reynolds ever addresses you, you should definitely bow your head and avoid making direct eye contact. Good servants are seen but not heard."

I could see that life in the Reynolds' home would be very different from life in our little Ukrainian homestead.

After a couple of long blocks, Stradbrook merged into Wellington Crescent, and we were suddenly walking in front of enormous homes with expansive lawns. Bea and I kept taking turns carrying my suitcase.

"This is where the richest people in the city live. The houses back onto the Assiniboine River. And remember, you're fourteen now!"

"Yes, Bea, I won't forget, but I don't like the dishonesty."

The minimum age at which one could work full time was fourteen, so I had to be twelve to take the train and fourteen to start working.

"I understand dear, but you're not hurting anyone by saying you're fourteen."

We finally arrived at the Reynolds'. A packed gravel lane led towards the house, where it split into an oval to enable cars or carts to pull up in front. It was a large rectangular red brick building, which was very impressive to a farm girl used to flimsy wood structures.

It appeared to be two and a half stories high, with large bay windows on the main floor and big wood-framed windows on the second floor. I imagined eyes looking at us from those windows.

We started up the lane towards the house, but Bea veered onto a smaller track on the right-hand side that appeared to lead to the back of the house.

"Where are you going, Bea?"

"To the servants' entrance. We never go in the front door. That's reserved for the master and his family, and their guests, of course."

When we got to the side of the house, Bea stopped and looked me up and down. Then she straightened my hat and brushed my jacket. "Now remember, you have to look neat and clean at all times. They won't stand for any sloppiness."

As we came around the corner, I saw that the backyard was an expanse of green grass with a neat stone walkway leading to a smaller brick structure, perhaps twenty yards behind the main building.

"What's that?" I asked.

"Those are the servants' quarters, and that's where you'll be sleeping and taking most of your meals."

Flowers bordered the outside of the servants' quarters, and white curtains fluttered in the windows—it was quite pleasant.

Bea led me up a few stairs to a small wooden landing and knocked on the back door of the main house. There was a delay of a minute or two, and then the door opened to reveal a severe-looking woman of about forty with dark hair and glasses.

"Oh, it's you," she exclaimed as if surprised at what the cat had dragged in.

"Yes, Miss Wilson," Bea bowed her head slightly. "As promised, I've brought my sister Sofiya."

"Pleased to meet you," I said and, imitating Bea, bowed my head.

She looked me up and down for a moment before sighing and saying in a definite English accent, "Well, you had better come in then."

Miss Wilson led us through a small foyer and a hall before we reached a kitchen that was about the size of the entire main floor of our little homestead. A huge wooden table stood in the centre of the room with an imposing gas range against one wall, an electric refrigerator humming in another corner, and various instruments arranged on the counters.

"Have you never seen a kitchen before?" Miss Wilson demanded.

The truth was I had never seen anything like this, and, of course, we didn't have electricity yet on the homestead.

"Only the kitchens that we have on the farms, ma'am," I replied.

"You don't have to worry about anything in here. This is the domain of the cook, Mrs. Murray, and the kitchen maid, Polly. Thank God you won't have any business in here. Your responsibility will be cleaning the rest of the house. You do know how to clean, don't you?"

"Yes ma'am," I replied, not liking her manner one bit.

"I don't suppose you have your own clothes?"

I must have looked confused because Bea quickly intervened and said, "No ma'am, she doesn't have her own maid's uniform. Anna told me that you had extras here."

"Hmph, I don't know if they'll fit your sister. She's thin as a reed. Are you sure you're fourteen, girl?!"

"Yes ma'am," I said with another half bow. I felt I better be respectful, particularly since we were treading on thin ice.

"Are you handy with a needle and a thread? You're going to have to take in your frock."

"Yes ma'am," I replied. This was true as I had spent countless hours helping Mama make clothes for my siblings and adjusting them for hand-me-downs as they grew.

"Since you took your sweet time getting here, it's too late in the day to start work. Take her out to the servants' quarters, introduce her to the others, and see if you can get a frock for her. Tomorrow morning I'll get you started on your duties."

With that, she dismissed us, and we headed out the back door.

"Goodness Bea, is she always like that?"

"Like what?" Bea asked.

"So bossy."

"You know I don't work here, but she seems pretty much like the head of the household at my place."

We walked along the stone path to the servants' quarters, where Bea again knocked. This time, a round, ruddy-faced woman in her mid-forties quickly answered the door.

"Aye, what is it?"

"Hello Mrs. Murray. I'm Anna's friend, Beatrice, and I'm bringing you my sister Sofiya who's starting as the new chambermaid."

"Aye, come in."

Mrs. Murray had a very different accent from Miss Wilson. She rolled her "Rs" in a most pleasing manner, which I later learned was typical of a Scottish accent.

We entered to find a cozy dining area to our left and a sitting area with a couple of divans to the right. Plenty of light poured in through the front windows, and I had an immediate impression of what, for me, was luxury.

"Mrs. Murray is the cook in the Reynolds' household," said Bea.

"And it looks as if I'll have a right fair job trying to fatten you up lassie," Mrs. Murray said to me. "You're nothing but skin and bone."

A younger woman with a pleasant round face and smooth complexion came out from a back room.

"And this here's Anna—you'll be working with her in the house."

Anna stepped forward, smiled, and shook my hand amiably.

"Bea's told me about you," she said.

Anna took me through to a bedroom at the back of the cottage, which contained a bunk bed on the far wall and a single bed on the near wall.

"I sleep in the bottom of the bunk bed," she said, and Polly sleeps in the other bed. "As the Johnny-come-lately, you'll sleep in the top.

"Where does Miss Wilson sleep?" I asked.

"She has a bedroom to herself," Anna answered, pointing down the hall to a second bedroom.

"I'd best be off now," said Bea.

I had a sudden moment of panic. Bea had been my one remaining tether to the homestead. When she left, I'd be truly away from home for the first time in my life.

She must have sensed my stress as she said, "Don't worry, you'll settle in just fine here, and I'll come round tomorrow evening to see how you're doing."

I followed her out the door and around the side of the house, where I broke down and started crying.

Bea turned and hugged me. "Don't worry, child. You'll be alright. They'll feed you well, and you'll make friends with Anna and Polly."

I calmed down, nodded, and finally let her out of my grasping hug. I watched her back as she walked around the house and down the sidewalk. I took a moment to compose myself and went back to face my new "family."

I unpacked my suitcase and found a place for most of my things in an armoire in our room. Polly, who turned out to be another Ukrainian girl from my neck of the woods near Gimli, came back from a walk and gave me a warm welcome.

The four of us, Mrs. Murray, Anna, Polly, and I, had a simple supper of soup, bread, and butter in our cottage.

"Where does Miss Wilson eat?" I asked.

"She normally eats supper in the big kitchen with the butler, Iain McAdam," said Mrs. Murray, whose first name was Joan. "But she usually has breakfast with us."

I went for a short walk after supper with Polly, and we spoke Ukrainian together and talked about our homes. The street was impressive, with magnificent homes and lovely flower bed gardens, but I already missed the heady aromas of the farm, the wild evening calls of songbirds, hawks, and ravens, and the squawking of the ducks and geese.

As I lay in bed on the first night in my new life, I reflected on my day. For the first time, I had travelled on vehicles not pulled by a horse—a steam train and a trolley car! Maybe I had only travelled sixty miles, but I felt as if I had been transported into another world.

Chapter 7

LIFE AS A MAID

The next day, I woke up as the sun rose, and heard Anna stirring in the bunk below me. I looked across and saw that Polly's bed was empty.

"Are you awake, Anna?" I asked softly.

"Yep, it's time we got up," she answered.

I could hear movement in the kitchen next door.

"Where's Polly?" I asked.

"Mrs. Murray and her get up early. They usually make some oatmeal, put breakfast out for us, and then head over to the big house to get breakfast ready for the family."

I slipped out of bed and hopped down to the floor, which was partly covered by an area rug.

"Can I use the bathroom?" I asked.

"You're supposed to wait your turn," Anna said. "Miss Wilson always has priority. Mrs. Murray and Polly are next because they have to be up first. Then it's me, and you're last. I'm ahead of you because I have seniority." And she stuck her tongue out.

"But I really need to go now!"

"You've got your chamberpot under the bed here if you need it," she pointed out.

There was no privacy in the room, and I hardly wanted to go pee in front of a girl I'd only met the night before.

Anna must have noticed a look of despair on my face because she said, "If you're really fast, I suppose it will be alright."

"But make sure it's clean!" she added.

I ran out into the little hall and into the bathroom.

For me, it was a treat to use a flush toilet. We only had an outhouse on the homestead and our chamber pots inside. I had used a flush toilet at the train station in Gimli a couple of times when we had gone to meet Bea at the station, but this was much neater.

I quickly washed my hands and stepped out into the hallway, where I ran into Miss Wilson, fully dressed and obviously heading to the bathroom.

"Get yourself dressed, and I'll see you at breakfast," she ordered.

I did as was told and was soon seated at the table. We had porridge with some fresh cream, sliced ham with bread, and, new to me, some mustard. There was also a pot of tea and some marmalade on the side. It seemed quite luxurious as we normally just had oatmeal and bread at home.

As I was stuffing some bread and marmalade into my mouth, Miss Wilson said, "If you want to work in a good English home, you must learn to comport yourself in a more ladylike manner."

I paused for a second, gulped, and mumbled, "Yes, ma'am."

"And, among other things, that means sitting straight at the table, chewing your food properly, and not acting like some ravenous dog off the street."

Suddenly self-conscious of everything about myself, I tried to straighten up and slow down my eating. I watched how Miss Wilson and the others ate, my enjoyment of the breakfast going down considerably.

"After breakfast, you and Anna clean the dishes, and then I'll take you over to the house to get you started on your duties," Miss Wilson said.

*   *   *

It was another beautiful late summer day, one of the best times of the year in Winnipeg. The plagues of mosquitoes had died down, and the high humidity had given way to a pleasant warmth.

I only had a couple of seconds to enjoy the air as we crossed over into the big house and entered the kitchen.

Mrs. Murray turned to Miss Wilson and said, "The family's all seated, so you had better hurry up."

Miss Wilson signalled for me to follow her, and Anna brought up the rear. She crossed the kitchen to a corner and opened a door. I had assumed it was a door to a larder in the basement, but, to my surprise, there was a narrow spiral staircase leading upwards.

I glanced back at Anna and raised my eyebrows. "The servants' staircase, dummy. We don't use the family staircase."

Emerging onto the second floor, Miss Wilson opened a door that gave onto a narrow hallway. We proceeded down the hall and did a sharp right turn.

Miss Wilson opened another door and said, "This is the master bedroom, and you'll always do up the bed here first because the master is usually the first up from breakfast."

The bedroom was large enough to sleep a family of twelve out on the homesteads. The floors were gleaming golden, and a couple of immaculate dressers stood against the walls.

The sheets, pillows, and a blanket were all jumbled up on the bed. Miss Wilson pulled them back and said, "We wash the linen once a week on Wednesdays. However, always give the sheets a good check, and if they're dirty, you change them right away."

As Miss Wilson turned her head, Anna poked me in the ribs and winked. "Don't worry, that doesn't happen much these days."

I didn't understand what she was talking about, but I noticed a wet-looking spot near the top of the bed.

"Ma'am, do we change the sheets because of that stain?" I asked.

"No, that's just a little wet spot, and it'll dry before the evening."

"It's from Mrs. Reynolds' drool," Anna whispered.

"Okay, quickly now, girls!" Miss Wilson ordered.

I wasn't sure what to do, but Anna said, "First, we shake out the pillows. Grab a couple."

She went to a window, lifted it open, and shook her pillows out.

"Whatever you do, don't drop 'em outside," Anna said. Now park 'em on these chairs while we make up the bed."

Anna went to one side and I went to the other.

"Now pull till it's tight and tuck the sheet under."

Although I thought I pulled hard, Miss Wilson said, "That's not good enough. Tighter!"

I couldn't imagine why this mattered so much. Surely the sheets would get messed up as soon as the Reynolds lay down on them.

Miss Wilson must have sensed my doubt because she said, "The reason that English people run this country is that we pay attention to every detail and do things right."

"Now the top and bottom," said Anna.

We repeated the procedure around the bed until the sheet was as tight as a drum top. We finished by pulling up the top sheet, smoothing the blankets, and replacing the pillows, after plumping them up a bit more.

While Anna and I made the bed, Miss Wilson straightened various things in the room.

"Anna, you know the routine. I'm going downstairs to see if everything is alright at breakfast. You show Sophie what to do."

Miss Wilson disappeared around the corner and down the little hallway to the servants' stairwell.

"What's in there?" I asked, pointing to a small room in the corner.

"That's the masters' private bathroom. We'll clean it later. Come on. There are three other beds we have to make up before the young ones come up from breakfast."

Anna led me to the back of the house, where we entered another huge bedroom, although smaller than the master. There was a messed-up double bed in the corner and a lot of makeup on one of the dressers.

"This is Cora's bedroom, the eldest daughter."

We went through the same routine with the bed when Anna saw me looking at the makeup.

"Cora's right pretty, and she knows it," Anna said. "She's a bit high and mighty but not too bad, really."

We proceeded down the hall and entered the next bedroom.

"This is Bobby's room, the only boy."

There was a funny smell in the room, but I couldn't put my finger on it.

"How old is he?" I asked.

"He's fourteen and full of 'imself." Anna pulled back the sheets to reveal a large yellowish stain in the middle.

"Yeww, at it again, he is!" Anna pretended to gag.

"What's that? Did he go pee?"

Anna burst into a high giggle.

"You're a right card, aren't ya, dearie! That's him playing with his kishka."

I had no idea what Anna was talking about. Frank, my half-brother, was quite a bit older than me and my other brothers were a lot younger, so I didn't have experience with teenage boys in the house.

"I guess we better change these sheets then," I said to cover up my confusion.

"I suppose so, but I'm gonna ask Miss Wilson if we have to do it every time Bobby gets his jollies."

We pulled the sheets off, and Anna thankfully carried them in a ball out into the hall. She opened the door to a storage closet and said, "We'll dump 'em in this basket till we're ready to wash 'em."

She opened another door to reveal a broad, shallow closet full of blankets and sheets.

"Here, grab one of these. They're the sheets for the single beds."

We made up the bed in Bobby's room and then proceeded to the last bedroom, which was the smallest. It had a single bed in the corner, with the nicest pink pillows I had ever seen and a large stuffed teddy bear sitting in the middle.

"This is Sally's room, the youngest girl."

When I looked questioningly at Anna, she said, "She's alright, even if she's a bit soft in the head."

"What do you mean?"

"I'm not quite sure, but there's something off about that girl. She's right friendly though."

We finished with Sally's bed and headed out into the hall, where I ran smack dab into a young man as I turned the corner.

"What the..!" he said, and then looked me up and down.

"Well, lookee here!" he said. "Have we got a new maid?" he asked Anna.

"Yes sir, this is Sophie, sir."

He looked at me with a half smirk, half leer, bowed, and said, "Pleased to meet you."

I half curtsied and said, "Pleased to meet you sir."

At that, he laughed in my face and pushed by us both, heading to his room.

"He doesn't seem very nice," I said.

"Hah! You sure have a way with words." Then, lowering her voice, she said, "But don't get caught saying anything bad about the family, or Miss Wilson will be on your tail."

As we headed towards the servants' staircase, a tall, elegantly dressed woman emerged from the family staircase, with Miss Wilson in tow. I knew it had to be Mrs. Reynolds.

"This is the new housemaid, Sophie," said Miss Wilson.

Mrs. Reynolds was probably the tallest woman I had met in person, and she held herself very erect. She was wearing some type of brocade dress with elaborate swirls that gave her a peacock-like appearance.

She regarded me through pince-nez glasses and said, "Welcome to our home. I trust you'll settle in satisfactorily."

This seemed rather ambiguous to me, but I curtsied and said, "Thank you, ma'am."

"Another Ukrainian girl, I take it?" Mrs. Reynolds asked Miss Wilson.

"Yes, ma'am. It's very difficult to find suitable English girls these days."

"Hmm, well, carry on," she said.

Anna and I stepped aside as she swept regally into the master bedroom.

We were going to continue about our business when the door to the family stairwell burst open, and a tall, gangly young girl sprung out of it and came skipping towards us.

"Good morning," she said in a high cheerful voice.

This had to be Sally, the youngest girl.

Anna introduced me, and Sally reached out, shook my hand vigorously, and said, "Very pleased to meet you!"

She was a breath of fresh air in the stuffy house.

"See you around," she said and continued skipping down the hall.

Anna and I grabbed Bobby's sheets out of the cupboard and headed down the stairs. We walked through the kitchen where Mrs. Murray and Polly were evidently bringing dishes back from breakfast, and Mrs. Murray was washing them.

A smallish and slender dark-haired man was sitting at the table, polishing silver. He was dressed very neatly in dark pants and a smartly-pressed white shirt. He was slightly balding and appeared to be in his mid-fifties.

"Hello, my dear," he said when he spotted me. "You must be Sophie."

"Yes, sir." I gave a little curtsy. "Pleased to meet you."

He chuckled. "I appreciate it, but there's no need to curtsy when you address me."

I blushed, and Mrs. Murray said, "This is Mr. McAdam, the family's butler. And you need not pay attention to a word he says," she added with a twinkle in her eye.

I had noticed a small room off the corner of the kitchen, and I must have glanced at it.

"Aye," he said. "That's where I'm a-bedding down."

"All the real men are off to the war. That's why we're stuck with the likes of 'im," Mrs. Murray said.

"That's her way of saying she's in luv with me." He winked. I immediately liked him.

"Oh, right, a scrawny little thing like that. Heaven help us!"

I wasn't used to this kind of banter on the farm, but I could see that they liked each other underneath the words.

"Enough chitchat," said Mrs. Murray. "The water's ready."

Anna explained that our next task was to do the day's laundry. That included serviettes and table linen from the previous day, accumulated clothes from the family, and, once a week, the bedsheets and the servants' clothes.

The Reynolds owned a hand-operated washing machine. Anna and I carried a big pot of hot water over to a metal bucket in another corner of the kitchen. We used ladles to scoop some of the hot water into the bucket before picking up the pot and pouring the rest in.

"Now ya always be careful doing that, ya hear?" said Mrs. Murray. "You don't want to scald yourselves, and, more important, I don't want any of that hot water wasted."

Anna took me to the dining room on the main floor. It was the most impressive room yet. Of course, I didn't know one type of wood from another but later learned that the gleaming floor was maple, while the enormous dining table and its ornately carved chairs were made of oak. Elegant glass-doored cabinets adorned the walls, and a huge bay window looked over the front yard and its flower gardens.

We gathered up the serviettes and the tablecloth from breakfast and carried them back to the kitchen. We put the table linen into the metal bucket, slid it on a couple of short rails under the washing machine, and closed the top. It had a crank that moved an agitator, which Anna started to work on.

She pointed to the clock on the wall. "We have to agitate this for twenty minutes. I'll do the first five minutes, and then we'll switch. In the meantime, go upstairs and grab a broom from the cupboard and sweep off the dining room table and floor."

When I emerged out of the staircase, I saw the Reynolds' children marching by the end of the hall. They were apparently heading off for morning riding lessons.

It was a bit of a sprint to follow Anna's directions and be back in five minutes. When I got back, I took over from her and soon found that turning the crank was hard work.

"Use both arms, and it's easier if you put your back into it," she said.

While I was taking my turn cranking, Anna slid another large bucket out from under a cupboard. She attached a hose to the kitchen sink tap and ran water into the bucket. So many new gadgets!

When the twenty minutes were up, we dunked the table linen into what I now perceived was the rinse bucket. Then we squeezed the excess water out with our hands before running each item between two rollers at the top of the washing machine. A little drain channel funneled the water back into the rinse bucket.

As each item emerged from the rollers, we laid it on a kind of flat clothes stretcher that Anna had put on one of the kitchen counters. Once the stretcher was full, we carried it out back and laid it down on a wooden table next to a clothesline. It was a fine day, and I could see that the laundry should dry quickly.

"What do you do during the winter?" I asked.

"We take everything up to the attic and string 'em up there. Of course, it takes longer, and nothing smells as good afterwards."

We went back and did the whole thing over with the rest of the kitchen things and then did a whole other basket of the family's laundry. It was hard work indeed, and I was already tired when we were done with the first batch. However, it was a sight easier than doing laundry on the homestead, where all we had was a tub, a scrubbing board, and a brush. I couldn't imagine doing all this laundry the way we did it back home.

"Now the cleaning," Anna said.

We went inside, up the stairs, and fetched brooms and feather dusters from the storage closet.

"We'll start with the sitting room."

The sitting room was another enormous room located opposite the master bedroom. It sported a couple of comfortable-looking divans, several easy chairs, a writing desk, a small piano, and a gorgeous view of the flower gardens in front of the house. I also noted a couple of bookshelves lined with hardcover volumes.

"This is where the family spends quite a bit of time in the afternoon, reading, talking, and sometimes playing music," Anna said.

We went around with our feather dusters, making sure we dusted off all visible surfaces. A huge area rug covered the centre of the room, and we used a stiff-bristled broom to brush it off.

"We carry this outside a couple of times a year to beat it and air it out, but it's too heavy to do that all the time."

We used softer brooms to sweep up what little dirt there was off the hardwood floors, and then we repeated the process in each of the bedrooms. Then we went back downstairs, where Anna guided me through a procession of rooms, each of which was more impressive than anything I had previously ever imagined.

First came the reception room, which was off to the right of the entrance for someone entering the house. Several comfortable divans were spread around, and paintings graced the walls, including a portrait of Mr. Reynolds. The floor was burnished birch, with what I later found out was a Persian carpet at one end. There were a couple of bronze busts on pedestals in one corner, and a glass cabinet displayed various curios, some of which were clearly First Nations.

"Careful with them busts, Sophie. You don't want to knock one of 'em over," Anna said.

5. Typical Wealthy Person's Home
Winnipeg, 1910s

I must have been gawking because she said, "C'mon now, we have to get a move on. We need to be extra careful before the weekends because that's when the Reynolds usually entertain. At least I don't think anyone's comin' tonight."

We continued through a sliding door to an equally large adjacent room.

"This is what they call the Entertainment Room," Anna said.

It was uncluttered, but a big piano stood against the outside wall, and a strange machine sat on a pedestal against the far wall.

"What's that?" I asked.

"That's a gramophone, dummy. It plays music on disc records. The family uses this room when they host parties, and the guests want to dance."

I noted a type of bar in one corner with a few high stools and some racks holding liquor up against the wall. Anna noticed where I was looking.

"A party wouldn't be a party without some booze now, would it?"

We gave this room a quick once-over as it was almost spotless anyway. Lastly, Anna led me through another sliding door to what she called the library, a long but shallow room. An enormous billiards table squatted at one end, and there were a couple of divans and a large liquor cabinet at the other end. The walls were mostly lined with shelves of books, so it merited its title as the library.

"This is where Mr. Reynolds entertains his male friends. As far as I can tell, they play billiards, smoke cigars, and drink whiskey."

Anna must have noticed the look of awe on my face.

"You'll get used to it soon enough," she said.

"Sorry, I've just never seen anything like this house."

"Yeah, a little ritzier than your house on the homestead, I bet."

That was an enormous understatement. All the buildings out on the homestead were rough primitive things in comparison to the luxury of the Reynolds' house. With my background on the farm, there was no way I could have visualized or imagined the opulence of the Reynolds' house, and I was left dumbstruck.

*   *   *

After a quick cleaning of the library, we headed back down to the kitchen where Polly was already seated, and Mrs. Murray had a welcome lunch for us. There was a soup with nice big chunks of beef, accompanied by fresh bread, butter, and cheese.

First, I had to use the washroom, and I was told to go to our quarters.

"What about in the winter?" I asked. "Do we still have to go back to our quarters to go to the bathroom?"

"Aye, normally you do," Mrs. Murray said. "But from time to time during the day, if most of the family is out, we can use the washroom on the main floor next to the dining room."

Mr. McAdam came in, and the five of us commenced an enjoyable lunch. About ten minutes later, Miss Wilson joined us, and I noticed that the air of conviviality was quickly stifled.

"Do you always take lunch here in the big house?" I asked.

"On weekdays, yes," answered Miss Wilson. "On weekends, or when the family has company, we normally take our lunch in our quarters."

I understood that we were to stay out of the way of the family as much as possible.

After lunch, Anna and I thoroughly cleaned the bathrooms, and I was introduced to new cleaning tools that I had never seen, for example, for the toilet.

Next, Anna led me outside to check on the laundry. The napkins and tablecloth from the dining room were already dry and ready to take inside. We folded them up and placed them on the stretcher-like board we had used before.

"Now we have to iron all of this," Anna said.

"And where do we do that?"

"In our quarters."

We took the linen into our little house, poured water from the tap into a pot, and lit the gas stove to heat some water. Then we sat down for a glorious few minutes.

"Did you grow up on a farm outside Winnipeg?" I asked Anna.

"Sure did."

"Then I bet you had to carry water from a well every time you needed water for drinking, washing, or whatever?"

"Of course!"

"And you had to carry wood for the woodstove, clean out the ashes and everything?"

"What do ya think, silly?"

"It sure makes things easier having running water and a gas stove. It's luxury."

"Yeah, it might seem like it at first. But ya soon get used to it, and there's plenty of work to do around here. The water's ready, so get off your bum!"

We filled two little irons with the hot water and spread the linen out. Anna used an ironing board, and I just used our kitchen table. Anna showed me exactly how to iron and fold each item—I was surprised by how everything in the household was done in such a precise manner. We spent a pleasant hour or so chatting while doing our work.

When we were done, we carried the linen to the big house and then fetched the rest of the laundry. We repeated the whole process, although there were more instructions on how to exactly iron the clothing so that the creases appeared in just the right places. Anna handled the more difficult items, but she showed me how to do them as she went along.

Once we had taken the family's laundry back in, I thought we might be done for the day, but we still had to thoroughly clean the servants' quarters.

"Miss Wilson would have a hissy fit if she found a speck of dust under her bed!" Anna told me.

We finally got a break when we finished cleaning up. Anna said she was going to lie down, but I wanted to get outside and enjoy some of the day.

I walked back along Wellington Crescent, admiring the well-kept gardens that graced each house. I soon came upon a small park, so I stopped and sat down on a little bench and looked up at the sun playing through the leaves of the elm trees.

Even the trees are better here, I thought. Back on the farm, we only had scrub poplar and spruce. The elms were majestic in comparison.

Thinking back to the farm and my family, I couldn't believe it was only yesterday that I had packed up and left. Already it seemed like half a lifetime ago.

It struck me that we don't mark time by the hours, days, and years of the calendar; rather, we mark the times of our lives by the significance of the events we experience.

Chapter 8

THE MOST SIGNIFICANT EVENT OF MY LIFE?

All things considered, the next few months went fairly smoothly. I had a lot to learn, and Miss Wilson was quite hard on me most of the time but, with Anna and Polly's help, I progressively became more proficient at my tasks. Soon I was a more or less accepted part of the household.

Since we were given room and board, and I had never spent money in my life, I could save most of what I was earning and send a good deal of it to my family. This pleased me enormously. The land on our farm was so poor that my parents were only able to eke out a meagre existence selling milk, eggs, butter, and the like in Gimli. However, since most of the other farmers also produced similar products, prices were generally low, and they appreciated the extra money they received from Beatrice and me.

Once Labour Day passed, the Reynolds' children went back to school, and it was pretty quiet in the house during the daytime, which made it easy to get the work done. I was glad because their son Bobby was usually rude when I ran into him. The eldest girl, Cora, treated me with indifference; after all, I was just another Ukrainian servant girl and she had probably seen several of us come and go during her life.

The youngest girl, Sally, was downright friendly, and it was generally a delight to run into her. However, when she got sick in late October, something happened that made it more memorable than just a pleasant encounter.

I remember it was a bright cold day, typical of Winnipeg, with the sun streaming in through the windows in the sitting room. Sally had stayed home with the sniffles, although as she herself had protested, she wasn't feeling too badly.

Sally was having some difficulties with her English classes, and the Reynolds had hired back their old governess to help her in the afternoons after school hours. When I came into the sitting room, Mrs. Penner, for that was her name, was reading to Sally.

"Oh, hi, Sophie," said Sally with a big smile.

"Hi Sally," I replied. "Please don't mind me," I added, looking at Mrs. Penner.

She spoke in an enchanting contralto, and as I dusted the bookshelves, I was mesmerized by her voice and the story. I slowed down and dragged out my work to the point that it must have been obvious.

Mrs. Penner looked at me with an inquiring glance. She seemed friendly, so I took a little risk.

"I'm sorry," I said. "It's just that the story is so interesting, and you have such a beautiful voice."

"Oh, can Sophie please join us?" Sally asked

Mrs. Penner looked from me to Sally and hesitated.

"I don't think it would be appropriate," I responded. After all, I knew my place was to be seen and not heard and, preferably, not seen either.

"Please, Mrs. Penner," Sally repeated.

"Besides, I still have more work to do," I said.

However, the idea of listening to this woman read to us had instantly captivated me, and something in my manner must have tipped off Mrs. Penner.

"Do you enjoy reading, my dear?" she asked me.

"I liked it very much at school, but we never had books in my home."

"Pretty please," Sally asked.

"Perhaps another day," Mrs. Penner responded. "Ah, Sophie has other business to attend to today."

"Well, tomorrow then!" Sally exclaimed.

Mrs. Penner paused again before asking, "What time do you normally finish your daily duties?"

"Nowadays, about 4:00, but if I really hurry, I can be done sooner if nothing unexpected comes up."

"We'll see then," Mrs. Penner said as she dismissed me with a nod of her head.

A couple of days later, Miss Wilson spoke to me after breakfast.

"I can't understand why, but Mrs. Penner wants you to join her and Sally in the sitting room at 3:30 this afternoon."

I could tell by her manner that she disapproved, so I suppressed my excitement and simply said, "Yes, ma'am."

"You better make sure you have all your chores done by then!"

"Yes, ma'am. I'll make sure they're done."

"And remember that today is the day that all the cabinets need polishing."

"Yes, ma'am."

"Harumph, alright then."

Each day we had a special task in addition to the regular cleaning and laundry. Some days we had to polish the crystal, another day we did the servants' laundry, another we had to apply wax polish to the furniture, and so on. Miss Wilson had worked out regular schedules so that we never really had any rest during the day, apart from our lunch breaks.

We worked full days Monday to Friday and a half day on Saturday. While Sunday was supposed to be our day off, we often did a couple of hours cleaning early in the day, particularly if the Reynolds had had a party the previous evening.

At the time, it never occurred to me, but when I looked back later, I realized that we had no contract, we could be dismissed at any time, and we had no worker protection rights whatsoever. However, that all seemed normal to me, and I was quite happy to have a job and earn some money.

I finished my chores a little before 3:30 that day and rushed back to our quarters to clean up a bit before I joined Sally and Mrs. Penner in the sitting room.

"Oh, goody!" Sally said when I walked in.

I'm not sure why Sally liked me so much and I was afraid it was because she was a bit "off." She was only a year younger than me, but she hadn't reached puberty and acted much younger.

"We're reading *Pride and Prejudice* by Jane Austen," Mrs. Penner said to me. "In this chapter, the two sisters, Elizabeth and Jane, are speaking with each other. Sally, why don't you read the part by Jane? And Sophie, you can take the part of Elizabeth."

She explained that she had two copies of the book and that Sally and I could share while she would read the narrator's part using the other copy.

I sat down on the divan next to Sally, and she wiggled up next to me and placed the book on our thighs. She smelled sweet, something like lily of the valley. It was very strange to be sitting so close to one of the family—the rest of them were so distant, so standoffish that I felt like I was breaking a taboo. We began our reading and soon came to the following.

I started with, "*Oh! You are a great deal too apt, you know, to like people in general. You never see a fault in anybody. All the world are good and agreeable in your eyes. I never heard you speak ill of a human being in your life.*"

And Sally responded with, "*I would not wish to be hasty in censuring anyone; but I always speak what I think.*"

"*I know you do; and it is that which make the wonder. With your good sense, to be so honestly blind to the follies and nonsense of others! Affectation of candour is common enough—one meets with it everywhere. But to be candid without ostent...a...tion or design—to take the good of everybody's character and make it still better, and say nothing of the bad—belongs to you alone. And so you like this man's sisters, too, do you? Their manners are not equal to his.*"

I stumbled over words such as affectation and ostentation, while Sally stumbled over a few words such as *censuring*. Mrs. Penner explained to us what these words meant, and Sally continued our reading.

"*Certainly not—at first. But they are very pleasing women when you converse with them. Miss Bingley is to live with her brother, and keep his house; and I am much mistaken if we shall not find a very charming neighbour in her.*"

Mrs. Penner then took the narrator's part. "*Elizabeth listened in silence, but was not convinced; their behaviour at the assembly had not been calculated to please in general; and with more quickness of observation and less pliancy of temper than her sister.*"

She stopped and asked us, "What can you tell about Elizabeth and Jane's character from this dialogue?"

I was completely taken aback by her question. No one had asked me anything like that in my life. Mrs. Penner was asking me to give an opinion on characters in a novel. All I was used to doing was following orders, doing chores, and taking care of the younger children. Even in school, we had been asked to learn things by rote, such as our timetables, but never asked to *think*!

Sally and I looked at each other, and I could see what amounted almost to panic in her eyes. She clearly wasn't good at this, and I felt I had to save her from any embarrassment.

"Well, Jane seems to be a nice person who sees the best in everybody," I said, stating the blindingly obvious.

"Yes," Mrs. Penner answered. "And what about Elizabeth?"

I looked at Sally again and could tell she would like me to continue.

"Elizabeth is more cautious," I said. "Maybe she sees people more like they are."

"Excellent!" Mrs. Penner said. "Do you think that Jane Austen is trying to say that Elizabeth isn't a nice person, but Jane is?"

I was amazed by Mrs. Penner's questions. She was asking us to analyze what we had read, to understand what the author was saying! I felt a thrill of excitement run through me—this was so much fun.

I looked at Sally again, and she seemed lost. I knew I had to try to bring her into the conversation.

"Oh no," I said. "I think both Elizabeth and Jane are good people, don't you, Sally?" I nodded at her.

"Oh yes!" she nodded back.

"Maybe they're just different, like you and your sister Cora are different?"

This seemed to make Sally think. After a minute, she said, "But Cora and I aren't like Elizabeth and Jane."

I looked at Mrs. Penner, and she caught my eye in a complicit glance.

"What makes you say that?" Mrs. Penner asked Sally.

"Because Cora and I don't talk closely like the sisters in the book."

"So you think Elizabeth and Jane are close to one another?" Mrs. Penner asked.

"Of course!" Sally said. "Isn't it obvious?"

Soon the three of us were talking about what it was like to have a sister, how it was different in each family, and how it was clear that Elizabeth and Jane supported one another.

We continued to read, and Mrs. Penner occasionally asked us questions. The experience was a revelation for me. I had never before used my brain in such a *detached* manner—to sit back, reflect, and interpret what we were reading. And on top of that, the story was compelling— would Jane and Mr. Bingley get married?

That was the day I fell in love with reading, and it was a day that changed my life forever. From then on, I became a voracious reader, and no matter all the storms I would face, it was to remain my one unchanging delight.

Mrs. Penner told Mrs. Reynolds that my presence seemed to help Sally engage in the reading, and it transpired that I joined in most days at 3:30. I was soon allowed to borrow books from the library as long as I signed them out like in an actual library. And so it was that most nights soon found me curled up with one or another classic of English literature.

The days with Sally and Mrs. Penner launched a lifelong love of reading, but also of learning and of critical thinking about the world around me. Of course, that didn't all happen on that one day...but it was the day it all started.

Chapter 9

WAR YEARS

Over the next several months and years, I spent most of my free time reading. I read the Bronte sisters, Thomas Hardy, and Dickens, and was mesmerized by all of it, although Elizabeth Bennett remained my favourite heroine.

Miss Wilson regularly obtained the daily newspapers from the Reynolds when they were done with them, and she grudgingly shared them with me. Although I preferred novels, I always scanned the news and read the articles that attracted my interest.

Sadly, most of the news in them days was about the so-called Great War. Late in the fall of 1916, the news trickled in about the slaughter at the battle of the Somme. Real information came in slowly, and we found out most of the truth much later because government censors didn't want the general population to hear bad news for fear it would sap public support for the war.

Still, when over a million men die or are seriously injured in a prolonged battle, there are limits on what censors can do. We eventually found out that almost 25,000 Canadian soldiers were killed in that most futile of battles, and countless others were injured. It was little comfort that the only gains during the entire five months occurred when the Canadian battalions took the lead in capturing the town of Courcelette.

Unfortunately for the other Ukrainians and me, war fever had gripped the nation, and there were numerous articles about the "enemy in our midst," meaning Ukrainian and other Eastern European immigrants. The general tone of these articles was that it was a damn good thing that the government had rounded up these "illegal aliens" and put them in work camps across the country. Frank had been caught up in the fervour to arrest these "enemies" and had been interned, so I could never shut the war completely out of my mind.

Every now and then, I would receive a letter from Frank, who was in an internment camp somewhere near Banff, Alberta. He couldn't write very well and wasn't prone to saying much. A typical letter might say something like:

Dear Sister,

I hope you and the family are doing well. I think of you often and remember the good times we had.

The life here is hard but we have enough to eat. The mountains are very beautiful and I hope you will see them one day.

Love to you, papa, mama, and all the family,
Frank

Every time I received a letter from him, which wasn't often, my heart leapt with love and pity for his plight. It was so unfair! And then I'd feel a surge of anger at our English bosses.

Frank wrote his letters in pencil and they tended to be smeared quite badly. I later found out that all ingoing and outgoing mail from the camps was censored, so there were many things he could not say. I sent frequent letters to Frank until he was released, trying to be cheerful, usually describing events in Winnipeg and our household. It was good practice for my writing.

* * *

Fortunately, the fighting ground to a halt with the onset of winter and we were spared more horrific news during the winter of 1916/17. I was able to return to my novels with some degree of equanimity.

The news occasionally held some interesting opinion pieces, as slowly, tentatively, some Canadian editors began to question Britain's leadership in the war. They suggested that Canadian soldiers shouldn't be put wholly under British command to be used as pawns in their horrible chess game. I didn't see too many of these articles in the Reynolds' household because they subscribed to the conservative *Telegraph*, rather than the more liberal *Winnipeg Free Press*. Fortunately, Bea would save some of these articles for me from her household, where they subscribed to both newspapers.

Although most of us didn't realize it at the time, Canada was forging an identity for itself and breaking free from the apron strings of Mother England.

I'll never forget the day when we heard the radio emission in April about Vimy Ridge, that fateful day when the Canadians' role came to the fore.

We had a radio installed in the servants' quarters in the spring of 1917 when the Reynolds upgraded to a newer version, and we got their hand-me-down. On April 12, we had finished work for the day and had all returned to our quarters. As usual, the radio was on, and Polly, Anna, and I were huddled closely around, listening to the crackling news.

"After three days of fighting the Canadian Corps has successfully pushed the Huns back and captured Vimy Ridge," the announcer proudly exclaimed. *"Vimy Ridge has been a key objective of the allies throughout the war, and the Canadians have succeeded where multiple attacks by British and French units previously failed."*

Anna, Polly, and I all held our breaths as we strained our ears.

"Sadly, the victory has come at the cost of the lives of several thousand of our brave boys. However, their victory brings hope that this horrible war can be brought to an end sometime soon."

We three girls looked at each other, and tears simultaneously flowed from our eyes as we spontaneously joined in a fierce three-way hug.

*   *   *

Mr. Reynolds had put up a big wall map of Western Europe in his study, and one day he walked in while I was examining it. I didn't know much about geography, and the map had piqued my interest.

"Sorry, Mr. Reynolds," I said as I curtsied and looked down.

He looked at me questioningly and, on an impulse, I said, "This map is very interesting, sir."

"Harumph." He cleared his throat and regarded me balefully.

I was just about to skedaddle when he said, "Interested in the war, are you, girl?"

"Yes, sir, of course, sir."

He approached me, and I froze, not quite sure what to do, as he had never said more than two words to me up to this point.

"I hear from Mrs. Penner that you're quite clever."

I didn't know how to respond to this, but I managed a weak, "Thank you, sir."

"But do you know anything about maps and geography?"

"No, sir. I'm afraid I don't."

For the first time, he softened and allowed himself a small smile, "Don't you worry yourself on that score. Most women can't tell north from south on a map."

I didn't know how to take that, but he walked up to the map and said, "Come here."

He pointed to places where he had put pieces of masking tape with arrows on them.

"These arrows show where the Allies are massed to attack the Huns," he said.

I was interested, but I didn't really have my bearings. He must have sensed my confusion because he relaxed and, speaking in an avuncular manner, explained the general north/south orientation of the map, showed me where the borders of France, Belgium, and Germany lay, and pointed out the sites of some of the most famous battles.

I'm not sure how much I grasped, but somehow the whole war suddenly became more real to me. Up to now, the place names had been meaningless, but now they seemed tangible and more connected.

He spent about five minutes, with me nodding and saying, "Yes, sir. Thank you, sir," when his mood suddenly changed.

"Harrumph, well off you go, girl!"

Despite my dismissal, I had learned enough so that each day that I passed through the study, I spent a little time examining the map and checking out the places I had heard about on the radio. As a bonus, the map showed England in quite some detail, and I was able to locate many of the place names from my English novels, such as Bath.

Although I can't claim to have fallen in love with maps, this encounter was a springboard for me to learn more about the geography of Manitoba and Canada. I did learn to read a map reasonably well, and although it's a little embarrassing to the female race to admit it, that was more than most of the women I knew in them days.

*   *   *

There was perhaps an even prouder moment for Canada when in the fall of that year, Canadian troops had a key role in the battle of Passchendaele, and the final push to take the town from the Germans was led by the Winnipeg Battalion.

"The 27th battalion of the Canadian Expeditionary Force, from Winnipeg, led the way into Passchendaele in another significant victory for the allies today."

I remember hugging Anna and both of us crying when the news came over the radio. I also remember looking over Anna's shoulder at Miss Wilson's sour face looking at us in silence.

"The Canadian Expeditionary Force has not yet lost a battle in which it has participated throughout the entirety of this bloody conflict."

While the war was raging in Europe, another kind of war was being waged in Winnipeg. The main combatants in this silent and mostly unacknowledged war were the Ukrainians (the Bohunks), the English, and a group that didn't really exist at the start of the conflict—the Canadians. It was a war for our hearts, a war for our allegiance.

In my case, the English clearly won the early stages of the battle. After Mrs. Penner introduced me to Jane Austen, I became immersed in English literature. While I admired the heroes and heroines of those great books, without realizing it, I also came to admire the English culture which had produced all these wondrous stories.

I was working in an English household and was exposed to some of the greatest English literature of all time. The English were my bosses. They were the ones who had built this incredible home, they were the ones who had built this amazing city, and they were the ones who had built an empire that straddled the entire world.

It was only natural that I took it for granted that the "English" were superior. This wasn't a conscious decision on my part—it was just an obvious fact of life.

In contrast, we Ukrainians were poor, uneducated, had no literature of which I was aware, and were clearly indebted to the English for letting us escape the poverty of the old country.

Perhaps the most striking thing for me in the Reynolds' household was the formality, the rituals, and the discipline imposed in all their activities.

It started from the break of dawn, or perhaps even the night before, when the servants laid out the clothes the family would wear the next day. The family would invariably descend at the appointed time, already dressed for the day in clothes finer than I had ever previously seen, just to take breakfast. Mr. Reynolds would have already had the newspaper delivered to his room and read the most important business and political news.

The table was, of course, set with polished silver, laundered serviettes, and gold-trimmed plates. And every meal consisted of a pre-set menu agreed upon between Mrs. Reynolds and Miss Wilson, who relayed it to Mrs. Murray.

And there was the daily "tea" at 5:00, which consisted of a variety of sandwiches, scones, preserves, and tea, all served in the reception room.

While weekends did offer some free time, there were frequently scheduled outings to City Park where the Reynolds would ride horses and Bobby played in a cricket league. Cora and Sally had tutors who came in for piano lessons and instruction in French. In addition to riding and cricket, Bobby also participated in fencing every Saturday morning. From my reading, I could plainly see that the Reynolds were attempting to maintain the trappings of a wealthy British family.

All this planning and pomp and circumstance impressed me a great deal. When I thought of our Ukrainian homestead in comparison, everything seemed so messy and disorganized. No wonder the English ruled the world, and we Ukrainians were servants or stuck in internment camps.

It's not surprising that I started unconsciously imitating my English "masters." I took Miss Wilson's admonishments seriously to sit straight, chew with my mouth closed, and be neat at all times. In the first instance, these were household requirements; in the second instance, I wanted to be more like the heroines in my English novels.

I recall one time when I went home for a weekend in the summer. Papa picked me up at the station and we had a pleasant cart ride back to the homestead. It was wonderful to smell the ripe crops, the plowed earth, and the fresh country breeze.

When we arrived, Mike, John, and Anna came running out, and I hugged them all at once. In contrast to the Reynolds' family, my brothers and sisters seemed dirty and wild, but I never saw such spontaneity at the Reynolds!

The contrast between our tiny, drafty house and the opulence of the Reynolds' was even starker than the contrast between our families.

But it was great that I could let my hair down and relax. I was aware that I was always on pins and needles at the Reynolds, whereas I could plop down in a chair at home and not worry about my posture.

Still, everyone sensed a change in me. We were sitting at the table eating some bread with tea when I must have wiped at my lips and brushed off some crumbs in front of me.

"So you think you're a British lord, now do you?!" Mama exclaimed.

"Pardon me?"

"You'll soon be getting too good for the likes of us, eh?"

Mama was always hard on me, but this was a slap in the face.

"No, Mama, of course not," I responded.

"Go easy on her, dear," Papa said. "She's not a little girl anymore; she's a young woman."

There had definitely been a shift in our relationship. I was making more money than they did on the farm, and there's no denying that earning power affects status, even within a family.

In the evening, some of the neighbours came by with their kids, including a fifteen-year-old "boy" named Danilo. I put "boy" in quotation marks because he was already considered a young man, just as I was a young woman. In them days, the concept of being a teenager didn't exist, and indeed we never used the term. We pretty much went directly from childhood to adulthood once we hit puberty and left school.

We were just considered to be young inexperienced adults.

Danilo had been in school with me, and I remembered him as a pleasant, if not particularly bright boy. I asked him about some of our schoolmates and was surprised to learn that two of the girls I had known had just got married, both at the age of fifteen. Fifteen was considered a bit young to be married, even then, but it certainly wasn't shocking. Nonetheless, I couldn't help but think that these girls were doomed to dull and tedious lives as farmers' wives.

I realized that my time in the city was changing me in many ways. Perhaps it was all those British novels and their enlightened heroines, but I couldn't possibly imagine getting married any time soon. There was too much to learn in life.

So when Danilo awkwardly started flirting with me, I was quick to turn away his shy advances. I'm sure that the word subsequently went out that Sofiya Lyszko thought she was too good for a local farm boy.

*   *   *

As summer turned to autumn in 1917, life continued pretty much the same for me, and, fortunately, I was still able to keep working my way through the Reynolds' library. I regularly spent time reading with Sally and, on occasion, with Mrs. Penner and Sally together.

One day, I got back to our quarters pretty late after spending some extra time reading with Sally in the sitting room. Miss Wilson wasn't around, and Mrs. Murray was serving some supper to Anna and Polly.

"Ah, miss high and mighty has deigned to join us poor servants, eh?" Mrs. Murray scowled at me.

I was shocked.

"Sorry I'm late," I mumbled. "Sally wanted to keep reading because the story was so exciting."

"Are ya sure yer wanting to sit down with the likes of us?" Mrs. Murray continued.

"Of course," I answered. "I don't know what you're talking about."

I looked at Anna and Polly for support, but they both averted their eyes and looked down at their meal.

"Anna, Polly, surely you don't feel like that, do you?" I pleaded.

I couldn't believe it when Polly said, "You didn't answer Mrs. Murray. Are you sure you're wanting to sit with the likes of us?"

At this, I couldn't suppress the tears. I jumped up and ran to the washroom, where I cried into the sink.

Anna and Polly had been the closest people to me in my life for over a year. We worked, ate, and slept together daily and had always got along. How could they talk to me like that?

I don't know what happened to me in that minute. Maybe it was the influence of the Bronte sisters, but I suddenly resolved to stop crying.

I didn't want to choose sides, but I decided that I wouldn't be ashamed just because I was fortunate to be learning. The sad thing is that even with that decision, I was, in a way, choosing sides.

I wiped my eyes, washed my face, fetched my jacket, and went through the kitchen.

"I'm going for a walk," I said. "Hope you enjoy your supper."

I walked down Wellington to my favourite little park. It was late October, and there was a chill in the air. But brightly coloured leaves still clung to the elms by the river, and they glowed as they caught the setting rays of the sun.

Despite my sadness, I couldn't help but think, *There's always beauty in this world.*

*   *   *

After the battle of Passchendaele, the war bogged down again as the winter of 1917/18 set in.

The day after the crying incident, Anna and I were in the dining room dusting when she said, "Sorry about yesterday. You know we don't really mean it."

My first thought was, *Yes, you do mean it,* but I managed to say, "It's alright, don't worry about it."

So a little truce was established in that particular battle in the ongoing war on the home front. Mrs. Murray didn't pick on me anymore either, but I'm not sure that things were ever quite the same again between us. For my part, I made sure that I did all my work diligently so there was nothing they could complain about. And the truth was that I had always done my work well without complaining, and I know they knew it.

With the approach of spring in 1918, we knew that the fighting would pick up again, and there would inevitably be more deaths. The official line from the government, which was largely reflected in the press, was that the allies could win the war over the summer. However, most of us had become inured to the authorities' platitudes and gave them scant credence. The battle lines had changed little since 1914 and it seemed that the war would go on without end.

When spring arrived, it was the Germans who went on the offensive. They launched a series of attacks and pushed the Allies back in several areas. The Germans had signed a treaty with the Russians, and this had freed up many of their soldiers to move to the western front. Although this news was also filtered, most of us got the picture—things weren't going well, and there didn't appear to be any end in sight.

And every weekend, whenever I ventured out in the city, there were more and more returned men hobbling about with horrible injuries, missing legs, arms, or an eye. The reports of deaths of Canadians in the newspapers also continued to mount.

Ironically, I didn't have to worry about anyone in my family or anyone I knew being killed or injured because no one that I knew from the homesteads had enlisted. Immigrants to Canada could become 'naturalized' after living in Canada for three years, and then going before a court and swearing allegiance. Many Ukrainians had already been naturalized prior to 1914 and, as the war dragged on and the demand for bodies continued, more and more of these Ukrainian Canadians were allowed to enlist. Sadly, this meant that many of them were killed or injured as well. While the majority of the names on the published lists of deaths were of English origin, Ukrainian and other Eastern European names appeared more frequently in the last years of the war.

The Reynolds were fortunate that Bobby was too young to enlist, but they had cousins in the city that were not so lucky. A nineteen-year-old nephew, the son of Mrs. Reynolds' sister, was killed by a sniper's bullet in July of that year. I had seen him once before he went off to the war, and he looked a confident, strong young man. What a useless waste of a promising life!

As it turned out, the Germans' offensive petered out. The Allies held firm and were eventually able to launch a counter-offensive with the help of newly arrived American troops.

With the Canadians playing a central role, the Allies scored a major victory at the Battle of Amiens on August 8, 1918. Mr. Reynolds marked it on his map with an exclamation mark. Although we didn't know it at the time, this turned out to be the first of Canada's glorious "Hundred Days."

Anna, Polly, and I found ourselves glued to the radio every evening, and I read everything I could on the war effort. Victory followed victory at the Second Battle of the Somme, the Battle of the Scarpe, the Battle of the Canal du Nord, the Battle of Cambrai, the Battle of the Selle, and the Battle of Valenciennes. The Canadians had a leading role in all of these battles, which cemented their reputation as a formidable fighting force. I followed each of these victories on the big map, and one day when Mr.

Reynolds caught me at it again, he exuberantly spent ten minutes pointing out the site of each victory—which was pretty easy to see as they were all marked with tape and red exclamation marks.

"Those Huns are finally learning that they bit off more than they could chew, eh girl?!"

"Yes, sir."

"They're learning about the mettle of an Englishman, hah!"

"And the Canadians too, sir," I ventured.

He looked askance at me, and I thought I was going to catch it, but all he said was, "Right you are, girl. Right you are."

As November neared, the Allies had recaptured almost all the territory the Germans had taken at the start of the war, but they had not penetrated into Germany itself. Winter was coming soon, and many of us despaired of total victory and an end to the war—we expected that the fighting would stop with the onset of winter, only to start yet again the next spring.

But we were unaware of the effect the series of Allied victories had had on the enemy's morale. Apparently, the rank and file were in despair and completely exhausted from fighting what they, too, saw as a pointless war. Much later, we learned of a serious mutiny in the German navy, and that a full-scale rebellion against the Kaiser was underway.

By early November, rumours started to circulate of an impending armistice. Our Canadian boys were actively engaged right to the very end as they pursued the retreating German army to the town of Mons, where the British had fought and lost their first battle of the war. On

November 10 and 11, the Canadians pushed the Germans out of Mons, finally liberating the townspeople who had been under German occupation for four full years.

Sadly, many Canadians lost their lives or were seriously injured in this final push.

And then, on November 11, the news came over the radio at breakfast time that the "Great" War had finally ended… on the *"eleventh hour of the eleventh day of the eleventh month."*

Polly, Anna, and I jumped up as one and hugged and hugged, all our little disagreements temporarily forgotten. Even Miss Wilson and Mrs. Murray engaged in a brief hug, after which Mrs. Murray embraced each of us girls in turn. Miss Wilson shook our hands and gave us an awkward pat on the back before excusing herself "to talk to the family."

When she returned, she said, "Mrs. Reynolds said you can all have the afternoon off to commemorate the victory. She hopes that you'll be leaving something for supper, of course," she added to Mrs. Murray.

"Yay!" we all cheered in unison.

We worked our butts off that morning and, after a quick lunch, Polly, Anna, and I headed for downtown. On the way, I stopped to pick up Bea and Helen but only found Helen. We jumped on the streetcar, everyone buzzing with joy and excitement.

As the streetcar rolled along, people in the streets waved to us and shouted, and we waved back. People were hugging each other everywhere, and smiles and tears mingled in all the faces as we rolled by.

We got off at Union Station, where a large crowd had gathered. Some people had instruments, and they blared on them as loudly as they could. Everyone shouted, and a chorus of "God Save the King" rose up.

Young soldiers seemed to be everywhere. One of them approached me and held out his two hands. I spontaneously took them, and he began to dance and sing crazily. When he tried to pull me towards him, I let go and held my arms out to push him away.

"Aw, missy, just celebrating a little. Can't you give us a little kiss?"

"Alright then," I said brazenly, "but only on my cheek."

6. Armistice Celebration
Nov. 11, 1918

Polly and Helen appeared to be scandalized, but Anna just laughed as I turned red. It was the first time I had ever been kissed by a young man. When he noticed Anna laughing, he, fortunately, turned his attentions to her, to which I was surprised to see she was only too willing to respond.

Soon an impromptu parade started up, comprised mainly of open-top cars with men waving flags. A few people who had instruments joined in, as did a lot of the soldiers. It was rather a ragtag affair, but that didn't stop it from being the greatest parade of my life.

We girls skipped along and followed the parade down Main Street. At one point, a young soldier passed around a bottle of whiskey. I had tasted whiskey before, but only with water, honey, and ginger as a cold remedy. I don't know what got into me, but I took a swig and gagged. Everyone laughed and we continued down the street, happier than we'd ever been in our short lives.

Little did we know what was soon to follow.

Chapter 10

ILLEGAL ALIENS

This is the story of my half-brother Frank's internment during WWI. I was only eleven when the war broke out and twelve when Frank was interned, and information was tightly controlled by the authorities, so I didn't understand too much of what was happening at the time.

At the outset of this history, I warned the reader that these stories are only as accurate as my memory. In this case, I suppose the story is only as accurate as Frank's memory and my memory of what he told me. However, I have bolstered it with what I discovered from various sources about really happened in those years, scant as those records were. I am confident that the story is correct in its broad strokes.

Frank and most of the internees were very tight-lipped about what transpired during those years. Fortunately, Frank and I visited the old homestead one warm August evening much later in life. We found ourselves sitting outside, watching the evening light fade away as the night sky came to life.

We couldn't help but reminisce about them days and, whether it was the comfort of the darkness or the whiskies that I kept pouring for him, Frank finally opened up and told me his story.

*   *   *

We came from the old country in a big cargo ship when I was five or six years old. I'm sure it was a cargo ship because we were jammed into a huge room with little cots laid out in rows. Nobody had a private room. There was Papa, Mama, and me; my real mother had died when I was a little boy, and I don't remember nuthin about her.

I grew up on the farm, and life must have been hard for Papa and Mama in them days. Mama was pregnant on the voyage over, and she had the baby that first summer, a little girl named Modra. I don't rightly know why, but Modra didn't make it through our first winter—all I know is that it was damn cold and food was scarce.

Mama kept havin' babies every year, and soon I had a bunch of baby sisters. There was Bea, Sophie, and Helen, before Mama finally had her first boy and Mike came along. It kinda fell to me to help Papa with all the farm work, and there wasn't much time for schoolin'. I went to school enough to learn to read and write and do my arithmetic, but that was about it.

By the time I was fifteen, jobs were good in the city, so Papa sent me there in the winter because there wasn't much to do on the farm anyway. I got a job in a steel mill feeding iron ingots into the rollers. It was hot work, but I made some good money for a while, and I learned to do a few different jobs in the mill, which stood me in good stead down the road.

In 1914, the economy wasn't too good, and I was laid off at the ironworks, although they recalled me now and then for a few weeks. Them farms around Gimli weren't any damn good, and there were oodles of young men like me coming off the farms, heading into the city looking for work.

Course, we wuz all poor and jammed into claptrap housing in the north end, while all the English lived in the posh parts in the south and west.

I remember when the war broke out in August 1914, the papers started sayin' that we were all a bunch of dangerous aliens, and somethin' had to be done about us. Now, this seemed downright strange because most of us had either been born here or had come over when we were really young, and didn't remember or care much about the old country. Our lives were here and all we wanted were decent jobs.

Papa had told me once that he had been forced to join the army in the old country. The Austrians, or some such people, had rounded up young Ukrainian boys on their farms and made them become soldiers. I think he'd spent 'bout five years in their army and, when he was discharged, he got some severance money.

I recall him once sayin' that the only good thing 'bout the army was that they gave him enough money to buy his passage to Canada and put the money down for a homestead. He wanted to get away from the old country and start a new life. But another time, he also said he learned a lot in the army about how to make things and get by.

When the war started and the papers in Winnipeg were sayin' all those nasty things 'bout us, someone got the idea that we better make it clear whose side we were on. A rally was called at the Industrial Bureau for Ukrainian men to show their support for Britain and the king. I went along, mainly because I had nuthin else to do, and thought maybe I could find out about jobs at the "Industrial Bureau."

There were a coupla fellas at the front of the room tellin' us that, with the outbreak of this war, we were in danger of being considered enemies of the king and that we'd never get jobs. They said that the purpose of the meeting was to make a declaration that we supported the British flag.

I think there were three speakers all tellin' us more or less the same thing. But it made sense. Then they started getting' us worked up.

"Do you all support the king in this war?!" they shouted at us.

"Yes," a bunch of us said or muttered.

"I didn't hear that. Do you support Britain and the Union Jack?" they shouted again.

"Yeah!" this time, it was much louder.

"One more time, people. Are you loyal to the king of England in this war?"

By this time, we were getting pumped up, and lots of us were in a mood to yell anyway, so there was loud cheering for the king.

"And do you support a public resolution that we Ukrainians support Britain in its war effort?"

"Yes!" we all cried.

A resolution was adopted, and it was sent to the governments in Ottawa and Winnipeg. *The Free Press* ran an article on it the next day, but it was buried on the tenth page. Strange to me, the article said that *"A group of Ruthenians"* had met and passed a resolution. For some reason, the press liked to call us Ruthenians, but we thought of ourselves as Ukrainians who happened to speak Ruthenian. I also heard that a group of Poles had met at Holy Ghost School on the same day as us and passed a similar resolution in support of Britain.

But all that didn't do us much good. Those were dark days indeed. We couldn't believe what was happenin' to the citizens of Winnipeg. They used to be mostly quiet, polite people, but now they were gripped by war frenzy.

As soon as war had been declared, parades were constantly springing up. Groups of British people would go marchin' down Main Street waving flags and singin' "God Save the King," "Rule Britannia," and even that French national anthem. Crowds lined the streets yelling support for the king and England. Naturally, fights were breaking out, and they usually ended up with some German or Ukrainian getting beaten up.

I managed to get a coupla weeks work at the back end of August at the ironworks, but the atmosphere wasn't so great. Guys with English names were always sayin' things like, "Do ya know which side you're on, buddy?"

The Government of Canada passed the War Measures Act around that time, under which anyone born in Austrian Hungarian empire lands were deemed to be "enemy aliens." Unfortunately, that covered most Ukrainian men in Manitoba at the time, including me.

Soon after, the comments started pilin' up.

"You know, we can lock your type up now, and ya don't get the right to a trial or nuthin, so ya'd better watch yerself."

"Hey boss, how long are we going to have to work with this enemy alien here?"

I tried to fight back. "Hey guys, I've been here since I was six years old. I'm a Canadian now."

But it didn't seem to help, and it was just a matter of time before my boss, who was a decent enough man, said, "Sorry Frank, there's not a lot of work to go round, and you don't have the right sort of last name right now."

It wasn't really a safe time to be in Winnipeg for a Bohunk, and harvest time was comin', so I headed back to the farm to help Pa. It was a poor harvest, but at least we were able to sell the bit of grain we reaped.

Later that fall, the feds passed some kind of law that all "unnaturalized immigrants" were to be considered enemy aliens, and anyone living in a city or within twenty miles had to be registered as such. I wasn't too worried because I'd been in Canada since I was a little boy, but the fact was that we'd never bothered to get my Canadian citizenship papers yet, so I wasn't "naturalized."

Starting in November, the government went around requiring all illegal aliens to register, but the farm was way outside the twenty-mile radius they had established, so Pa and I never got registered. When I went into Gimli a few weeks later, I read in the papers that some Ukrainians and other Eastern Europeans were getting arrested and put into an internment camp in Brandon.

There wasn't any work in Winnipeg, so I spent the winter on the farm, helpin' Pa fix fences, take care of the animals, and make improvements to the barn, the chicken coop, and the pig house. I went back into Winnipeg once but, as I didn't find any work, I came back home.

As spring approached, I needed to get off the homestead. Mama was always complainin' that I should be out working, and I felt trapped. I wasn't her son and we never got along real well. She also was always on top of Beatrice, tellin' her it was time for her to start working.

After I helped Pa with some spring plantin', Bea and I headed to Winnipeg in May. I found a crummy place for us to stay for a few weeks in a room in a small house in the north end. Bea had been given some contacts by some other Ukrainian girls and, luckily, she quickly found work in an English home south of the river. I wasn't so lucky.

Around the third week of May, I heard there was going to be a meeting of unemployed Ukrainians at a downtown park. So, having nuthin to lose, I headed down there early in the morning.

I can't remember the main speaker's name, but he was a real rabble-rouser.

"Let's face it, the English are prejudiced against us and aren't going to give us jobs!"

"They're all twisted up in their bloody war, and they can't see straight anymore!"

"The only thing we can do is get outta here! There's jobs in the US, and they're not at war. We gotta head south!"

All the men started nodding in agreement, saying that he made sense.

"I'm headin' for the border right now!" he yelled. "Who's with me?"

The men around me starting yellin', "Let's go, let's go!"

When I look back, I gotta admit it seems pretty stupid, but at the time it seemed to be a bright idea. I didn't have nuthin for me in Winnipeg, so why not?

A big group of us, close to 200 men I'd say, formed up and starting walkin' south. We headed down Salter Street and then headed west on Portage to avoid attracting the attention of the police and the Fort Osborne Barracks. We strung out a bit, so we weren't so obviously one big group of angry men.

We crossed the Assiniboine over the Maryland Street Bridge and were soon headin' down Pembina, leavin' the city. I don't know how we did it, but we didn't seem to attract the attention of the police or anyone who cared.

A few miles south of the city limit, I looked back and noticed some of the men were droppin' out. I'd heard a coupla 'em say things like, "Where are we going anyway?" "Do we really know if there are any jobs there? This is a dumb idea."

After we got rid of the doubters, though, we kind of coalesced into a coherent group. I fell in with another young fella by the name of Andrew.

"What kind of work are you lookin' for, Andrew?" I asked.

"I'm a railroader. Me and most of the boys here been working in railroading."

"Winnipeg should be a good place, with three railway companies."

"Yeah, you'd think so, but they laid off all of us Bohunks."

"Think it'll be any better in the States?"

"Can't be any worse. At least the Yanks don't think we're their enemy. Those British bastards have it in for us."

We'd all charged off with whatever we had on our backs. It was crazy, but I really didn't have anything in the rented dump in Winnipeg, except my shaving gear and some extra socks and underwear. Maybe Bea would go pick my stuff up and, if not, I supposed I could easily replace those things if I got a job.

It was a beautiful spring day, but after a couple of hours walkin', we started to get thirsty and a bit tired. We passed a farm that had a pump in the yard. One of the lead men went in and explained what we were up to, and soon we were all linin' up to drink water out of our hands or our hats.

That refreshed our spirits and soon we were marching along with renewed energy, singin' songs from the old country. It was soon clear that almost all of us were Ukrainians, united by our background and the simple desire to find work.

There weren't many paved roads in them days and the road was gravel. It probably wasn't very good for driving as plenty of potholes showed up after the spring thaw, but it was fine for walking. It had been raining the previous days, so it wasn't too dusty, but the gravel was a bit hard on our feet.

We made it to Ste. Agathe that night, a distance of about twenty-five miles. Most of us hadn't carried any food, so we were hungry and thirsty. There was one little general store that was fortunately still open, and we all lined up and bought what we could afford, which wasn't much. The proprietors were French Canadian and spoke

French between themselves but had enough English so we could get by. Andrew and I pooled some of our money and were able to buy a kubasa, which tasted like heaven, and washed it down with some milk.

Someone found a grassy open field near the Red River, so we all headed over there and flopped down in the grass. The river was calm, meadowlarks were calling, and I remember the most serene feeling settlin' over us as the sun set.

Andrew and I hunted along the river bank, and we found enough deadwood to build a decent-sized fire. As dusk melted into night, the men crowded around watchin' the red sparks fly into the air. Turned out that Andrew had a harmonica and was a damn good player. Soon, we were singin' more songs from the old country, some that I knew and some that I didn't.

A coupla men had small flasks of whiskey that they passed around to those of us nearest the fire. We were all beat from the long march, and soon we were drifting away, staring up into the endless night sky, wonderin' what life was all about.

*   *   *

The next morning we were all awake before the sun rose. Hundreds of birds were calling, and their songs carried strong and clear in the still dawn air. I moved my hand and it got soaked. There was a heavy dew on the grass, and we were all wet from it.

Some of the men were feeling itchy and found ticks on their bodies. We shoulda thought about that, but we were so doggone tired that we had just flopped down in the grass. Fortunately, the mosquitoes weren't out yet, or it would've been a rough night.

We had about forty-two miles to go to the border, so we kind of got organized and, after relievin' ourselves in various spots along the river, headed off. We ate the little bit of food we had leftover from the previous night and stopped at another farm to get water.

We made good time in the morning as we were refreshed from the sleep, and there was definitely strength in numbers. Walking as "comrades in arms" sure made that march a lot easier.

Around nine a.m., a car drove by us comin' from Winnipeg that had a couple of Mounties in it. They stopped near the front and asked the lead men where we were going, and then they continued on.

It turned out to be a hot day for springtime, and we started to flag after a short lunch break. My feet were swellin' and I could tell I was getting blisters. I wasn't the only one, as several other men had to stop to take care of their feet. I ended up by cuttin' some of my handkerchief and wrapping my right foot with it to reduce the rubbing.

By late afternoon, most of us were exhausted, hungry, and achin' all over. I'm sure a lot of us were questioning the wisdom of what we were doing, but a lot of the men had worked in the States previously and told us that it would be worth it.

"Down there, they don't treat you like you're scum," one man said. "Everyone is an immigrant and they don't much care if you're from England or Austria."

"Yeah, they're not like these uppity Brits who think they're better than everyone else," another said.

"What's the pay and working conditions like?" I asked.

"Depends, but it's pretty much the same as Canada."

"Someone told me the pay's not that good," I said.

"Yeah, well, what do you prefer? No job with no pay, or a job that doesn't pay that well? At least we'll be able to survive. And there's always the chance of working yer way up."

The days were long in mid-May, and it was a good thing because we needed almost the whole day to get to the border town of Emerson. Although there were a few stragglers, we managed to arrive more or less in one group.

As we filed through the town's main street, we were suddenly met by half a dozen North West Mounted Police. Four of them were in cars, and two of them were on horseback.

"Now, where do you think you're going?" one of them on horseback said.

"We're just heading down to the States to look for work," one of our men said.

"Oh yeah? And would you happen to be a bunch of illegal aliens?"

"I don't know about that, but we don't want to make any trouble. We're just looking for work, and there isn't any in Winnipeg."

"You expect me to believe that? It's more likely that you're going to meet up with some of your Kaiser friends and stir up trouble, right?"

"No sir, none of us would do that."

More of our men had come up, and there were at least 100 of us facing the Mounties at that point, with more arriving every minute. We must have looked a desperate bunch—unshaved, dirty, sunburnt—no doubt we looked like outlaws.

With more men arriving from behind, the ones at the front were being pushed forward without meanin' it.

The Mounties in the car stepped out with guns drawn, and horses appeared from a side street with more armed Mounties. Although I didn't see it, a coupla more Mounties rode up from behind, and we were suddenly surrounded.

One of the Mounties on a horse produced a bullhorn and started yelling instructions.

"None of you men are going to be allowed to cross the border! We're at war right now, and illegal aliens don't have the right to cross borders."

We all started jostling and grumbling, and again there was a bit of a push forward. In response, several of the Mounties pointed their guns at us.

"You just listen to what we tell you and no one will get hurt!" the Mountie blared again.

I looked around, and it was pretty obvious we were trapped. We were unarmed, dead tired, and had no gumption for a fight with the police.

One of our lead men raised his hands and said, "We don't want any trouble."

"That's it, you heard him," yelled the Mountie. "Now, you all raise your hands and just do what I say."

There was more grumbling, and some of the men yelled things like, "We're not doing anything wrong. You can't stop us!"

But everyone fell in line and followed their orders. They made us march back down the main street, across an open field to a pasture enclosed with a fence with an open gate.

"Now, you men go in, form lines, and sit down."

I realized that the car that had passed us in the morning had tipped off the Mounties at the border, and they had all day to plan what they were going to do with us. They also had plenty of time to bring in reinforcements on the train.

"You men must be tired and hungry," the same Mountie yelled. "So the first thing we're going to do is feed you, and then you're going to sleep in barns under armed guard."

I had to admit that they were damn clever. At that moment, most of us were dying for some good grub and a decent place to sleep. Even though we were all angry, you could feel a collective sigh run through the group. It was a sigh of giving up the fight, a sigh of relief that someone was taking care of us.

It was getting dark and they knew they had to be quick, or there'd be no stopping us from sneaking out in the dead of night and crossing the border. The lure of food was the best way to keep us from making a run for it.

When it was our turn, Andrew and I were led with a dozen or so other men to a community hall where they had a kind of soup kitchen set up. There were women ladling out stew with bread onto plates, and tables were set up for us to eat. I noticed a couple of Mounties stationed at both exits with guns.

"You've got five minutes to eat, and then you exit through the back door where you'll be taken to your posh sleeping quarters," the Mountie laughed.

Andrew and I sat and wolfed down the food—and I gotta say that it was one of the tastiest meals of my life. As soon as we were done, our plates were gathered up and quickly washed for the next group. It was a real slick operation.

After we'd finished eating, our group was escorted to a barn.

"Now, you men go on in there and have yourselves a good rest. In the morning, we'll go through your papers and decide what to do with you. And remember, there'll be guards with rifles at each door, so no funny stuff!"

It wasn't easy to see in the barn, so we just found ourselves a corner with some hay and lay down.

"What do you think they're gonna do with us?" Andrew asked.

"I don't know, and right now, I don't care." I think I was asleep in less than a minute.

*　　*　　*

The following day, we again woke at first light. The barn was full of men needing to relieve themselves, and we somehow all agreed to use the same corner. It didn't smell that great, but most of us had experienced a lot worse, growing up with animals on farms and working in hot, crowded iron mills and the like.

The Mounties were up just as early, and they soon opened the door and told us to come out in groups of ten.

When Andrew and I staggered out, we could see that they had a table set up not far away with two men sitting at it. They made us line up about ten yards from the table and then called us over one at a time. I soon got called up.

"Registration papers?" the Mountie barked.

"I don't have any."

He looked at me for a moment and then said, "Name?"

"Frank Lyszko."

"Nationality?"

"Canadian."

"Oh yeah? You look and sound like a bohunk to me."

"Okay, so I'm Ukrainian Canadian."

"That's more like it. Age?"

"It's my nineteenth birthday today."

He looked up and exchanged a grim smile with the other Mounties.

"Occupation?"

"Steelmill worker and farmhand."

"What iron mill did you work at?"

"Vulcan Steel and Ironworks."

"Address?"

"I've been bunking in a little place on Alfred street, but I was living on my father's farm near Camp Morton all winter."

While I was being questioned, the other Mountie took notes in a type of ledger. A third Mountie stood nearby with a rifle slung over his shoulder.

"So, where the hell are your registration papers?"

"I was livin' on the farm, so I didn't need to get registered. It was only folks livin' in the city or close to the city that had to register."

"You just told me that your address is on Alfred street, and you worked for Vulcan Steel. Far as I know, there ain't any steelworks out at Camp Morton."

"Well sir, it's as I told ya. When they did the registration, I was outta work and livin' on the farm. I just moved into the city a coupla days ago."

"Yeah, right."

He wrote something down next to my name, but I couldn't see what it was.

"Put him with the rest of them," he said.

They walked me around the edge of a small bank where there were a couple of other Mounties waiting.

"Hold out your hands," one of them said.

"Is this necessary?" I asked.

One of them pushed me in the back and said, "Do what you're told."

I held out my hands, and they tied them up with some rope. Then they walked me down the main street to the train station. They took me out to the platform where a Grand Pacific train with four passenger cars was waiting. They told me to board the rear car on the train, walk to a seat, and sit without getting up.

Armed Mounties stood on either side of the car.

A few minutes later, Andrew joined me, with his hands similarly bound. They repeated this process until all of us were on board. Maybe someone got away, but I don't think so.

An hour later, the train was on its way back to Winnipeg, where we were met by more Mounties. They herded us over to the Canadian Pacific Station and, without going into all the details, an hour later, we were heading west, most of us not knowing where or what for. What we did know was that we had lost our freedom.

Anyhow, that's the story of how I came to be arrested and put into an internment camp during WWI.

Chapter 11

✦

INTERNMENT

The only internment camp in Manitoba during the war was in Brandon, so I figured it was a pretty certain thing that's where we were heading. The good folks of Brandon had lobbied hard to have the internment camp situated in their city, and, sure enough, that's where we ended up.

The main thing I remember from those first days was being treated like an animal. We were herded onto the train in Emerson, poked and prodded and herded onto the train to Brandon, and then herded into the internment camp. Even our complaints sounded in my ears like so many sheep bleating.

They put us in the Brandon winter fairgrounds, which, lucky for us, was a pretty new building. It even had electric lights.

The men who were already at the camp weren't too happy to see us. Not that they had anything against us because we were all Bohunks, but it meant more crowding. I think there were close to 900 of us in that camp after our group arrived, and there were only a couple of washrooms.

It was a large building, but it wasn't meant to house anyone, never mind hundreds of prisoners. The main floor had been used mainly as a stable, along with a big central area for showing livestock. The second floor was made up of a series of rooms that had been used for meetings, conventions, and the like.

The one big convention room was converted into a giant bedroom for all of us. It was jammed full of cots right next to each other, and you often had to climb over men to get to your cot. We were essentially confined to the second floor of the building, although they let us down to the stable area to walk around twice a day.

Since the building had displayed livestock for sale, the whole place smelled like a giant barn. Only instead of cows, we prisoners were the animals in the barn.

7. Brandon Internment Camp Facility
circa 1912

Unlike the other internment camps across the country, we weren't given any work. Not that we knew it at the time, cause we weren't told a thing. I s'pose it was because the camp was situated in the heart of Brandon, and they would've considered us a danger to the local inhabitants if they let us out.

The first few weeks didn't seem so bad, maybe because of the novelty of the situation. But pretty soon life began to be pretty monotonous and, for some, unbearable.

We had nothing to do all day long, so we'd mainly sit and play cards, talk, and complain. Most everyone had similar stories.

"My brother and I were out of work back home in the old country when an agent for Canada came to recruit us. He told us that Canada welcomed immigrants, especially Ukrainians. We was only here for about eight months before we was laid off our jobs—we was told the company didn't want alien "scum" working for them anymore."

"Yeah, I know what you mean. When I first started working on the railroad, it was okay—long hours, but good pay and they treated ya decently. But once the war broke out, it was a different story. Suddenly, all of us Ukrainians were shit. We got the worst jobs, the foremen picked on us, and then we got fired."

Some of the men had been beaten up by English Canadians, and many had been arrested for no reason other than "vagrancy."

"Seems like it's a crime if you don't have a job, but they won't give you a job. Where's the justice in that?"

Every now and then, the guards would take us out in the town in shifts for a walk around the fairgrounds, which was nice, but the townspeople would gawk and yell insults at us.

"You scum don't deserve what you're getting! Our boys are in Europe fighting for Canada and you're getting free room and board! You should all be ashamed of yourselves."

We hadn't done anything to hurt them. Why did they hate us so much?

As I said, the worst thing was the feeling that you were just an animal. We had all been given numbers, and we weren't individuals anymore.

It started to affect Andrew badly.

"Frank, I don't think I can't take it much longer. I've got to escape."

"How are you going to do that? The guards are watching us all the time."

"You know when we get taken out for a walk in the town, there's a spot where we turn a corner round the building, and there's a side street right there?"

"Yeah, I think I know the place you mean."

"Look, we're strung out by that point with a couple of guards at the front and a couple at the back. As we go round the corner, the guards at the back can't see ya for a minute. I think I can make a break for it down the side street, and they won't even see me."

"That's crazy, Andrew. They have rifles, you know!"

"Look, if you don't want to come with me, you can help me. Make sure that you're at the back of the line, and just before we come to the corner, fall down and mebbe grab someone else as you fall. You'll cause a distraction, and the guards will focus on you. I'll be around the corner where they can't see me, and that'll give me my chance."

I reluctantly agreed to do it.

The next time they took us outside, it was a fine sunny day in early June, and it was good to be out of our prison. Crabapple and lilac trees were still in bloom, and we got tantalizing brief glimpses of them on the sides streets as we trudged along.

I did as Andrew had asked and made sure I was near the back of the line. There were about 100 of us in the group, walking four abreast, but we were strung out pretty good when we came to the corner where Andrew planned to make his break for it.

I pretended to stumble, fell forward, and grabbed onto the legs of a man in front of me, dragging him down as well.

This caused a minor commotion as all the men turned to look at us, and the guards behind us came up.

"What are you doing? Get up now!" they barked.

"Yes, sir. Sorry, sir, I just stumbled," I mumbled.

We heard some yelling from around the corner, and then a shot was fired.

"Jesus!" I said. And then to myself as a little prayer, "Please don't let Andrew be shot."

"Sit down now!" the guards yelled. "And put your hands on your heads."

We all sat down and did as we were told.

I looked up to see a guard with a rifle pointed right at me.

"The first one who tries any funny stuff gets it!" he yelled, looking me in the eye.

After about ten minutes, we were allowed to get up again and were quickly marched back to our quarters.

I didn't see Andrew anywhere, but the rumour quickly went around that they caught him trying to escape, and had thrown him into the "black hole."

A couple of guards came round to talk to me.

"You were helping your buddy trying to escape, weren't you?"

"No, sir," I said and hung my head.

"That weren't no coincidence when you fell. So don't lie to me!"

I was a bad liar, so I didn't say anything.

"You're lucky we only have one solitary. Otherwise, you'd be in there. But there's no food for you today."

I was lucky to get off so lightly. When Andrew got out of solitary, he told me what had happened.

"The plan almost worked, but one of the guards at the front turned to watch as we went around the corner. He saw me bolt and took a shot at me. I don't think he came close, but I turned around to see what was happening, and I ran right into some fat butcher that had stepped out into the street."

"Bad luck, eh?"

"Yeah, I fell down and twisted my ankle. By the time I got up, the guards were on top of me."

Some of the prisoners were angry at Andrew because the guards stopped taking us outside for walks. But they understood his urge to escape, and they didn't hold it against him.

Life went on, but surprising to me, Andrew's escape attempt seemed to embolden the other prisoners.

"I gotta get outta here," I heard more than one say. "I'll go crazy if I have to spend another week inside."

One Friday night, a guard got drunk and wandered into our quarters as we were playing cards. He started yelling at us and told a group of men to get up from their table. When they were slow to stand, he fired a couple of shots from his revolver into the floor at their feet.

They quickly jumped up, and the guard giggled.

"Now that's what I like to see. I speak, and you jump!"

Fortunately, a couple of other guards came running over to see what was happening.

A man named Nick was picking up the cartridges from the guard's gun.

The drunk guard pointed at him and said, "That fella was acting up and talking back."

That was a damn lie, but the guards took him and slammed him into the black hole for two days.

After they left, Andrew went back to playing his harmonica, several men sitting close and listening. Andrew was good, a sensitive soul, and was meant to be a musician or a poet. The confinement seemed to affect him a lot worse than me.

"I tell you, Frank. I don't care if I get shot. I gotta get out."

The next day, a couple of men tried to escape during the changing of the guard. They had used a table knife to loosen the putty around one of the windows so they could open it. At 9:00 p.m., they pried the window open and jumped outside, hoping they wouldn't be noticed as the guards changed up.

But ten minutes later, they were dragged back in, and each ended up spending a couple of days in the black hole.

Perhaps the guards did it on purpose, but a couple of days later, a copy of *The Brandon Sun* was passed around. Amongst a slough of statements about the dangers of "*aliens living in their midst*," the editorial stated that "*It is the duty of the authorities to punish these men so severely that others contemplating a dash for liberty will be deterred from doing so."*

Nonetheless, later that week I heard about a plot between a bunch of men who had hidden a good table knife and filed it down into a little saw. They were cutting a hole in the floor where they figured it led to the boiler room on the main floor because it was always warm there—the boiler wasn't turned on during the summer, but some of the men had been there since the winter, so they knew the spot. When Andrew heard of the plan, he was quick to join in.

I thought they were crazy, but Andrew kept at me.

"Come on, Frank. Do you want to spend the rest of your life in here?"

"Course not, but I want to have a 'rest of my life,' which I won't have if I get shot and killed. Besides, they'll let us out when this war's over."

"And who the hell knows when that'll be?"

We prisoners had precious little idea about what was going on in the outside world. Letters were allowed, but they were censored by the guards, both going in and out. I wrote a letter to Pa so my family would know where I was, but I hadn't heard back from them yet.

We weren't officially allowed newspapers, but occasionally one of the kinder guards would "accidentally" leave one around. Many prisoners couldn't read English, so normally one of the better readers, like Andrew, would read the news about the war to the rest of us.

In the spring of 1915, there had been a lot of bravado that the English and their allies would soon crush the

"Huns," but summer was coming to an end, and there was no end in sight, so we had no idea how long we might spend in prison. I think the uncertainty was as hard as anything for a lot of us—it was tough having no control over our lives. Even regular prisoners had a release date.

In the end, I agreed to try and escape with Andrew and a bunch of other men. The plotters had positioned a table over the floorboards where they were cutting a hole. They played cards in a large group in the evenings, making a lot of noise, while we took turns ducking under the table and sawing away with our little knife.

By the next Saturday, it was almost ready, and we had planned to make our break for it at 9:00 p.m. when the guards were changing. A man named George pulled out the floorboard pieces at about a quarter to nine, so we were ready to make our break.

My hands were sweating, and I was shakin' pretty bad at that point. I just couldn't stop imagining takin' a bullet in my back.

As the guards in the room started to head out, men slipped under the table and dropped to the floor below. Andrew was one of the first, and I was about the eighth man. My heart was pounding as if it were going to explode out of my chest. When it was my turn, I lowered myself down, hung for a second, and then fell as my sweaty hands slid on the wood. I crash-landed with a thump, but I didn't hurt anything.

I scrambled up, looked around, and saw some of the men who had dropped down before me, running out the boiler room door. It seemed to be going well, but then I heard a shout, and I could see guards arriving in the stabling area. One of them was knocked down by the escaping men, but there was clearly no escape that way, so I looked around and hid behind the boiler. A couple of the other men joined me.

A minute later, guards started arriving in the boiler room while a few prisoners almost jumped down into their arms, which was kind of pathetic. I had briefly hoped the guards would go chase the men who had got out and give us a chance to escape, but no such luck.

One of them looked around and yelled, "Any of you back there, come out now with your hands up, or we'll come in with our guns!"

Realizing the hopelessness of our situation, we each did what they said. We were marched out to the stable area and ordered to kneel down.

"Think we should shoot a couple to give 'em a lesson?" one of the guards barked.

"Yeah, that'd teach the bastards," answered another.

"Lookee here, this is the one that tried to help his pal escape outside."

I almost pissed myself as I was sure I would get shot in the back.

I could hear the guard step up right behind me, and I yelled, "Don't shoot!"

My back crumpled, but fortunately, it was from the butt of his rifle as he shoved me face-first into the dirt.

"Now, you just lie there like a good boy until we tell you to move."

We had our hands tied behind our backs one at a time and were eventually marched back upstairs. We were herded to a small room, where we were pushed in, and told that we'd be spending the night there. There was no furniture, so we were forced to lie down on our sides on the bare floors for the night with our hands tied up.

The next morning they got us out one at a time, took down our details, and informed us we'd each be getting a couple of days in solitary. They told us one of the men trying to escape was shot and was in the hospital, but they wouldn't say who he was.

All in all, I guess we got off pretty lightly, but I was worried sick it was Andrew who had been shot. And once we returned to our quarters, we realized that Andrew wasn't there. One of the men first down the hole said he was running across the stable floor with Andrew when the guards saw them and ordered them to stop. He stopped, but Andrew kept running, and they shot him in the back.

A deep gloom settled over the camp, and we lost all desire to escape. Our gloom deepened when we were informed about a week later that Andrew had died of his wounds.

Everything got stricter for a while, but at least we were allowed to have a mass the next Sunday, and words were said in remembrance of Andrew. But the preacher made a point of noting that good Canadian boys were dying every day over in Europe.

I can't rightly remember much for the next several months. I know that more prisoners arrived and that we were at our peak numbers in late August. We prisoners seemed to accept that we weren't going to escape, so we settled into a routine and gradually tried to make life more bearable.

Some guy started a reading club and, although I wasn't really interested, I joined just to keep busy. The organizer was a socialist, and when he could, he selected books that talked socialist ideas about equality. Lookin' back, I'm surprised that them books weren't censored because they sure got us thinking about the injustices of capitalism.

8. English Class for Ukrainians in the
Brandon Internment Camp, 1916

The same group organized some Sunday night dances and mock weddings. The local Ukrainian women donated clothes and books to us, and some of the younger guys without beards would dress as women for these events. I guess we were all badly missing the company of women, but I can't say that was much of a substitute for me.

I think that Colonel Clark, the camp commandant, felt badly about Andrew's death, and I believe he directed the guards to make life easier for us. A lot of the men were really good at carving, like Pa, and the guards provided us with wood and small carving knives. That was a real show of trust.

The carvers made a bunch of things, like necklaces and picture frames, but the most beautiful were the violins. I never did learn to carve really well, so I was mighty impressed. So were the guards, and they allowed the men to purchase strings and get their violins working.

Soon, playing our instruments, listening, and singing became our major occupations. We'd sing songs in Ukrainian, and we eventually all learned the lyrics, so it could get real loud when hundreds of us were singing in unison.

In one of our smuggled copies of *The Brandon Daily Sun*, we saw that the nearby residents complained about the noise and said prisoners should be treated like prisoners, not like they were at a whoop-up. Fortunately, Colonel Clark ignored these complaints. He seemed to understand that we needed things to do to keep us from going crazy.

One other good thing that happened was that I started to get letters from my family. I found out later that Sophie was writing them, but Pa and even Ma told her some of the things to say. Even then, Sophie had a way with words, and tears came to my eyes as she described the simple daily chores they did around the farm. I remembered that I used to grumble and complain to Ma about the things she'd tell me to do—now it seemed like paradise lost.

My reading and writing really improved while I was in prison—not that I ever became very good. But being forced to write letters and joining the reading club were good things that helped me later in life.

Despite these small mercies, time just seemed to drag, each day pretty much the same as the previous one. When I look back, I know it seemed like an eternity, but at the same time, it went by in a flash. It doesn't make sense that both those things are true at the same time, but there it is. Life is strange, innit?

*   *   *

The only other event during that time that stands out in my memory is Ukrainian Christmas. We received a lot of parcels from family members, including tobacco, apples, paper and pens, and dried fruit. I think some of the parcels contained whiskey, but the guards confiscated it for their own use.

We were allowed to celebrate Christmas with a concert, and a priest came in to say mass for the first time since Andrew had died. We even had a Christmas meal brought in to us that the local Ukrainian women had prepared. It was all very lovely and reminded us that there was another life beyond the walls of our prison and that we might be able to rejoin it one day.

For a brief time, we seemed to be humans again, but when it was over, it was back to the monotonous routine, feelin' like animals in our big closed-in barn.

The war continued to drag on during the winter of 15/16, with neither side making progress. More Canadian boys were being sent over, and, as they left, a labour shortage started to develop. The citizens of Brandon wanted to put us to work building roads and such, but the authorities didn't think it was a good idea for us to work in the town.

They agreed that it was a good idea to put us to work, just in more remote locations where we couldn't escape so easily. Unbeknownst to us, the commandant and other higher-ups were making plans for us to become more useful.

In February of 1916, about 200 men were sent to Jasper to work in the internment camp there. As spring approached, a number of men who had been farmers were released to work on area farms, on condition that they maintained good behaviour and stayed on the farms. In June, about seventy men were sent east to work on railway construction.

The camp was shutting down as men were transferred to places where they could work and contribute to the war effort one way or another. On the one hand, many of us were glad to get away from the boredom and relished the chance to be outdoors again. On the other hand, it was a harsh reminder that we had no control over our lives and could be dispatched to wherever our English masters thought appropriate.

It was strange to see men with whom I had lived and slept next to for months on end suddenly leave, with hardly time for a handshake good-bye. As I watched their backs walk out the door, it was the last I ever saw of most of them.

At the end of July, I was in the group of the last men to be sent away from the Brandon prison. About 100 of us were sent to Castle Mountain, Banff. Apparently, the Brandon camp was officially closed the next day, and for the rest of my days, I never returned there.

*   *   *

Once again, we were herded onto a train and shipped west. It was pretty incredible to arrive in the Rocky Mountains, and it might have been one of the best experiences of my life if I hadn't been a prisoner.

The train stopped briefly in Banff, but we weren't allowed to disembark and were then taken directly to Castle Mountain. It wasn't a regular stop for the train, but it stopped to let us off.

The first thing we noticed was the fresh, cool air and the delicious scent of pine trees. As we crossed the Bow River, we all stopped to stare at the shockingly clear blue water gurgling along. I'd never imagined that a river could be so pure and clean—prairie rivers were always full of sediment.

"You can drink straight outta the river," one of the guards said. "And if you want to freeze your balls off, you can jump in." He laughed.

We were driven into a stockade with a twelve-foot barbed wire fence all around it. Big canvas tents were set up in the middle of the stockade, and those were our sleeping quarters. An extra-large cook tent stood in the middle of the grounds while the guards had their separate tent outside the fence.

The very next day, we were set to work on extending the road from Castle Junction to Lake Louise. It was hard manual work, hacking out stumps, shovelling dirt and rocks all day, and hauling the waste off to the side and dumping it in the bushes.

One of the men who was already there when we arrived from Brandon, a guy by the name of Peter, said, "You guys have it lucky. This year we have a steam shovel. Last year we did everything by hand."

The steam shovel was clearly a great help as it could dig and pull up roots and stumps in a fraction of the time that it would have taken us to do it by hand.

At the end of the day, I was dog tired and had a headache.

Peter said, "It's your first day here. The altitude is getting to you, but you'll get used to it in no time."

He was probably right, but the fact was that we men from the Brandon camp hadn't done any labour in a year, and our bodies weren't used to it. All I know is that I had one of the best sleeps of my life that night.

We were told that we would be paid twenty-five cents a day for our labour and we could spend three dollars a month in the canteen on things like cigarettes. The rest of the money would be held and given to us on discharge if we stayed on good behaviour. If we tried to escape or anything, we would forfeit our wages.

"Bah!" Peter exclaimed. "Don't believe they're ever going to pay youse!"

9. Internees Leaving Castle Mountain Camp
Summer 1916

I wasn't sure what to expect. Things between the prisoners and the guards had improved over the last six months in Brandon, and the guards here didn't seem so bad.

When I said this to Peter, he said, "Last year they used to hang us by the wrists for nothing!"

"For nuthin?"

"They called it 'insubordination,' but it was usually next to nothing," he said.

Most of us who had come from Brandon were ready to work reasonably hard, but the men who had been there for a year told us to take it easy.

"They'll work ya to death if ya let 'em," Peter said.

We weren't used to the hard work anyway, and we had to work six days a week, ten hours a day, so we learned to pace ourselves.

The weather in August was pretty nice, although I was surprised at how cool it got at night, which was okay because it was good for sleeping.

"Just wait till October comes. You'll freeze your asses off," Peter said.

Peter kept talking about escaping, but after what had happened to Andrew, I wanted no part in that. The others who had come from Brandon were of the same mind, but not the men who had been at the camp when we arrived.

"You know, these guards either can't shoot, or they don't really want to hit us. Every time someone makes a break for it, the guards shoot at us, but they've never hit anyone. It's worth taking the chance," Peter said.

Sure enough, the men made a number of escape attempts but were usually caught soon afterwards. One day, Peter and two others tried to make a break for it, simply by running into the bush when the guards weren't looking. A couple of guards saw them and fired. Peter was shot in the leg and fell over. The other men stopped running and were caught.

Peter was screaming blue murder like he was dying, but fortunately the bullet hadn't hit anything fatal. He was taken to the hospital in Banff, and we didn't see him until the end of October.

Just like in Brandon with Andrew, after Peter was shot, the men settled down and stopped trying to escape. We worked at a pretty slow pace, but we worked steadily, so the guards let us be. It was as if we had reached an unspoken truce. We wouldn't try to escape, and in turn, the guards wouldn't push us too hard.

Peter sure was right about freezing our asses off when October came. Growing up north of Winnipeg, I was used to the cold, but the tents we were sleeping in had no heat. We had to sleep with our coats on, and we were pretty grubby all the time. Any water left out would freeze overnight, so we had to go down to the river to get running water to wash in—and that water was always damn cold.

By early November, the days were getting shorter, and it took us an hour to walk to and from the worksite. The ground was frozen, so it was almost impossible to get any work done. Eventually, the superintendent saw that it was pointless to continue, so we spent a few days cleaning up the camp, and in mid-November we were packed off to the winter quarters at the Cave and Basin in Banff.

Most of us were happy to get into quarters with heating after the bitter cold of the tents. Peter was back from the hospital and told us that things were much better this year than the previous winter. Then, there had been almost 100 more men, and they had apparently been packed together like dead fish, but now we had adequate space between our cots, and they had even freed up a separate room for reading and playing cards.

"Luxury!" Peter exclaimed when he saw it.

The previous year had been bitterly cold and the men hadn't done much work, but it was milder this winter, so the authorities had us out working almost every day. But they say that a change is almost as good as a rest, and as we were given a number of different tasks, it didn't seem so bad.

The town used us as its handymen to do all the odd jobs it wanted to get done. We did a bunch of brush clearing at the Banff recreation grounds and spent a lot of time cutting timber and sawing logs for firewood. We did some road straightening on Tunnel Mountain Drive and worked on the road to Bow Falls.

The coolest job was building an ice palace with an interior maze for Banff's winter carnival. It was an amazing piece of ice art, over twenty feet tall in the centre, and I believe we all took some pride in it when it was done. I'll always remember looking up at it, gleaming in the sun, with Mount Rundle in the background.

The other luxury those of us who had been on good behaviour were permitted was the use of the Cave and Basin hot pools on off-hours when it was closed to the public. The authorities accepted that we needed to wash from time to time to prevent the spread of disease and the hot pools were right there.

Ice Palace at Banff, Alberta: built by interned aliens. 1916-17

10. Ice Castle Built in Banff by Internees

Soaking our tired bodies in the hot water on a cold winter's day was a treat like no other!

It wasn't all fun and games though. In Brandon, almost all the prisoners had been Ukrainians, and the remainder were mainly Poles and other Eastern Europeans. None of us had anything fundamentally against each other, and we all got along.

In Banff, though, there were a good number of German prisoners, although they were in the minority. I never understood exactly what went on, but a lot of them had been excused from regular work duties as "prisoners of war." Someone told me that the Canadian government believed it had to treat prisoners of war according to some international convention, but that it could do what it wanted with us "illegal aliens."

Not surprisingly, that didn't sit well with us Ukrainians. As far as we could see, the Germans had started this bloody war and were responsible for getting us into this horrible mess. And then they were excused from hard labour because they were prisoners of war. As Peter said, "What kind of bullshit is that?!"

Tempers sometimes flared, and, more than once, a couple of the Germans ended up taking a beating. Some of the guys didn't take to a Romanian guy, and he took a licking as well. He asked to be given protection from the rest of us and was put in a different building. He must have been in a pretty bad way because he slit his own throat on Christmas Eve.

I think that shook everyone up pretty badly. The guards put the Germans in separate quarters, but they also noted who the troublemakers amongst us were.

The authorities seemed to realize that things were tense, so they gave us holidays on Ukrainian Christmas and Ukrainian New Year, but there was no big dinner or anything like we had in Brandon the previous year.

* * *

The war machine in Europe kept calling for more men. As a result, by the spring of 1917, there were serious labour shortages in Canada. Apparently, the railways and some factories and mines were asking if they could get us prisoners to work for them.

In April, the Canadian Pacific Railway came and scooped up over 100 of us to work on railroad projects, and I was one of them. We all had to sign papers that said we would be faithful to Canada and the king, that we would work for at least a year for the railway, and that we would obey all laws. We also had to report monthly to local police authorities to show that we were living up to the terms of our "release."

As things turned out, working for the railroad wasn't that much better than being in prison. Our wages were painfully low, the work was long and hard, and we didn't have much freedom because we were shuffled from one work camp to another at the CPR's whim. Still, we were never locked behind barbed wire, had some money, were free to write letters, and do what we wished on days off. But that didn't mean much because we were usually working in some camp in the middle of the BC bushland.

Afterwards, I heard that the Banff internment camp was completely shut down in July of 1917. The last job the men had been working on was an extension of the Banff Springs Golf Course.

I also heard that many of those men weren't released and were sent to another internment camp somewhere in northern Ontario. For sure, I didn't envy them, even if most of them were apparently Germans.

When I look back, I can see that we prisoners were thrown together into a situation where we were as close or closer than we'd be with anyone in our lives. We ate, worked, and slept side by side under tough conditions day after day. We had had no choice in this.

Then we were suddenly thrown apart, and with the exception of a few, I never saw or heard of those men ever again. We had no choice in that either.

At the same time, if someone asks me today what the best time in my life was, the first image that comes to my mind is lying on the banks of the Red River with

150 other men, dog tired, listening to the plaintiff notes of Andrew's harmonica drift along the still evening air.

*   *   *

So that's Frank's story of being interned during WW1. The only time he really talked to me about it was on that beautiful August night. Otherwise, it seemed that it was something he'd rather just be forgotten… as if it had never happened.

Chapter 12

———✦———

THE "SPANISH" FLU

When we first heard of the Spanish flu, it was largely ignored by most of us. After all, when the initial reports came through in the fall of 1918, Canadian boys were fighting valiantly and dying horrifically as they brought WWI to a close.

So when I saw a piece in *The Telegraph* about how a type of influenza was killing thousands of people in Spain, it didn't make much impact on me. After all, Spain was a long way away, and I had never met anyone from Spain in my life.

Of course, the truth is that by the end of the war, we knew the flu was terrible and we knew it was almost certainly coming. But few of us, if anyone, was really prepared.

What is it about the human psyche that denies the danger in these situations? Is it because the danger is unseen? Is it because it is only hypothetical before it actually arrives? Or, in our case, was it because we had endured so much suffering during the war that our minds refused to believe that anything as bad as the war could be coming along?

In any event, as the greatest slaughter in human history was coming to an end, our government decided it had not had enough of war. There were fears that the Bolshevik Revolution in Russia could spread and that it should be contained before it threatened other bastions of free enterprise. Accordingly, a Canadian Siberian Expeditionary Force was formed that eventually sailed from Vancouver to the port of Vladivostok, with the idea that it would help the White Army defeat the Bolsheviks.

A train carrying soldiers from Eastern Canada for this "expedition" arrived in Winnipeg at the end of September. Unfortunately, some of the soldiers carried the flu with them. Although they were immediately quarantined in a hospital, within a few weeks, several cases of the flu were reported in the community.

The authorities reacted swiftly—the schools and universities were closed, and public meetings of more than six people were banned. But, for whatever reason, these measures were not enough to stop the spread of the worst pandemic in modern history.

No doubt the spontaneous parade that took place on November 11 didn't help matters, but by that time the flu already had the city in its grip. I'll never forget the events that followed that brief day of exultation.

One morning, Miss Wilson addressed us at breakfast.

"From now on, you girls will have to wear these masks whenever you are in the Reynolds' house," she said, pulling a number of white medical masks out of a bag.

"Why, is anyone sick?" asked Anna.

"No, no one is sick yet," she responded. "But these masks will help ensure that you don't spread any germs if you get the flu. And it will help protect you if any of the family members get it."

"Are the Reynolds' wearing masks too?" I asked.

"Don't be silly, girl. They're not going to wear masks in their own home. And further, you won't be doing any reading with Sally from this point on."

"So they're afraid we'll give them the disease?!"

"Sophie, everyone's afraid right now," she said.

"Since the Reynolds won't be having guests in the near term, you only have to give the reception and entertainment rooms a quick dusting," she added.

"Thank God for small mercies," Anna replied.

The next couple of days, we went about our duties as quickly and quietly as possible. The Reynolds' children were home since the schools were closed, but we were told to interact with them as little as possible.

I ran into Bobby in the upstairs hall the next day.

"Well, well," he smirked. "I can't say that mask does you any harm. Gives you a little air of mystery, eh?"

"Excuse me, sir," I said as I quickly passed by.

When I stopped by Sally's room, she jumped up when she saw me. "Oh goody, are you going to read with me now?" she asked excitedly.

Mrs. Penner was sitting with her at the desk, also wearing a mask. "I'm afraid she can't, Sally. Not at least until this flu is over."

"How silly," Sally said. "Of course I'm not going to get that flu!"

However, the next day I heard coughing coming from her room when I was cleaning the bathroom. When I tried to go into her room, I was met by Miss Wilson.

"I'm sorry, Sophie, you can't go in. She needs rest," she said.

I looked at her, the masks unable to cover the fear in our eyes.

"Yes," she said, responding to my unspoken question. "It looks like the flu."

That night as we took supper in our quarters, we whispered to one another.

"The doctor came this afternoon."

"I don't think it looks good."

"I heard Mrs. Reynolds crying! Can you believe it? That woman actually crying?"

"What do you think'll happen?"

"Who knows? She's in God's hands now."

"Aye, she's in God's hands," said Mrs. Murray. "And we should all say a prayer for her now."

Mrs. Murray reached out her arms, and the four of us, including Polly, Anna, and me, held hands. I don't remember the exact words she used, but it was something like this:

> "Dear Jesus, our beloved shepherd,
> Ever caring, ever watchful over your flock,
> One of your lambs is lost and sick,
> She is innocent and in need of your healing love.
> Dear Jesus, comforter of souls
> Please hear our prayer for your little lamb,
> And spare her so that she may live out her days
> And honour your grace with good works.

Our Lord Jesus Christ, amen."

I burst out sobbing as soon as the prayer ended.

"Now, now, Sophie," Mrs. Murray said. "We all need to be strong at a time like this."

I wiped my eyes and nodded, but I just couldn't believe that Sally might be dying.

That night for the first time in a long time, I prayed to God. I'm not sure how pure my prayers were, as I always had difficulty believing in God.

"God, if you really exist and you really are a god of love, then prove it and save Sally!"

I don't think that's how you're supposed to pray, but at the time, that was the only way I knew how.

11. Winnipeg Free Press Paper Boys with Masks
October, 1918

The next day I was cleaning in the sitting room when Mrs. Penner saw me.

"Sophie, please come with me. Sally wants to see you."

I followed her into Sally's room, which smelled dank.

Sally was propped up on pillows in her bed, and looked only half-alive. Her hair lay in disheveled wet strands, seemingly glued to her pillows. Her eyes were hollow, and they glistened with fever.

Mrs. Reynolds sat in a chair by her bedside, holding her hand.

When she saw me, Sally started and managed a half-smile. She tried to sit up and call my name, but a coughing fit overtook her, and she collapsed back onto her pillow. The coughs racked her body for a couple of horrible moments, and then she rasped for breath, wheezing and wheezing.

Finally, she seemed to get her breath back, and she whispered, "Hi, Sophie. Come here."

I looked at Mrs. Penner and Mrs. Reynolds, and they both nodded. I approached the bed, and Mrs. Reynolds stood up and motioned for me to take her place in the seat.

I sat down, and Sally reached her hand out to me. I hesitated ever so slightly, and then I took it in mine. It was hot and clammy.

"How are you?" she asked in a whisper.

It was all I could do to stop myself from crying and forced a little smile.

"I'm fine, thank you," I managed.

"Strong and wise, just like Lizzie Bennett, eh?" she smiled weakly.

She was tearing me apart. She was always fun and enthusiastic, if a little silly. But at this moment, she was a sage and I was the little girl.

"I don't think so," I responded. "But I can always try."

"Sophie, if I die, you won't forget me, will you?"

She spoke this in the most straightforward manner, with no pleading or whining. She just wanted to know.

"Of course I'll never forget you, Sally," I said, squeezing her hand. "But don't talk like that!"

She smiled and started to say, "We had some good…" when she was interrupted by another coughing spell and wrenched her hand away from me. It went on longer than the last one, and she had even more difficulty getting her breath back. She tried to speak again, but an awful gurgling sound came out of her chest.

I looked at her in despair as I took her hand back in mine. The colour drained from her face, and she turned a faint hue of blue.

At that point, a nurse entered the room, and I was asked to move away.

"Good-bye, Sophie," Sally said as she gave my hand a last weak squeeze.

I squeezed back and patted her hand as I fought to hold in my tears.

"Get better, and I'll see you soon," I managed to whisper.

"You should go now," Mrs. Reynolds said, not unkindly.

Later that night, we got the news via Miss Wilson that Sally had passed away.

I cried into my pillow until Anna stood up and hugged me.

"She's in heaven now," she said softly. "Please don't cry anymore."

I realized I was keeping her awake, and I forced myself to calm down.

"What kind of god kills innocents?" I asked myself again and again. "It's just not fair."

*   *   *

The next morning when I got up, Miss Wilson, Mrs. Murray, and Polly were already in the big house preparing breakfast for the family. Anna was still in bed and whispered to me that her throat was sore and asked if I could please make her a cup of tea with some honey.

"Oh no!" I thought. "Please don't let Anna get sick too!"

I got dressed and went into the kitchen, poured some water into the kettle, and grabbed a match to light the gas stove. I turned the dial on the front burner, struck the wooden match against the side of its box—and BOOM!

The next thing I knew, I was looking up from the floor on the other side of the room with Anna looking over me—or what seemed through my eyes to be three Annas.

Her mouth was moving, and she was obviously saying something, but I couldn't hear her.

"What happened?" I mumbled.

I could see Anna's mouth moving again, but all I heard was ringing in my ears and a muffled sound.

In actuality, she was screaming, "Oh my God, you're alive! You're alive!"

I tried to sit up, but the room spun so badly that I put my hand up against Anna's chest and lay back. She must have understood because she gently placed my head on the floor. Her mouth moved again, and she disappeared for a moment before returning with a pillow for my head. I let myself fall back into the pillow and closed my eyes, sensing nothing but the continued ringing in my ears.

To make a long story short, the gas hadn't been properly turned off by either Mrs. Murray or, more probably, Polly. In them days, gas was odorless, and you couldn't smell it. The gas had probably been slowly filling the room after they went to breakfast in the big house, and it was just waiting for me to light a match and almost blow myself to Kingdom Come.

Amazingly, apart from temporary hearing loss, I seemed to be fine. I had been literally blown across the room against the opposite wall, but I hadn't hit anything sharp, and nothing had hit me. Anna had gone to get Miss Wilson and, after they checked me out, Anna cleaned me up with a damp cloth and they put me back to bed.

A doctor was fetched, and he duly checked me out. He decided that I had had a very lucky escape and that all I needed was rest in a dark room until my head felt better. I suspect that I had a concussion, but they weren't diagnosed in them days.

I must have fallen asleep because the next thing I remembered, I was lying in bed, with the afternoon light filtering through the window, reflecting on the events of the last twenty-four hours. Two days ago, Sally had been a healthy, happy young girl with her whole life in front of her, and by the end of the day yesterday, she was dead. And, except for Providence, good luck, or fate, just that morning, I had woken up totally fine and could have easily been killed in a flash.

Was that it then? Our lives were nothing of importance and could be extinguished at a moment's notice? Did we live or die according to God's whim? If so, once again, I thought, what kind of cruel god was that? Was there any reason I was spared and Sally was not?

At that moment, lying in the darkness of our bedroom alone, the stories of so many of the veterans became much more real. How many of the returned men had recounted stories of their comrades falling by their sides while they were somehow miraculously spared? I got a glimpse now of how they must have felt and of some of the guilt that must seep into their souls. Lord, why not me?

The randomness of it all was incomprehensible.

*   *   *

Sally's funeral was a simple affair, held at an Anglican church. People were not supposed to congregate in groups, and this applied to funerals as well as all other gatherings. The number of people at the funeral far exceeded the rules laid down by the city, but the church was still fairly empty, and people spaced themselves apart from one another.

I had recovered sufficiently to attend, but I found it was really difficult as Sally was like a sister to me. I tried to hold myself together, but at one point, I couldn't contain myself, and I broke down until Anna whispered to me that Sally wouldn't want to see me unhappy.

Mr. and Mrs. Reynolds had had a reception prepared at their house, but almost everyone begged off.

"What a horrible disease! People aren't even allowed to mourn properly," I said to Anna.

I don't think the servants had been intended to come as guests, but Mrs. Reynolds came and asked us to please join the family. I think she needed to have some people around to provide a feeling of a true ceremony in honour of Sally. It was the saddest affair I ever attended.

*   *   *

Over the next few weeks, thousands and thousands of people contracted the flu, and hundreds died in the city every week. Macabrely, it preyed on young and healthy people.

The city had quickly gone into a lockdown, and all restaurants and places of entertainment had been immediately closed. It didn't make much difference to us servants as we normally didn't go anywhere anyway. But on the short walks I took, it was strange to see people crossing the sidewalk as I passed—they often waved or said "hi" to show that it was not personally directed against you.

There were stories in the newspapers and on the radio of hundreds of women who had formed a volunteer society and were spending their time helping the sick, at risk to their own health.

The sickness and death toll was much worse in the north end, where all the Eastern European and Jewish immigrants huddled together. Many of them still had to work to earn their daily bread, and they were forced into crowded conditions both at work and at home. Just like the war, it was mainly people from poorer families who died. Sally was a sad exception.

*   *   *

Over 1000 people died in the city in the month of November, and it seemed no family was completely untouched. However, as Christmas approached, the number of new cases dropped off suddenly. We had no clear idea why but it seemed as if the pandemic was ending in the city as suddenly as it had started.

I had been given an entire week off at Christmas, so on the 21st, on a bitterly cold day, I found myself on the train back to Gimli. Papa came to get me even though it was below minus thirty degrees Fahrenheit and there was a biting wind from the north.

He had two horses hitched to the cart, which was highly unusual and, also unusual, they had blankets draped over them and cinched underneath their bellies. I saw that he had the sleigh, which slid over the snow much more easily than a cart's wheels would turn.

"No one should be out in this weather, malenka kit. Even the horses can freeze if they're out for too long."

We stayed at the same cousin's house that we had used when I moved to Winnipeg because it was too cold to try and make the trip in one go.

The next morning, we headed out right after breakfast. Unfortunately, the weather had not improved. Papa had brought several extra blankets, and we piled them under, around, and over ourselves. Even so, it was a bitter ride back, and I was losing the feeling in my feet when we were still a few miles from home.

"Papa, I think my feet are freezing."

He pulled the sleigh over and came to a stop.

"Here, let me have a look."

He bent down and slowly pulled off my boots and my socks.

"We need to warm them up," he said.

He lay down on the floor on his back, opened his coat, and placed my feet on his bare stomach.

"Papa! You don't need to do that! You'll freeze."

"Don't worry about me, malenka kit. We need to do this."

He wrapped the blankets around my legs and covered himself so that my feet were completely protected.

"Papa, don't freeze yourself."

"Just tell me when you can start to feel some warmth coming back into your feet."

After about seven or eight minutes, I did feel my toes again, although the pain was horrendous as the blood seeped back in.

"Yes, yes, I feel my feet again," I said, trembling from the pain and the penetrating cold.

"Okay, good. A couple of more minutes, and we'll be on our way."

I was gasping and tears were flowing involuntarily down my cheeks, freezing on my skin as my feet slowly warmed. After his promised few minutes, Papa put my boots back on but did them up loosely so as not to constrict the blood flow, and we recommenced our journey.

The days were at their shortest, so night had fallen by the time we started up again, and the stars progressively came out as we slid along. Our breath froze in the air as soon as it escaped our mouths, and when I had to spit once, I'm sure it froze before it reached the ground.

Despite the bitter cold, the night sky was awe-inspiring. There was as of yet no moon, but the brilliance of the stars and the reflective power of the snow provided more than enough light for the horses to see their way.

Here and there, we could see lights peeking out from farmhouses. This comforted me as I knew we could stop at any of them if need be. But we somehow managed to make it home, Papa depositing me in front of the house while he went to stable the horses in the barn.

When I staggered in the front door, I was overwhelmed by the children. Mike and John gave me quick, perfunctory hugs, as befitted their impending manhood, but with real warmth in their smiles. Annie and Nicholas clambered on me, squealing with delight.

"Sophie, Sophie, it's so wonderful that you're back!" they exclaimed in unison.

Mama came and gave me a big hug and said that it was nice to see my face again. The stove crackled with heat, but it was nothing compared to the warmth emanating from my family.

Soon Papa came in with my bags, and Nicholas started singing, "What did my big sister bring for me? What did my big sister bring for me?"

I always brought candies and little treats that were hard to come by in Gimli, and soon I was placing them on the table, to all the children's delight. In them days we didn't know about dental hygiene and the problems with sugar, so I watched them happily stuff themselves.

Nicholas noticed that I had some other bags.

"Sophie, Sophie, do you have more presents in there?" His eyes shone with excitement.

"Maybe I do, but you'll have to wait till Christmas to find out."

*   *   *

As Ukrainians, we would normally have celebrated Christ's birth during Ukrainian Christmas, which followed the orthodox calendar, and would be twelve days later. However, we had no orthodox churches close by, and the Roman Catholic priests all observed Christmas on December 25. Besides, our English employers observed Christmas at the same time, so we didn't bother fighting back.

In any event, we didn't make such a big fuss about Christmas in them days, other than it being a time for the family to get together. Beatrice and Helen had both also got the time off and came back the day after me, so the whole family was together again, except for Frank, who was working for the railroad out west. Fortunately, a neighbour had been able to fetch them from Gimli, and the weather had warmed up considerably, so they didn't have to deal with the same death-defying ride back that Papa and I had faced.

On Christmas morning, we managed to bundle into the sleigh for the ride to church, the kids all sitting on top of one another. Nicholas sat on my lap, and Annie snuggled up close to me under a blanket on my left.

"You boys are all growing like weeds!" I said as I bounced Nicholas on my knee, and he poked Annie.

"I'm as tall as you now," said Mike, who was now twelve and looked like he'd be the tallest in the family.

"It's so nice to have you here, Sophie," Annie smiled and gave me a hug.

Annie was the warmest and most affectionate of us children. Beatrice was always more reserved, and I suppose I was somewhere in between. I suppose I was an observer of life, but at times like this, I'd get caught up in the moment and forget my analytical side.

I looked at Annie, her perfectly smooth skin, pink cheeks glowing in the winter chill.

"You're so beautiful," I told her and hugged her back while Nicholas blew a raspberry.

It was difficult for the young ones to sit through the mass, but I believe they were a bit awed by the Latin liturgy, and especially by the incense pouring out of the thurible as the priest walked up the aisle and swung it from side to side. Just as I had when I was younger, I saw Nicholas's eyes open wide as clouds of pungent smoke poured out of it.

After the service, there were a lot of greetings and hugs with neighbours who had all been cooped up in their homes, sheltering from the bitter prairie winter. Then it was off back home, everyone's stomachs growling in anticipation of the feast to come.

The stove was blazing, and the new house was warm, with all of our bodies heating it up. While Mama, Bea, Helen and I finished getting Christmas dinner ready, Papa played songs on his fiddle and the young children played on the floor.

Soon we started bringing out the dishes. The centrepiece was a roast ham that had been smoked in the chimney earlier that fall. The boys' eyes shone at the sheer size of the pork leg, glistening with its fat juices. Next came the holubtsi, potatoes, and buckwheat wrapped in cabbage leaves and covered with gobs of homemade sour cream—heaven on earth!

And of course, we had that most well-known of Ukrainian dishes, perohe (perogies), covered in bacon bits, fried onions, and more sour cream. We also had a mound of fried cabbage with more bacon bits, drenched in homemade butter. Next, the hot bread came out of the oven, delicious with or without butter or sour cream.

After lunch, I pulled out the rest of my "presents." The most important were two fruit cakes filled with nuts and dates. I had things like dice and cards, and a cribbage board for the boys—I would have to teach them how to play—and a little alphabet book for Nicholas to help him get on his way to reading.

Bea and Helen had also brought various knickknacks and sweet treats, so we had plenty of dessert to snack on all afternoon.

A couple of our closest neighbours came by on their sleighs for a visit and some Christmas cheer. Although Papa wasn't much of a drinker, he did keep a bottle of whisky on hand to offer guests. I saw that they helped themselves to it liberally and made a mental note to get a bottle for Papa the next time I came back (although I would have to get Mrs. Murray to buy it for me).

In the late afternoon, we all went out with Papa and walked around as he fed the animals, gave them water, and made sure everything was in order. The cows had been let out into the corral in the morning because it wasn't such a cold day, but we herded them back into the barn for the night. Papa had more cows now than ever before, and I was pleased to see that he seemed to be doing well.

All in all, it had been a perfect day and the happiest time we had ever had together as a family.

*   *   *

It started the next afternoon when Nicholas suddenly coughed loudly. Everyone turned their heads and looked at him.

"Are you feeling alright?" Mama asked.

"I don't know," he answered. "I think I have a sore throat."

We all looked at each other anxiously as Mama went over to him and put a hand on his forehead.

"Hmm, you're a bit hot. You better lie down."

"But I don't want to go to bed. I want to be here with everyone."

I glanced around, and I could see everyone was thinking the same thing—if he has the Spanish flu, he should be isolated.

"I think it's best if you go to our bedroom," Mama said. "You can lie down on our bed, and I'll leave the door open so you can hear everyone."

Mama soon had him lying down, snuggled in with some blankets. But it wasn't long before he was coughing more and more regularly.

An hour later, Annie started to cough.

Mama insisted that she lie down in the other bedroom, and soon she was also ensconced in bed. The older children—Bea, Helen, Mike, John, and I—all looked at each other, dread staring out of one another's eyes.

Fifteen minutes later, John started to cough.

"No, no, please no!" I cried to myself. "Don't let this be happening."

By the time our little supper was over, there were four sick children in the house—Nicholas, Mike, Annie, and John. For some reason, the oldest of us, Bea, Helen, and I, were all fine.

Why was that? Was it because we had been exposed to it in Winnipeg and had either already fought it off, or were the three of us immune? Was it possible that one of us had brought the disease into the house? Oh God, was it possible that I had brought this horrible disease to my family?

Papa and Mama tried to force the three of us, who seemed to be fine, to go to sleep upstairs. Normally no one slept upstairs in this house, and the room there was just an attic, but it was warm enough with the heat that rose from below. Bea protested, saying she wouldn't be able to sleep and wanted to help.

Mama finally relented and said that Bea's help would be enough, and I'm ashamed to say that I readily consented. It wasn't that I was afraid to help; it was that I knew it would break my heart to watch my brothers and sister suffering. I didn't think I could take it. But I don't know which was worse, actually watching them or imagining their suffering as I tossed and turned while listening to their coughing through the long dark night.

The following day all four of them were worse, but no one else was sick. They all seemed to be having difficulty breathing, a sure sign it was the Spanish flu.

Mama let us go into their bedrooms, and I sat with Annie for a long time, holding her hand, staring at her beautiful face, flushed red not from the cold this time but from a ferocious fever. After coughs racked her body, I couldn't help but bend forward and hold her close to me.

"Don't, Sophie, you might catch it," she whispered.

"Annie, don't worry about me. I won't get it."

She tried to speak again, but she wheezed and gasped, and no words came out. I squeezed her hand tightly, and she closed her eyes.

A couple of minutes later, she re-opened them after seemingly seeking the strength to speak. Her eyes shone with a supernatural brightness.

"Sophie, will you promise me one thing?"

"Yes, Annie, anything."

"If I die, will you always say a prayer for me each year on the day I died?"

Tears welled up in my eyes, and it took all my strength not to sob.

"Of course, Annie, but don't talk like that. No one's going to die."

She squeezed my hand and whispered, "Thanks, Sophie. I knew I could count on you."

Before I could say anything else, I heard the front door opening and closing and loud voices. In a minute, Mama came tramping in with two nuns from St. Mary's convent.

"Can you leave us for a moment, please," they directed me.

I looked at Annie, and she nodded weakly. I gave her hand another squeeze and left the room. A few minutes later, Mama and the nuns came out and visited each of the sick children in turn.

"I'm afraid it doesn't look very good," said the older and larger of the two. "We'll have to take all four to the hospital in Gimli."

"But it's too cold for them to travel," Mama said. "They'll freeze."

After a few days of respite, the bitter cold had returned.

The same nun dropped her voice. "If they stay here, they'll die. It's best that we take them to the hospital where they can be properly treated."

"No, I'm not going to let you take the children. They won't even make it to the hospital," Mama hissed.

The nuns argued and argued, saying that if the children died, it would be on her conscience and that Jesus would be the witness to her sin.

"That's not fair," I blurted out. "Mama just wants what's best for them!"

"Hush, Sophie," Papa said. "Let us sort this out. You three girls go upstairs until we settle this."

I wanted to argue, but Papa had spoken quietly and firmly. He rarely gave us orders, but when he did, we knew he was serious, and we always obeyed him. The three of us climbed upstairs and listened to the conversation as best we could.

We heard the discussion go on for about ten minutes, after which it seemed a decision had been made.

"I'm going to see what they've decided," I said.

Bea tried to stop me, but I shrugged free and clambered down the stairs. Papa was in the kitchen.

"Well?" I asked.

"We decided that Annie and Nicholas will go with the sisters to the hospital. They're younger and may need oxygen or something that they can get at the hospital. We're keeping Mike and John here. Hopefully, they'll be able to fight it off on their own."

And so it was that ten minutes later, Annie and Nicholas were bundled and propped up in the kitchen. We each gave them a hug good-bye in turn and wished them well, everyone saying that they would get better soon.

"Thanks, Sophie," Annie said. And in a whisper in my ear, "I love you, big sister."

Papa had gone outside to hitch one of his horses to the nuns' sleigh so it would be faster. He came back and helped the nuns escort first Annie and then Nicholas to the sleigh, where they were wrapped up as well as possible. In a minute, the sleigh was sliding away from the house and out to the road.

The nuns couldn't make it to Gimli that day, so they told us they would stop at Camp Morton, where they promised they would take good care of the children before going on to Gimli the following morning.

We passed another horribly anxious night in the farmhouse. We didn't have a phone in them days, so we had no way of knowing how Annie and Nicholas were doing.

Thank God, if I can use that expression, Mike and John were a little better in the morning.

It was time for me to go back to work while Bea and Helen had two more days off. After a very early breakfast, Papa hitched up the cart, and I said good-bye to everyone and hugged the boys tightly. Papa and I hardly spoke on the long, grim ride back to Gimli. We were both consumed with dread while clinging to hope.

The sleigh flew across the snow on our journey as conditions were perfect. Indeed, when the snow was just right, it was faster to travel by cart in winter than in summer because the snow offered far less friction and made the horses' job a lot easier.

However, as we approached Gimli in darkness, I had the sense that Papa slowed down as if he was anticipating bad news and wanted to delay it as long as possible. When we finally arrived and entered the reception area at the hospital, we were told to wait a moment while they fetched the doctor. As soon as he emerged, we could tell it wasn't good.

He told us that Annie and Nicholas had both died earlier that day, within hours of arriving at the hospital, suffering from pneumonia and unable to get enough oxygen into their bodies.

Tears welled up in Papa's eyes, and I burst out sobbing as we fell into each other's arms. I don't know how long we clung to each other, but Papa was the first to get control of himself. He apologized to the doctor and asked if we could see them.

The doctor, who was young, said that wouldn't be possible right away because they had died of an infectious disease. Although Papa was shaken to his core, he suddenly showed a resolve of steel.

"Young man," he said. "We have been with my children for the last few days, and they all have this flu. We've already been exposed, and we are not leaving until we see them."

The doctor hesitated, but whether it was something in Papa's eyes or the logic of what he said, he relented. He told us we would have to wait a bit, but that he would bring us in as soon as he could.

About fifteen minutes later, a nurse came to fetch us, and we were taken down a hall to a small room at the back of the hospital. The room was freezing and barren, except for two metal cots placed side by side.

Annie and Nicholas lay on their backs, sheets covering them except for their dead faces. We gingerly approached and, although I initially held back my tears, I broke down again.

Papa held me while I sobbed, crying, "Why? Why Papa? It's not fair."

"Hush, hush, malenka kit."

"Papa, do you think that it's my fault? That I brought it from Winnipeg? Maybe Mama's right, and trouble follows me everywhere I go!"

"Hush, hush, that's not true. No one knows why these things happen, but none of it is your fault." Papa hugged me while I continued to sob.

Eventually, I managed to get control of myself again, and looked down at Annie, still with her beautifully smooth complexion, now devoid of life. The two of them were the picture of youth and innocence.

It was beyond belief that just two short days ago, they were both laughing and enjoying Christmas. Was there no end to the cruelty of this life? Was there no permanence to anything?

*   *   *

I had missed the last train back to Winnipeg, so we ended up staying in Gimli's little hotel for the night. Papa wanted to go straight back, but I convinced him that he needed to rest, and I didn't want to be left on my own. Besides, the horses needed a rest as well.

That night, unable to sleep and going over and over the events of the last couple of days, was one of the worst of my life. Not for the first nor the last time did I ask myself "What kind of god would do this?"

I'm sure Papa didn't sleep either. He was up and gone by 4:00 a.m., giving me a kiss and a hug before he left. I couldn't imagine how awful the ride back for him would be, knowing that he had to impart such terrible news and no doubt being worried out of his mind about Mike and John.

I wanted to go back to the farm with him, but Papa convinced me that the best thing to do was to go back to my job for a couple of days and then return for the funeral. I was afraid for Mike and John, but they had shown signs of improvement that morning.

Ever since Didus passed away, I had accepted it as a fact that we have souls. I clung to that thought and did my best to pray for Annie's and Nicholas's souls—I certainly wasn't going to pray to any god who had ordained their deaths.

Chapter 13

MIKHAIL

One Sunday afternoon in early April in the spring of 1919, I had returned from church and was sipping a cup of tea in the servants' quarters with Anna while Ms. Wilson did some knitting in our sitting room. (And, yes, despite my doubts, I continued to go to mass most Sundays, mainly because I would meet up with Bea and now Helen.)

While at church, I would always pray for Annie, Nicholas and Sally. Although I was still depressed about their deaths, I think the prayers helped me.

Mercifully, Mike and John had fully recovered from the flu.

As a sixteen year-old young woman, I still had my own life to live, and something was about to happen that would rejuvenate me. A knock came at the door, and Anna jumped up to answer it.

"Sophie, there's someone here to see you," she said.

The next moment, Frank appeared in the doorway.

I squealed with delight, jumped up, and ran to him for a big hug.

"Frank, it's so great to see you!"

"Little sister, how are you?" he asked in Ukrainian.

"Duzhe dobre, dyakuyu," I answered, but catching Miss Wilson's eye, I quickly added, "We're fine, thanks."

"I was hoping to take my favourite sister out for lunch," said Frank, switching to English.

"That would be nice," I answered, and I introduced Frank to Anna and Miss Wilson.

Anna enthusiastically shook Frank's hand and said, "I've heard a lot about you!"

In contrast, Miss Wilson stiffly said, "Pleased to meet you," without extending a hand.

Frank removed his hat and gave her a quick bow. "The pleasure is all mine, madam," he said with a thin smile.

"I have to get back to my duties," Miss Wilson said and headed out to the main house.

"So that's your boss, is it? Seems like a typical stuck-up English bitch."

"Frank!" I said, honestly shocked. "When did you start using such language? And she's not all that bad."

"There's my little Sofiya. Always seeing the good in people, even when it's not there."

"But I believe it is there, although it's true that sometimes you have to look hard."

"Let's go. I have a friend I want you to meet. I think you're going to like him."

I turned to look at Anna, but she immediately understood.

"You haven't seen your brother in years. You two should have some time alone."

I rushed to my room, combed my hair, put on my one good hat, grabbed my light coat, and was down in a flash. Frank had been released from the Banff internment camp in the spring of 1917 to work on the CP railroad, which he did for a couple of years. However, he had recently returned to Winnipeg and found work at the Vulcan Ironworks, thanks to his previous good reputation there. This would be the first time we would be in the city together—he had already been interned when I arrived in 1916.

It was a beautiful day, with apple and crabapple trees in bloom in the yards of the mansions along Wellington Crescent. I took a deep breath, savouring the scent wafting along the spring breeze.

"What a glorious day!" I said, speaking in Ukrainian.

"Yes, it is, but there aren't any apple trees in the north end."

Winnipeg was strictly divided along class and ethnic lines. As Bea had told me the day I first arrived, the wealthy English mainly lived south of the Assiniboine River, and the middle-class English lived just north of the Assiniboine and west of the Red River. The poor Ukrainian and Jewish classes dwelled well away from the English in the north end of the city, on the other side of the downtown and industrial areas.

"Frank, the sun shines on all of us equally."

"Right again, sister. Unfortunately, the benefits of the corrupt system tend to rain down mainly on the capitalist pigs."

"Frank, what's gotten into you? So much rancour!"

"Sofiya, if you had spent two years in a concentration camp, you might be a little rancorous yourself."

And then he launched into a passionate speech.

"The current system is designed to benefit the capitalists at the expense of honest hard-working men. As long as things stay as they are, we Ukrainians will only be slaves to produce wealth for the English capitalists."

I glanced at the mansion we were passing, its beautiful expansive lawn bordered by tulips springing out of the recently frozen ground, and I thought of the people inside. Although I didn't know them, I could be certain that the owners were English and the servants were likely Ukrainians.

We strolled along Wellington until we came to the Maryland Street Bridge, where we crossed the Assiniboine River to the north side. The river was still running high from the winter melt, but it was no longer threatening to run over its banks.

"There's a couple of cafés on this side of the river where we can relax without being surrounded by hoity-toities," Frank said.

There were a lot of inexpensive cafés in them days, perhaps partly because so many single men did not cook for themselves. Besides, they were great meeting places. It wasn't easy for us servants to entertain guests, so cafés were ideal for meet-ups with friends.

We soon came to a little café, and Frank opened the door for me. It took a second for my eyes to adjust to the lower light, but I soon spotted a very good-looking young man getting up from a table and approaching us.

"How good to see you, my brother," he said, embracing Frank.

Frank turned to me. "This is my comrade, Mikhail." And to Mikhail, he simply said, "This is my younger sister, Sofiya."

"Ahh, a goddess of wisdom!" Mikhail said, taking his hand in mine, bending down, and kissing it.

He looked up at me with shockingly bright blue eyes from under a mop of thick brown hair. "And please feel free to call me Mike if you like. Everyone in this country does." As he spoke, he revealed strong white teeth in a wide mouth.

I was still revelling in the feel of his lips on my hand but managed to say, "I quite like Mikhail."

We sat down in a little booth, and Mikhail ordered some lunch for us. Surprisingly, they had some borscht, and we had chicken sandwiches. As we waited for our food, Mikhail switched back to Ukrainian.

"Frank, the moment is rapidly approaching when the workers of this city are going to stand up and demand their rights."

"Do you think there will be a workers' action soon?" Frank asked.

Mikhail dropped his voice. "Yes, the Labour Council has been meeting with the various trades, and they're organizing a general strike."

"Wow, when will it happen?"

"Shhh, keep your voice down. This needs to be kept quiet." And turning to me, he smiled and said, "You understand that you can't repeat any of this?"

I nodded, thinking that I was ready to do anything this impossibly charming man asked of me.

"A date hasn't been set. To have impact, it has to be sudden so that we cause maximum disruption for the capitalists."

Frank nodded and said, "It's time we showed them that they can't do whatever they want with us."

"That is true," said Mikhail reaching across the table and patting Frank's hand. "But remember, my friend, that this will only be one action in a long struggle for equality for all."

Our food arrived, and a middle-aged woman unceremoniously plunked our bowls and plates down with a grunt. However, I felt as if I was in the Ritz, wherever that was.

"This strike may gain us workers better wages and fairer working conditions," continued Mikhail. "But as long as the capitalists own the means of production, they will always be rich, and the workers will always be poor. The only way forward to a just society is for the workers to take over ownership of the means of production."

"You mean like the Bolsheviks in Russia?" Frank asked.

"Yes, but of course we don't want any violence," answered Mikhail. Looking at me, he said, "We want to create an egalitarian society, but we do not believe in violence to achieve our aims."

"What do you mean by an, er, eagle-tarian society?" I asked.

"Egalitarian." He smiled without a trace of condescension. "It's a society in which all men are brothers and all men are equal. There would be education for all, and there wouldn't be the great differences in wealth that we see today."

I had never heard anyone speak of such ideas in my life. The only talk I was used to on the farm was about the health of the pigs, cows, and chickens, and the weather. And the talk amongst the servants in the Reynolds' home was either about the dishes and the food, or gossip about the family.

"And does your egalitarian society mean equality for women as well?" I asked, surprised at my own brazenness.

Mikhail smiled broadly. "Of course it does, my sweet."

No one but my father and Frank had called me by little endearments. No doubt I had a grin from ear to ear.

"When I speak of comrades, I mean all men and women," Mikhail continued. "We are all comrades. We use the word comrade because it shows we are all equal. There are no 'sirs' or 'lords' like the English have."

"We'll never have equality when the English run this country," Frank exclaimed.

"I'm not sure you're right about that, my friend. There are many English in the labour movement here in Winnipeg that are also striving for a just society."

"Can we trust them to look after our interests, or are they just like the capitalists?"

"I think we can trust them. The English lords in the old country sent their young men to be slaughtered in the war, and it was the same thing here. A lot of the younger and poorer English are tired of being the whipping boys for the rich."

"I hope you're right."

"For better or worse, they're the real leaders in the workers' movement here."

The conversation continued over tea, me listening to everything like a deer in the forest, especially every word that fell from Mikhail's lips. Whereas Frank's talk smacked of bitterness, Mikhail focussed on his vision of an egalitarian society.

Afterwards, Frank and Mikhail walked me home, although I think I just floated.

Chapter 14

LOVE IS IN THE AIR

Over the next few weeks, we settled into a routine in which Frank and Mikhail would fetch me on Sunday, and we'd have lunch and then go for a long walk if the weather permitted.

On the fourth Sunday after I had met Mikhail, Helen joined in. The four of us walked to City Park, which later became known as Assiniboine Park, after the original Indigenous people in the area. So far, it had been a glorious spring, with rain falling at night and sunshine pouring down each day. That Sunday was a gorgeous early May day, with the delicate fragrance of spring flowers wafting on gentle breezes.

In contrast to the sweetness of the air, Frank and Mikhail were engrossed in a serious discussion.

"A moment of truth is fast approaching, comrade," Mikhail said. "All the unions under the Building Trades Council voted to strike on Thursday, and the unions under the Metal Trades Council voted to join them on Friday. Tomorrow, none of them will be showing up for work—the spring is the time for construction, and the capitalists can't get any of their money-making schemes off the ground if no workers are willing to do their dirty work."

"Yeah, that'll show 'em that they have to give us decent wages," answered Frank.

Mikhail nodded. "My friend, that would be a good step in the right direction. But remember, what we're really fighting for is fundamental change. That'll only happen if and when the workers have real political power."

"What does that mean?" I asked.

"Ultimately, we need a form of communism in which the workers own the means of production. But a good first step would be to form a labour party, like in England, that can get legislation to better the lot of the working class."

As always, when Mikhail spoke, I was enraptured by his eloquence and passion, but even more by the fire in his eyes. His ideas were so heady, so beyond my realm of experience, that I hardly dared speak for fear of showing my ignorance.

It was about three miles from the Reynolds' house to the park, but we were used to walking long distances around the farm, so it wasn't a problem. We entered the park via the southeast entrance and were soon in the Formal Garden section.

"Wow, it's beautiful," I said.

"Look at how neat the flower beds are," Helen answered.

The garden was laid out in triangles, circles, and stars. Tulips were in their full glory, with spectacular mixtures of red, pink, and white mixed in with yellow daffodils. Many of the other flowers had not yet begun to bloom, but Helen and I were still impressed with the orderliness of it all.

We sat down on some benches to rest and admire the gardens for a while before Frank said, "Who wants to go to the pavilion and get some ice cream?"

"I do!" Helen said brightly.

I'm not sure what came over me, but I said, "Why don't you two go on ahead, and we'll join you in a bit?"

I don't think I consciously planned it, but I clearly wanted to be alone with Mikhail.

Frank and Helen did go on ahead, and Mikhail and I were left sitting side by side on a park bench in the most beautiful garden I had ever been in. Before I knew what was happening, Mikhail had my hand in his and was telling me that I was very beautiful.

I blushed and said, "Mikhail, I know I am not so very beautiful. Helen is much prettier than I am."

"Ah, you are partly right but mostly wrong, my sweet. You are very intelligent, and intelligence is always beautiful."

I don't know if he was some kind of wizard who read my mind, but he knew exactly what to say to win my heart.

"And it would be a very foolish man indeed who could look into your eyes that shine with intelligence and not see the beauty there."

My heart was fluttering, and I'm sure I was grinning like the proverbial Cheshire cat, but I said, "We better catch up with Frank and Helen."

We got up and walked along a dirt path between a little copse of trees, which momentarily shielded us from the view of other park visitors. My hand was still linked with Mikhail's when he suddenly stopped and pulled me back.

I turned to look at him and said, "What is it?" But he was already pulling me towards him, putting his arm around my back and bending down to kiss me.

I didn't resist, and the next minute our mouths were locked together, our lips and tongues eagerly searching each other out. It was a moment of magic.

Up to this point in my life, I had been told that sex was a woman's duty and part of the curse of being born a woman. Mama had always complained that women have to work, work, work, satisfy their man's lust...and get pregnant and fat for their reward.

Girls in them days didn't talk much about sex but whispered rumours at school had given me the impression that men were animals in the bedroom and sex was something to be endured, not enjoyed. And the oblique references to sex in church always equated it with sin and the basest of human desires. I had always imagined that I would never fall prey to such "base" temptations.

So that blissful kiss with Mikhail was a life-changing moment. It was like nothing I could have imagined—an intoxicating brew of tenderness and hidden strength waiting to be unleashed.

Somehow, I pulled away, let out a big breath, and said, "Please, Mikhail, we should go."

But I smiled up at him while his shining blue eyes burned deep inside me. He smiled back, took my hand, and we continued along the path.

When we emerged from the copse, we could see Frank and Helen far ahead approaching the pavilion. We continued on our way, hand-in-hand, when we passed three men sitting on a bench smoking. Mikhail nodded at them and kept speaking to me in Ukrainian.

"Hey, you Bohunks. Don't you know how to speak English?" one of them yelled at us.

Mikhail paused for a second, looked back, and calmly said, "Yes, we speak English."

Two of the men got up and stepped towards us. The closest one, an unshaven tough-looking man in his early twenties, said, "Then why the hell aren't you speaking it now?"

Mikhail let go of my hand, held out his own hands to either side, and said, "Comrades, we are just enjoying a little walk through a beautiful park on a sunny day."

"Comrades!? So you're Bolshies, are ya?" said the second closest man.

On closer inspection, the three of them looked like they could be returned soldiers.

"I believe that all working men and women are equal if that's what you mean," said Mikhail calmly.

"Yeah, well, some of us don't have jobs because you scum have taken them from us."

"I am sorry if you do not have a job, but you shouldn't be calling us scum," said Mikhail calmly but with an edge to his voice.

"Oh yeah? Well, you listen to me because I'm telling you and your little Bohunk girlfriend scum that you should go back from where you came from."

"Mikhail, please let's go," I said, pulling on his arm.

"You can call me what you like, but if you are a gentleman, you will apologize for what you just said to my friend," Mikhail said.

"Did you even fight in the war, blue eyes?" said the second one. "Or should I ask what side did you fight on?"

"I asked you to apologize to my friend," insisted Mikhail.

By this time, the third man had joined the first two, and they half-surrounded us.

"Please, Mikhail, let's go," I pleaded

"I'm saying it again," the first man said. "You Bohunky scum come here and take our jobs while we were risking our lives fighting your goddam Kaiser. Go back to your shithole of a country and take your skinny bitch with you!"

Mikhail swung with lightning speed, and his fist cracked into the man's face, sending him staggering back. Mikhail quickly turned to face the other men, but they must have been seasoned soldiers, and they were too much for him.

While one feinted to his right, the other jumped on Mikhail from his side, wrapped his arm around his neck, and pulled him back. Before Mikhail could respond, the third man stepped forward and drove his fist into Mikhail's midsection. Mikhail doubled over, and the first man, recovering, stepped forward and hit him with an uppercut in the face that sent him flying back.

The man who had been holding him used his momentum to throw him down, and in a flash, all three men were on him like a wolfpack on a deer. They began kicking him while Mikhail tried to roll out of the way, at least succeeding to avert the worst of their kicks.

I screamed, "Please, no, don't hurt him!" and tried to step between Mikhail and his attackers.

One of them turned, grabbed me by the collar, and roughly pushed me away.

"Stay away if you know what's good for you, you little slut!" he yelled.

The other two were still kicking at Mikhail, and I was terrified. When the one who had pushed me turned towards Mikhail, I ran and jumped on the first man's back, reaching my hands around and scratching his face.

He screamed and threw me off like a rag doll. He and the second man turned to look at me, and the first one said, "Touch me again, and I'll beat you senseless."

Mikhail used the brief break to scramble to his feet. All three men turned towards him again, and I saw blood streaming down Mikhail's beautiful face.

Fortunately, a whistle rang out, closely followed by shouting. I turned and saw a policeman racing towards us from the direction of the pavilion. Everyone froze in position.

The policeman blew his whistle again and came running up.

"What's going on here?!" he demanded.

"Nothing much, officer," said the first man quickly. "This Bolshie was disrespecting the king, and we was just learnin' him a lesson."

"That right?" the policeman barked, staring at Mikhail. "Are you a Bolshie?"

"I'm just an honest working man, officer. We were walking in the park when these men attacked us."

Although Mikhail's English was good, it was obvious that he was a Ukrainian. The policeman looked at the other three men.

"We're returned men, sir," said the second man. "We all saw action at the front, not like the Bolshie."

The policeman looked from the three men to Mikhail and I. Mikhail's face was covered in blood, he was bent over in pain, his clothes were all messed up, and his shirt was torn. It had to be obvious what was going on. But the policeman screwed up his face, apparently having made his decision.

"You'd better move on now and don't cause any more trouble, or I'll run you in," he yelled at Mikhail.

"But officer, these men attacked us for no reason and assaulted Mikhail," I said as calmly as I could.

"Maybe you dinna hear me, lassie, but I said to move on!"

"Come on, Sofiya, let's go," said Mikhail, limping over to me and taking my hand.

I bit my lip, tears coming to my eyes, but I went with Mikhail, not looking back. We caught up with Frank and Helen. I told them what happened, and burst out crying.

"I'm fine," said Mikhail, putting his arm around me. "Please don't cry."

"I'm sorry," I said. "It's just so unfair, and are you sure you're okay?"

We found a washroom in the pavilion where Mikhail could wash up. His nose had been broken, and it took a while for the bleeding to stop. He also had some nasty bruises on his ribs where he had been kicked, and a couple of them were undoubtedly broken because he was in pain for weeks afterwards, but luckily there was no permanent damage.

*　　*　　*

On Saturdays, I was only required to do my primary chores before I was free for the rest of the day. Mr. Reynolds was usually at home Saturday, and it was better if the domestics were out of his way.

The Saturday following that magical, yet horrible day at City Park, I fetched Helen a little before noon and talked her into going to see Frank and Mikhail.

"But Frank always says not to come visit him," said Helen.

"Pfftt, that's just Frank being a sourpuss. Once we show up, I'm sure he'll be happy."

Helen didn't seem so sure, but I talked her into it. We walked to Osborne, where we caught the trolley, travelled over the bridge, up Broadway, and onto Main Street, continuing past Union Station until we came to Higgins Avenue.

The Vulcan Ironworks was located just east of Main street in Point Douglas, and Frank had explained that he lived in some housing just past the end of the ironworks.

As Helen and I approached the ironworks the clang of metal and loud hammering rang out from the enormous worksheds. The ironworks had a reputation as a hellhole amongst the workers, and as we could see occasional flashes of red through cracks in the wall, it was easy to imagine that it was indeed hellishly hot inside.

Once we passed the ironworks, we came to a row of shoddily constructed shacks. Helen and I were taken aback for a moment. We looked at each other with the same thought.

"This can't possibly be where Frank and Mikhail live."

A long row of connected shacks constructed on a low platform of wood formed one continuous construction, a kind of townhouse row of shanty shacks. Most of the "homes" had no paint on them, and it was obvious that there were no bathroom facilities. An electric cord ran along the roof and, here and there, splitters lead into the shacks—so I supposed that they must have some electricity.

There would be no running water, however, and I noticed a couple of shabby outhouses around the side that must have served all of the shacks.

A group of rough-looking men stood around at the near end of the shacks, and when they saw us walking up, they quickly surrounded us.

"Hey, Bo Peep, have you lost your sheep?" one said to Helen, and the rest of them laughed raucously.

"Have you girls come up here to keep us men company?" another leered.

"Yeah, come into my place, and I'll fix you some tea, and maybe I'll give you a few extra treats while I'm at it," said a third.

Helen cowered, but I stepped forward and said as bravely as I could, "We're looking for our brother Frank Lyszko and our friend Mikhail Shevchenko."

"Are you now, missy? But since they don't seem to be here, mebbe you'll spend some time with a couple of us instead?"

At that moment, I heard Mikhail's voice.

"Comrades, what is happening here?" he ordered rather than asked.

"We're just chatting with two little hussies who've come our way," said the third man.

Mikhail took a step towards him and asked quietly but clearly, "Excuse me, but what did you say?"

His blue eyes were blazing. The other man looked strong, but Mikhail was taller, younger, and clearly infuriated.

"Nothing, nothing, just having a bit of fun, is all," the third man said.

Mikhail looked at him, seemed to calm down, and stepped towards us.

"These two girls are Frank's sisters. They are very good, hard-working girls, and they deserve our respect," said Mikhail, looking around and defying anyone to contradict him.

One of the men nodded, doffed his hat, and said, "Sure, any friend of Mikhail's is a friend of ours."

The other men all mumbled various forms of agreement and stepped away from us, saying things like, "Have a good day, miss," and "No disrespect meant."

At that moment, Frank came up. "What are you doing here, sisters?" he asked, half incredulously, but mainly angrily. "I told you never to come here!"

"Sorry, brother," I said. "We just wanted to visit you and Mikhail, and see where you lived."

"Well, you can see it's not a place for decent girls," he said.

Helen and I looked at each other again, both heartbroken to see the poverty the men were living in.

"Yes, it doesn't seem very nice, Frank," I said. "I thought you had better living arrangements."

"What the hell did you expect!?" he half shouted. "The Ritz?"

12. Typical North Winnipeg Home
early 1900s

"Calm down, Frank," said Mikhail. And turning to me, he said, "It's good that you see where we honest working men are forced to live while the factory owners live in those big houses on Wellington Crescent."

Witnessing the abject condition of the shacks, I could see clearly what Mikhail was always talking about—the injustice in the great difference in the lives of the factory owners and the workers who made the owners rich.

"Are you going to invite us in, Frank?" I asked.

"No, I'm not inviting you in. What do you think this is? A fancy tea parlour?"

Mikhail looked carefully at me and said, "Frank, let's invite your sisters in for a moment. I think they have the right to see where you live."

Frank protested, but a few minutes later they escorted us to the shack that the two of them shared.

Mikhail opened the door, and Helen and I entered, squinting in the darkness. Mikhail stepped in and pulled on a string hanging from a single bare light bulb.

The light showed us two small cots on either side of the room, with chamber pots visible underneath them. There was no closet, and some sundry clothes hung from nails on the walls. A rough table stood against the far wall with a washbasin on it, and a couple of ragged towels hung from nails. There was a small cracked mirror on the wall, which the men must have used for shaving. Lastly, against the near wall there was another rough table with a gas cook stove and a small pile of dishes next to it.

"Where do you get your water?" I asked.

Frank scowled and looked down, but Mikhail said, "There's a well with a pump out back. We have to fill our pot and our washbasin there and bring the water back in. Unfortunately, the water is not of the best quality."

"Are you satisfied? Now that you've seen it, can we go?" Frank said.

I had to fight hard not to let tears come to my eyes, but I managed to say, "Yes, where would you like to go?"

We agreed to go to a small Ukrainian café off Main Street on Selkirk Avenue that served borsch, perohe, and kapusta.

When we were seated, I looked across at Mikhail and his now bent nose.

I reached across and stroked his cheek.

"Are you okay? Does it still hurt?" I asked.

"I'm fine, Sofiya. Don't worry."

"Yeah, makes him look less like a pretty boy and more like a man!" Frank nudged Mikhail in the ribs.

"Oooh, careful there," Mikhail winced.

"Frank, watch it! Mikhail was injured by those horrible men!" I almost screeched at him.

"Really, it's fine. As long as no one hits me in the ribs, I don't feel a thing," Mikhail winked.

After we ordered, I said I'd pay, but Mikhail wouldn't accept that.

"What kind of man do you think I am, my sweet?" he asked.

After seeing how they lived, it seemed reasonable that I should pay, but the norms of the time held that the man pay or lose respect. That seemed silly to me, but I was the only one who appeared to think that way in them days.

"The results of the strike vote should be in soon," said Frank.

"What's that?" asked Helen.

"The Trade and Labour Council has polled all of the other unions in the city to see if they would be willing to support a general sympathetic strike," said Mikhail.

"And if they do, what's going to happen?" I asked.

"Then all workers with all unions in the city will stop working," said Mikhail, his blue eyes piercing into me.

"That would mean almost everything in the city would shut down!"

"That's right, my sweet."

"But do you think the authorities will stand for that?"

"No doubt they are going to fight back," said Mikhail.

"What will it mean for us domestics?" asked Helen.

"Ahh, that depends on what you want to do," said Mikhail.

"But we don't belong to a union," I said. "We'd have no protection and we'd lose our jobs for sure."

"That's true," said Mikhail. "Sad, but true. It will be more difficult for you to join in with the workers' action."

"But how will you all do without wages?" I asked. "How are you going to live?"

"Just like we've always survived," said Frank angrily. "We'll scrimp by, tighten our belts, and get by on a meal a day, if we can get it."

Mikhail regarded Frank sombrely.

"What your brother says is true," said Mikhail. "But we'll all be supporting one another. That is the key. If we stand strong together, we will prevail."

"I can't leave my job, that's for sure," said Helen.

"I don't think you need to worry about your jobs," Frank said. "No one's going to expect you to go on strike, are they, Mikhail?"

"No, our aim is to hit the capitalists where it matters most to them—in their factories."

Then, turning his blue eyes on me, he added, "But an action like this will test everyone's resolve and will reveal what each person is made of."

I held his eyes, knowing that he believed that I was made of the "right stuff."

Chapter 15

WINNIPEG RISES UP

The following Thursday afternoon found me in the Reynolds' dining room, cleaning the glass on the cabinets. I could hear Mr. and Mrs. Reynolds next door in the parlour.

"Can you believe it?!" boomed Mr. Reynolds. "Those bloody unions have called a general strike, and everyone in the city has walked off their jobs! Everything has come to a standstill."

"Unbelievable, dear. What do they think they're doing? What do they think they'll gain from it?" asked Mrs. Reynolds.

"Civil disobedience, that's what this is. And they're living in a fantasy world if they think they're going to get higher wages. Since the war ended, the economy has slowed down, and business just isn't that profitable these days. There's no money to pay them any more."

"Sit down, dear. I can see you're stressed. Let me pour you a glass of your favourite sherry."

I could picture her fussing about him, perhaps stroking his head as he sat in his upholstered chair with his chin up and his legs crossed.

"How will it affect us, dear? Will we be okay?"

"I think we'll be just fine. Fortunately, farmers still need to plant their crops and bring in their harvests. But depending on how long this damned strike goes on, it'll affect all of us. We might have trouble delivering our products."

"Seems like they're trying to bite the hand that feeds them."

"Damn right! Who do they think built this country? Most of those workers are Johnny-come-lately Bohunks who didn't even fight in the war. And now they want to take advantage of those who have put in years of hard work building this place up from nothing."

"Doesn't seem right to me. What are the business owners going to do about it?"

"We're going to fight back alright. We're forming a citizens' committee to organize ourselves. But keep that under your hat, eh dear?"

Suddenly it went silent, and I took that as my cue to exit. I didn't want to get caught eavesdropping. I wasn't sure which way to go, so I scurried out the opposite direction and quickly went up the stairs. I decided not to go into their bedroom in case Mrs. Reynolds had heard me and was following upstairs, so I went straight down the hall and opened the door to Bobby's bedroom with the idea of cleaning up.

I didn't expect him to be home yet, but he was sitting on his bed with his shirt off.

"Oh-ho, what do we have here!?" he said. "Have you come up to get a little treat?"

He stood up and came towards me. I couldn't help but notice his bare chest, and for a moment, I froze.

"Here, give us a kiss," he said, as he tried to put his arms around me and pull me towards him.

The leer on his face disgusted me. I put my hands on his chest and tried to push him away.

"No sir, please sir, don't!"

"Aw, come here. I know you want it," he half-whispered.

He pulled me close to him, and I looked down, averting my face. He put his hand under my chin and turned my face up to him, but I had seen exactly where his feet were. As he pulled me towards him, I lifted my right foot and stomped down hard with the sole of my shoe.

"Oooh, you little bitch!" he screamed as he let go of me.

Before he could do anything else, I turned and ran out of the room.

"You'll pay for this, you skinny little Bohunk," he shouted after me.

I was already halfway down the stairs and didn't stop as I sprinted through the kitchen and out the back door. I quickly crossed the backyard and made it into the servants' quarters.

Flopping down onto the sofa, I burst into tears. What had I done? Had I just lost my job? How would I be able to help Papa and Mama if I didn't have a job? If the Reynolds fired me, how could I get another job if they didn't give me a good reference?

I lay there crying for a few minutes, wallowing in my misery. But then I thought of Mikhail. Of course he'd say that this was just another example of the capitalist pigs taking advantage of the poorer classes—and he was right. What gave Bobby Reynolds the right to think he could do as he pleased with me? He was just a rich spoiled English brat.

I stopped crying and wiped my face. I was in the right and hadn't done anything wrong, so there was no need to feel ashamed. Mrs. Reynolds and Miss Wilson were the ones who made the decisions about the domestics, and when I thought about it, I doubted that Bobby would say anything to either of them. He might try to make my life difficult, but I had almost no interaction with him, so hopefully things could go on as they were.

And then I remembered that the city was on strike.

"Wow," I thought. "I've got to see what's happening."

I had pretty much finished my chores for the day, and I could probably get away. I straightened my hair in the mirror, went outside, and re-entered the house via the servants' back entrance. Fortunately, I ran into Miss Wilson, and after I told her a white lie about Helen being sick, she agreed to let me go for the day.

It was another gorgeous spring day. It had continued raining during the night, so there was plenty of moisture for new growth, while the days had been mainly sunny.

Evidence that nature is blind to the travails of mankind, I thought.

I wended my way along Westminister Street, Balmoral, and then to Granite Way before arriving at the legislature. Looking across Osborne Street, I could see a fairly large crowd of people mingling on the grounds.

The legislature was without doubt the most impressive and beautiful building in all of Manitoba. The entrance was adorned by six enormous Greek-style columns, with two broad wings flanking either side. The grand Tyndall Stone exterior radiated authority, and the soaring dome in the centre made it clear that this was the seat of power in the province.

The crowd was made up mainly of men, but I saw a couple of young women animatedly chatting amongst themselves, and boldly went up to them.

"What is it? Can you tell me what's happening?"

Two of them gave me a disdainful look, perhaps because it was obvious from my accent that I was Ukrainian.

But a third smiled and said, "Don't you know, dearie? We're on strike. The whole city's on strike!"

"You walked off your jobs? Where do you work?" I asked.

"We're all sales clerks at Ashdown's," the same woman replied.

"But you're not part of a union, are you?" I asked.

"No, but we've all got to stand together now," one of the others responded.

"Good for you!" I said.

"What about you? Where do you work?" one of the disdainful ones asked.

"I'm a domestic for a family on Wellington Crescent."

"So no doubt you're going to keep working, eh?" she sneered.

"There's no way I'd ever be hired back if I don't show up every day."

"Yeah, so you'll keep getting paid while we girls are out risking our livelihoods. And then afterwards, if we get higher wages, you'll probably get a raise."

I didn't know what to say, and I just looked down at my feet.

"Don't give her such a hard time," the friendlier one said. "It's tough all around right now."

"I really admire your courage," I said.

"Fat lot of good that'll do us," the last one said. "Come on, girls, let's go chat with some of the good-looking men here."

And with that, they turned their backs on me and wandered off in the direction of a small group of young men.

I was sad that they didn't see me as one of them. It was clear that the battle lines were being drawn up, and most everyone was going to be forced to take sides.

*　　*　　*

The days of the Winnipeg General Strike were the most intense of my life. They were both wonderful and terrible at the same time—excitement and awe, fear and despair all wrapped together in an inextricable ball of emotions.

Next Sunday found Mikhail, Frank, Helen and I at our favourite spot, the Downtown Café, discussing the most recent events.

"You must be happy that all of the unions agreed to go on strike, eh?" I asked.

"And not only that, most of the unorganized workers have joined in as well," Frank said.

"Yes, I know. I met some girls from Ashdown's that walked off the job on Thursday afternoon."

"Where did you meet them?" Mikhail asked.

"At the legislative grounds."

"What were you doing there?" he asked.

"As soon as I heard the strike had started, I had to get out and see what was happening." I smiled.

Mikhail smiled back and took my hand in his, sending a wave of pleasure through my body.

"You're really with us, aren't you?" he stated.

"Of course I'm with the workers. You've opened my eyes to the injustices in society. I suppose I knew they were always there, but I just accepted that that was the way things were. I didn't really think about it until you showed me a vision of a different world."

Mikhail smiled and stroked my hand, but Frank humphed.

"I told you many of the same things, so why didn't you listen then?"

I probably turned a bit red and didn't know what to say.

"It's not important, Frank. What's important is that now she sees the injustices for what they are."

Rose, the young lady who owned and operated the café with her husband, had given the men coffee before Helen and I arrived, but now she came over to take our orders.

"So you boys on strike now?" she asked with a smile.

"Darn right!" said Frank.

"Don't tell me. You're against capitalism, right?"

Mikhail, quick on the uptake, responded. "It's more important what we're for, and that's a fair deal for the working class."

"And does that include me, or am I capitalist too?"

"Of course it includes you. You're not a big factory owner as far as I can see." Mikhail smiled.

"You've got that right." Rose grinned.

She took our orders, and we continued our conversation.

"Have you heard about the Citizens' Committee of Two Hundred?" asked Frank.

"I overheard Mr. Reynolds saying something about the businessmen forming a committee, but I don't know what it's about," I said.

"Yeah, a bunch of the capitalists have formed a big committee to fight the strike," Frank said.

"No doubt they're going to take every possible measure to defeat the workers," said Mikhail. "And they'll have a lot of financial resources to do it."

When the bill came, I insisted on paying it.

"After all, I'm working right now, and you're not. You men are making sacrifices for the greater good, while Helen and I are working for the capitalists! It's the least we can do."

Frank quickly accepted before Mikhail grudgingly gave in.

*   *   *

It's difficult to describe the excitement in the air at the time. An invisible electric current rippled through the hearts, bodies, and minds of most of the working class. And for sure, it was rippling through my body.

Everywhere you walked in the city, groups of workers congregated, and spontaneous cheers and chants would break out. The downtrodden were finally speaking out and the hope for better times was alive in the fresh spring air.

After lunch, we took the trolley partway to City Park and walked the rest of the way. When we got to the park, I managed to whisper to Helen to take Frank away and leave me alone with Mikhail. We'd been to the park a few times now and had found a couple of favourite secluded spots. I'm embarrassed to say that I almost dragged Mikhail to one of them.

As soon as we were alone on a bench, I threw my arms around him. I definitely wasn't being very ladylike, but I was in the bloom of my youth, and I guess I can be forgiven.

"Whoa, Sofiya," he said, pushing me away after a particularly passionate kiss. "We have to maintain some decorum in public."

I knew he was right, but I wasn't really interested in decorum. I wanted badly to be alone with him.

"Sorry, Mikhail, but everything is just so exciting right now. And being with you excites me even more," I added boldly.

"I'm glad, I'm glad, but we should go softly. You and I have lots of time."

"I know Mikhail. As usual, you're so wise."

Given the morality of the day, I was close to acting like a cheap tramp, and I didn't want Mikhail to see me that way, so I forced myself to calm down.

But that night, as I lay in bed, I couldn't stop thinking of Mikhail, re-imagining his arms around me, his sky-blue eyes boring into me, and the molten sensuality of his kisses.

Polly and Ana were quietly snoring, and that night I discovered the pleasure that my own body could give me, which only drove me crazier to be with Mikhail. I was obsessed with him, and I fell into the same routine every night, biting my pillow to muffle the sounds welling out from me. I don't know what images came to my mind, as I still only had a fuzzy idea about how lovemaking would actually work, but whatever they were, it was more than enough.

Although what I was doing seemed natural, I couldn't help feeling guilty about it. Were women supposed to enjoy this kind of pleasure, or was it another example of Mama's refrain that I had the devil in me?

On the other hand, life had repeatedly shown me how impermanent everything was. What was the point of waiting when your life could be snatched away from you tomorrow?

* * *

The tension in the Reynolds' household was palpable. Anna and Polly weren't what you would call political, but their sympathies clearly lay with the strikers. Mrs. Murray and Mr. McAdam were both older and accepted the traditional order of things, so they were less sympathetic, but you could see that they were interested. Miss Wilson, on the other hand, represented the British upper class, even though she was just a higher-level servant.

One morning we were listening to the radio while finishing breakfast in our quarters.

"*Two of the highest-ranking ministers in the federal government cabinet, the Honourable Arthur Meighen, Minister of Justice and Senator Gideon Robertson, Minister of Labour, arrived in Winnipeg yesterday,*" the announcer stated. "*They've met with the Mayor, the Premier, and several prominent members of the business community, but they'll not be meeting with members of the Strike Committee. The stated purpose of their visit is to help expedite a quick and peaceful end to the strike so that business can recommence.*"

"That's hardly fair," I said. "They're only meeting with one side!"

Miss Wilson walked in as I was speaking and looked around at us.

"I haven't said anything formal to you about this strike yet, but it's clear that I need to," she said, looking directly at me. "You're all expected to do your duties as you regularly would, and anyone who supports strike activities will be dismissed."

Nobody said anything, but I stared at her with what she must have interpreted as brazen insolence.

"And let me remind you that the economy is slow, the Reynolds' business isn't doing as well as it has in the past, and there are plenty of women out there who would be more than happy to have your jobs. So we won't hesitate to let someone go if need be."

Mrs. Murray was the first to speak. "Yes, ma'am." Polly and Anna joined in, and both mumbled, "Yes, ma'am" as well. I didn't say anything, so she turned to me.

"Well?" she asked.

"You can count on me to do my work as well as I always do," I said.

She stared at me for another moment and said, "Well then, carry on, and I'll see you in the big house shortly."

*   *   *

Next Sunday, the four of us were back at the Downtown Café. Helen liked to go out, so she was always keen to join us. Bea preferred to go to church, and she had made friends with people there, so she usually spent her Sunday time with them. But she was also a nature lover, and she would often take long walks into the countryside by herself.

"How are you holding up?" I asked Mikhail and Frank.

"Fine," Frank answered. "We've got enough money and food to keep us going for a while yet. And we're used to going without."

"It's incredible to see the solidarity in the city," Mikhail said. "All the non-unionized workers are showing a lot of courage to support us."

"Yes, and a lot of those workers are women!" I said.

Mikhail smiled. "You are right, of course, my sweet. Have you heard that the provincial government has given an ultimatum to all the telephone operators to return to their jobs by tomorrow or be fired?"

"Yes, it was on the radio this morning."

"And Senator Roberts has given a similar ultimatum to the postal workers," added Frank.

"There's a meeting of the workers at Victoria Park this afternoon. Let's head over there," Mikhail said.

The streets were full of people milling about, mostly dressed in their Sunday best. For us women, that meant a simple cotton dress that hung down near our ankles, with full sleeves and a bodice that revealed our collar bones but was well above our breasts. In them days, it was common to refer to a women's fine ankles or neck bones—not surprising, I suppose, as that was about all that was revealed. In a way, I suppose I was lucky because I was considered to have excellent cheek and neck bones, as well as fine ankles. I wouldn't have been so lucky if the emphasis had been on breasts.

Since I had been making money and wanted to look pretty for Mikhail, I had purchased a necklace of imitation pearls and a new summer hat. I had adorned it with a flower in the hatband that morning, so I was feeling quite smart. The only makeup I wore was a little rouge rubbed into my cheeks for colour. Anything more could have been considered tarty, although, of course, some women wore lipstick.

The men mostly wore dark wool suits with white shirts, a tie, and a fedora. The men who did hard labour, like Frank and Mikhail, generally wore a tweed flat cap.

When we got to Victoria Park, there were thousands of people milling about, creating a sea of hats, bobbing about like so many waves on a choppy day on Lake Winnipeg.

"Are you sure we should be here?" Helen asked. "It's mainly men."

I was getting to enjoy the company of men, but I said, "Look over there—there's quite a few women as well."

There were a lot of telephone operators in the crowd, who were all female, and someone said they were going to decide whether or not to stay on strike.

A couple of different speakers addressed us, and I remember one, who I think was Fred Dixon.

13. Strikers Meeting at Victoria Park
June 1919

"Friends, citizens, tell me. What was Jesus's father's occupation?" he asked the crowd.

"He was a carpenter!" various people shouted.

"Yes, Jesus's father was a carpenter. Whose side do you think Jesus would be on in this strike?"

"Our side! He'd be with us!"

"Of course he would be. The so-called Citizens' Committee is using their churches as recruiting stations to hire thugs as strikebreakers. Does that sound like God's work to you?"

Shouts of "NO," and loud boos reverberated back.

"You know what it reminds me of? The Pharisees that Jesus chased out of the temple!"

People cheered and yelled, working themselves up.

"Are the churches really being used for that?" I asked Mikhail.

"Of course, but it's the Anglican and Catholic churches. The United Churches are with the working man."

"For years, the feds have been promising that civil servants, including postal workers, will get the right to form unions who will advocate for your rights," Mr. Dixon boomed through his bullhorn. "Has this happened yet?"

"No, no. Liars!" came the response.

"I say the time is now to stand firm. Are the postal workers going to give in and go back to work?"

Shouts of "NO" came back, mixed with more boos intended for the feds.

"Are you going to stand in solidarity with your brothers and stay on strike?"

"Yes, yes!"

It was thrilling to feel the collective excitement ripple through the crowd. I had never known anything like it. Mikhail squeezed my hand, and I squeezed back.

Mr. Dixon confirmed that the postal workers would stay on strike and then moved on to the telephone operators. The result was the same—all the operators would stay off the job and damn the consequences.

There was another round of loud cheering, and I was proud to see the women being cheered by the men, even though I wasn't one of them.

The "meeting" continued, with various speakers informing the crowd about the next steps in the strike and recommendations on keeping up the pressure on the business committee. A fiery woman got up and told everyone about a soup kitchen she had organized at which all hungry strikers could get a meal. There were big cheers for her, and it warmed my heart to see a woman taking a leadership role.

I later found out that her name was Helen Armstrong—she became a heroine amongst the workers for standing up against the authorities throughout the strike and was thrown in jail a couple of times for her efforts.

The pressmen had mostly walked off their jobs at the main newspapers, so the strike committee had started its own paper. Young men walked through the crowd handing out copies of the second edition of *The Strike Bulletin of the Western Labour News*.

Representatives of the Strike Committee explained how they were authorizing deliveries of milk to families with babies and allowing other essential services to continue.

"We are not insensitive. We are not brutes. The brutes are the business elite who live in luxury while we barely survive day to day!"

A collection was sent around to help the Strike Committee with its activities, including publishing the *Strike Bulletin*, and I gladly threw in the change I had in my pocket. It looked like most everyone was contributing something.

On that Sunday afternoon, it seemed that everything Mikhail had been talking about was coming true. The workers were rising in unity, and a new world of fairness and egalitarianism was dawning.

It was, for a short while, a glorious time.

Chapter 16

THE EMPIRE STRIKES BACK

On Saturday, May 31, there was a huge march by over 10,000 returned men supporting the right to collective bargaining. They marched to the legislature, where Premier Norris came out on the steps and listened to their demands. From there, they marched to city hall and similarly met with Mayor Gray, and afterwards, they marched to St. Boniface city hall. It was all very peaceful, and according to the news reports, they calmly presented their case to the political leaders, but nothing was resolved.

On Sunday, we headed out to meet Mikhail and Frank for our usual Sunday lunch meeting. Sometimes we walked, but it was drizzling that day, so we rode the streetcar.

"It's a good day to see a moving picture show," Helen said. "I'd like to see *Broken Blossoms*. It's supposed to be a beautiful picture."

"Sure, we'll tell the men."

"Should we really do that? Shouldn't we wait to see what they want to do?"

"What are you talking about? If you want to see a movie, just say so."

"But what we want doesn't really matter. We should do what the men want. They're the bosses."

I wanted to scream at her.

"Haven't you heard anything that Mikhail has been saying? Men and women should be equal!"

Helen smiled and said, "That's nice talk, sister, but you don't really believe it, do you?"

I was flabbergasted, but it showed me just how deeply entrenched our traditional ideas were.

When we got to the café, Mikhail and Frank were talking about the returned men's big march the previous day.

"It's wonderful that so many soldiers are supporting the strike," I said.

"It's an impressive demonstration of solidarity," Mikhail replied.

"Yeah, but not all of them support us," Frank said. "A lot of them think that we Ukrainians have been stealing their jobs."

"It's important that they see the real enemy is the capitalist system," Mikhail said, "and not other poor workers."

Helen timidly ventured, "The strike committee has allowed the movie theatres to re-open."

"It's rainy," I said. "Let's go see *Broken Blossoms*."

The men quickly agreed, and I gave Helen what I hoped was a meaningful glare.

"We'd better get over there in a hurry," I said. "The theatre will fill up quickly on a rainy day."

I signalled to Rose, jumped up, and paid her before Mikhail could protest.

We rushed over to the Royal Theatre on Main Street, and, sure enough, there was already a line-up outside. Movies were extremely popular in them days, and in fact, there were three theatres on the block.

For twenty-five cents, we got to see two full-length features and a short live vaudeville act between the films. Of course they were silent movies.

It was always exciting to go to the theatre, but I was extra excited to be sitting next to Mikhail in the dark. I managed to position myself so I was next to him with an empty seat beside me, with Frank and Helen at the opposite end. Mikhail and I spent a lot of the time kissing and whispering little things to each other during the darkest scenes. He put his hand on my thigh a couple of times and lightly rubbed it, driving me crazy.

Although the whole show lasted almost four hours, I could easily have stayed another four.

When we emerged, Helen said, "That was beautiful but so sad!"

I could see that she had tears in her eyes.

I had hardly paid attention to the films, but I squeezed Mikhail's hand. "Yes, it certainly was beautiful."

Mikhail managed to say, "It's excellent to see a film that shows a connection between poor people across different races."

The plot of *Broken Blossoms* involved a Chinese man caring for a young British woman who was abused by her father, although, of course, his love for her was purely platonic. They would have never shown any physical love between people of different races in them days.

That afternoon stands out for me as an island of normality in the tempestuous sea of war raging between the classes in the city.

*　　*　　*

In retrospect, I could see that there were two distinct phases to the strike. The first phase covered the weeks from the start of the strike on May 15 up to and including Sunday, June 1, the day we went to the movies. In that phase, there was boundless optimism and an almost universal feeling of brotherhood amongst the strikers and their supporters. We were confident that we would prevail and that temporary sacrifices would lead to long-term gains for the working class.

The second phase of the strike started in early June and continued to the end of the strike, during which business and government mercilessly struck back.

Things were getting pretty tense in the Reynolds' household as the strike progressed. I found it hard to care about the work I was doing for the "capitalists," and since Sally had died, my currency with Miss Wilson and the family had waned a bit.

Later that week, when I came into the common area where we had our breakfast, a copy of the *Winnipeg Free Press* was on the table. It was open to a page with a huge ad, urging the government to "DEPORT ALL ALIENS WHO SUPPORT THE STRIKE!"

I suspected that Miss Wilson had left it open at that page so we girls would see it when we got up. Two days later, a copy of the *Winnipeg Telegram* from the previous day was left on the table with a similar ad on display for us.

"*It is time the government deported…the undesirable alien and land him back in the bilgewaters of European Civilization from whence he sprung and to which he properly belongs.*"

My blood boiled when I read this, but at the same time tears came to my eyes. They were talking about people like Mikhail and Frank. How could they have so much hatred in their hearts?

*   *   *

The following Sunday found the four of us outside our usual meeting spot at the Downtown Café. We couldn't go inside because the strike committee had asked that all restaurants close their doors, and most had complied. The movie theatres had been closed again as well.

"There's a big service planned by the Labour Church at Victoria Park this afternoon," Mikhail said. "Let's go there."

We quickly agreed and headed off to the park.

Helen and I were walking a little behind the men when she said, "See, you just do what Mikhail wants. Anyway, it doesn't matter what we want. We don't count."

Again, I wanted to scream at her, but I gritted my teeth and managed to control myself.

"We DO count," I said. "I just happen to agree that we should go to Victoria Park."

Helen only smiled enigmatically.

"Why are the papers making this sound like a revolution?" I asked when we caught up to Mikhail and Frank.

"Because the business elite will get more sympathy from the federal government if they can convince them that the strike is really the start of a revolution," Mikhail answered.

"All the strikers are asking for is the right to bargain collectively!" I said.

"That's true, Sofiya, that's true, but the capitalists are afraid they'll lose control, and they don't want that to happen."

"Did you see the news yesterday?" asked Frank. "The feds have passed amendments to the Immigration Act that let them deport anyone not born in Canada without a trial."

"That's terrible," Helen said. "Both of you were born in the Ukraine."

"Don't I know it!" Frank responded.

"Did you see the news about the soldiers supporting the Committee of One Thousand who organized a counter-parade?" I asked.

"What?" asked Helen. "I've heard about the Committee of Two Hundred, but what's this one?"

"It's been expanded," Frank said. "There are a lot of business people lining up to make it clear whose side they're on."

"Pffft," Mikhail said. "There are some soldiers against the strike, but that's because they don't see the bigger picture. They're hungry because they don't have jobs and think if they support business, they'll get jobs once the strike is over. Besides, half the people in that so-called parade were business people, not soldiers."

"Yeah, and I heard that a lot of them got paid to march," Frank said.

"Everything is getting so much more serious," Helen said.

Mikhail regarded her calmly and said, "This is a fight for the dignity and rights of the common man. What could be more serious than that?"

"Have you heard that the city has hired a bunch of 'special police'?" Frank asked.

"No, who are they?" Helen asked.

"I think they're mainly a bunch of thugs that are going to be used to beat up strikers," Frank answered.

I didn't want to say it, but Helen was right—everything was getting more serious.

*   *   *

Victoria Park had become the centre of all the strikers' public meetings and was the place everyone who sympathized with the strike went to mingle, discuss events, and generally have a good time. On weekends, there were often bands playing along with a variety of talks.

That Sunday, James Woodsworth was giving a combination of a talk and a sermon to a huge crowd of people. He seemed very well informed and talked at length about the general economic situation in Canada and the unfairness of working conditions everywhere.

"Who is he?" I asked Mikhail.

"He was a Methodist minister but was kicked out because he's a pacifist and didn't support sending any men to the war."

He spoke like an old-time revivalist gospel preacher, exhorting the crowd to accept Jesus into our hearts as the path to salvation. But he also spoke a lot about social justice. I don't remember his exact words, but they ran along the following lines:

"Only when the capitalists have accepted Jesus into their hearts will we have a just society. Today, their hearts and minds are corrupted by greed that blinds them to the true equality of all mankind!" he boomed through his megaphone.

"I commend all of you honest working men for the restraint you have demonstrated throughout this action you have taken and for maintaining the peace at all times—actions that are no doubt blessed in the eyes of God as a fair protest for your deserved rights!

"Not only is peacefulness the right and correct action in the eyes of Jesus, but by being peaceful, you avoid playing into the hands of the conspiracy between business and politicians in this city and across this country. The authorities are looking for an excuse for clamping down hard on you, and you must not give them that excuse!"

"He seems very clever," I said.

"Yes, I'm not in agreement with his references to Jesus, but he's very perceptive," Mikhail said.

"You don't believe in God, Mikhail?"

He turned to me, his blue eyes searching my own, and said, "I believe in goodness and fairness to all mankind, Sofiya."

As usual, he knew exactly what to say to me. I realized that he avoided answering my question, but his answer satisfied me, at least as far as his beliefs. But it bothered me that he didn't ask me what I believed.

"Aren't you going to ask me if I believe in God, Mikhail?"

He scrutinized my face carefully for a moment and said, "I can plainly see that you are a good person, that you are intelligent, and want fairness for all. You do not accept the preaching of the authorities without question, whether those authorities be the church or the government."

He was able to articulate things about me that I could never have said myself!

"Just so you know," I said, "I can't accept the idea of God, but I do believe that we have a soul."

"Once again, you're living up to your name, Sofiya."

I stood, quietly basking in his praise for a moment, before returning to the sermon.

"What he's preaching makes more sense to me than what I heard in the Catholic church," I said.

"For most of its history, the church has been an instrument of oppression of the poor. We're better off without it," Mikhail answered.

As usual, I was out of my depth when speaking with him, but what he said had the ring of truth to it, and I squeezed his hand tighter.

After Mr. Woodsworth had spoken for about an hour and a half, other speakers, including Fred Dixon, took the podium. The common theme was the need for a fairer society, the end of huge differences in wealth, and the harmony of these objectives with Jesus's teachings.

There must have been about 10,000 people in the park and, incredibly, almost everyone stayed for close to three hours and listened to every speech.

*   *   *

The next day the city fired the entire regular police force and replaced them with the "Specials."

At breakfast on Tuesday, as this news was announced on the radio, Miss Wilson said, "Maybe now we'll have some law and order in this city!"

"Why do you say that, Miss Wilson?" I asked, fighting to keep my voice level. "Haven't we had law and order all along?"

She scowled at me and said, "All these people striking is illegal. Postal workers and other public servants don't have the right to strike."

"And neither should they," joined in Mrs. Murray.

Anna and Polly wouldn't speak against the older ladies, so I was clearly on my own.

"The workers are just asking for fairer wages," I said, perhaps a bit lamely.

"Hmmph!" said Miss Wilson. "I've told you before, if you don't like your wages, you can go somewhere else. And if the Reynolds' business doesn't pick up soon, you might be let go in any case."

I was increasingly resenting my job, particularly cleaning toilets and picking up after the family. Mikhail's ideas were affecting me—what made the Reynolds superior to me anyway? I really didn't like being trapped inside all day when most people were out on strike and there was so much activity in the city. I was missing so much!

For example, that Tuesday afternoon, there was a big incident on Main Street. The new Specials made an appearance in public, walking around with what the conservative press called "emblems of democracy." These emblems of democracy were sawed-off wagon yokes in the shape of a baseball bat—definitely a sad day for democracy.

A few of the Specials were trying to direct traffic, but they made a mess of it, and the crowd started heckling them. Soon the crowd spilled out into the street and blocked traffic, which prompted the new "chief" of police to send in mounted Specials to disperse the people. Some of the people started throwing bottles and stones at them, and a couple of the Specials lost control of their horses.

The Specials who had been trying to direct traffic ran and hid in a couple of stores, and apparently chaos ensued. Fortunately, no one was hurt except one of the Specials who sustained a mild injury, but who turned out to have been awarded a Victoria Cross for bravery in the war.

The next day, the press, who were firmly in the pocket of the city's business people, screamed that there was anarchy in the streets. According to the *Free Press*, the Victoria Cross recipient, Mr. Coppins, *"Narrowly escaped death at the hands of aliens."*

The press characterized the incident as a riot, and the editorials called for the police to smack down the strikers and teach them a bloody lesson. Of course, the Strike Committee had nothing to do with the whole incident, and, in fact, it was exactly the type of thing they had been trying so hard to avoid. They didn't want to give the authorities an excuse for clamping down with violence.

It was frustrating to me to have to read the accounts in the press because I knew they were biased. And I wanted to be out on the streets participating in peaceful protests.

Since the evenings were long at this time of year, I usually slipped out after work or after supper and caught the streetcar downtown. It was "Ladies Day" at Victoria Park on Thursday evening, and I managed to get down there on time for the tail end of the daytime festivities.

There was a huge crowd, and, for once, there were more women than men. James Woodsworth was speaking again, and he gave an impassioned speech for the emancipation of women and the equality of the sexes.

"In the days to come," he said, "women will take their place side by side with men, not as dependents or inferiors, but as equals."

A roar of cheering greeted this.

"This strike is much more than a simple strike for higher wages. It is part of the great movement for equality and the emancipation of women!"

At the end of his speech, we cheered wildly and shouted, "We'll fight to the end!"

It was thrilling beyond measure to feel that I was participating in the birth of a great change in society.

I couldn't help but think of my poor mother on the farm. I doubted that she would have ever heard of ideas like equality between men and women and, if she did, she would probably have dismissed them. And my father, God bless his soul, would certainly wave them aside as foolishness.

In fact, progress had already been occurring, and Manitoba had been the first jurisdiction in Canada to award the vote to women in 1916. As I was underage, I had not yet been able to exercise my enfranchisement rights, but I was looking forward to it.

The meeting continued after the supper hour, and I was eventually able to find Mikhail and Frank. It was a beautiful summer evening, and the speech about equality emboldened me. If the sexes were equal, did I have to wait for Mikhail to take the initiative to kiss me?

As the light faded, I dragged Mikhail to an out-of-the-way park bench. "You should have heard Mr. Woodsworth's speech about the emancipation of women, Mikhail. It was wonderful."

Before he could even answer, I wrapped my arms around him and kissed him passionately. I was definitely losing control.

As usual, he stopped the proceedings and talked me into going home before it was too dark and the trollies stopped running. I agreed, but I didn't know how much longer I would be able to hold on.

* * *

As spring turned into summer, it became hotter and hotter, further stoking the heat inside me. I was such a jumble of emotions: excitement about the workers' uprising, awe at the potential for women, and my passion for Mikhail. It was almost more than I could stand, and I was wound up all day, every day.

The next Saturday, the hottest and most humid day yet, I met Frank and Mikhail at the entrance to Victoria Park after I had finished work in the early afternoon. Helen had gone back to the farm for the weekend, so it was just the three of us. I brought food that I had scrounged from our kitchen, and we had an early picnic supper in the park when the speeches wound up.

By late afternoon, the heat was getting unbearable, but the weather threatened to break. Sure enough, soon deep rolling thunder sounded, and flashes of lightning arced across the sky to the west.

"We should get you home, my sweet, before the skies open up," Mikhail said.

I quickly agreed and, fortunately, Frank had met some friends of his and went off with them.

As the trolley gently rocked along, the flashes of lightning became more brilliant, and the thunder louder. Electricity shot through the air, and I literally felt sparks fly when I touched Mikhail's hand.

As we descended from the trolley, day turned to night, and an eerie stillness fell over the street.

"Come on. We'd better run!" Mikhail yelled.

Mikhail grabbed my hand, and we ran straight down the middle of the street. We had gone a couple of blocks when an enormous gust of wind hit us, and I stumbled forward onto the ground. Mikhail held me by one arm, but I put my other hand down and scraped it on the pavement.

The trees next to us shook wildly, and, with a loud crack, a huge branch sailed in front of us and smacked into the ground.

Mikhail pulled me up and yelled again to keep running.

We were within 100 yards of the Reynolds' when another huge gust hit us, this time accompanied by a wall of water. We were drenched within seconds.

We kept running, the air full of flying branches, leaves and debris, lightning flashing, and thunder cracking. We made it around the house and to the door of the servants' quarters, where we tumbled in with a rush of wind and rain.

Mikhail slammed the door and quickly put his arms around me, asking, "Are you alright, my sweet?"

I leaned back into him and began laughing uncontrollably. He thought I was sobbing and whispered, "It'll be okay. It'll be alright."

Mikhail still didn't seem to get it until I turned around and faced him, tears of laughter streaming down my face.

"I can't remember when I've had so much fun!"

"My crazy little girl," he said, stroking my face.

The next moment we were locked in a passionate embrace.

After a few minutes of bliss, we separated and, looking at him, I said, "You need to take off that wet shirt."

He smiled and obliged, slowly unbuttoning his shirt and then pulling his undershirt over his head.

I almost gasped when I saw his rippling physique. Mikhail and the other men did hard labour in the factory, which had the benefit of building up their muscles.

I put my hands on his chest, revelling in the feel of his maleness, and he pulled me towards him again. It was a whole different matter kissing him with his naked chest against me, and I was turning to butter in his arms.

Lightning was flashing over and over again, thunder was booming—and the air inside our quarters was electric.

He pushed me gently away and said, "Where is everybody? Are we sure we can be alone?"

"Miss Wilson usually visits friends on Saturday nights, and they play bridge, Anna must be with her boyfriend, and Polly visits her friends. Besides, no one is going to come back in this downpour."

"In that case, you need to get out of those wet clothes as well." He smiled.

I suddenly felt shy. I had never undressed in front of a man, and I was unsure about my body. I wasn't voluptuous like some girls, and that's what I thought men liked.

I looked down at the floor, and, sensing my shyness, Mikhail said, "Here, let me do it."

He reached around and undid the tie at the back of my dress and then proceeded to undo the buttons at the back. When it was sufficiently loose, he pulled it over my shoulders and let it drop to the floor.

He looked me up and down and then met my eyes.

"Sofiya, you are truly beautiful."

Of course, in them days I still had on a slip and a petticoat, as well as my knickers, so I was hardly naked.

Mikhail put his arms around me, and I must have shivered. He might have thought it was because I was cold when it was really a frisson of excitement, but he insisted on getting me a towel.

I told him I would get the towels because I knew which ones were mine, so I ducked into the washroom and returned with one bath towel and one face towel. He took the large one out of my hands, wrapped it around me, and started to pat me down.

I didn't care about being dry though, so I took his hand and led him to the couch. He sat down beside me, but I laid back and pulled him forward half on top of me.

We were soon searching each other's mouths, and I was lost in ecstasy. I could feel his maleness which both shocked and thrilled me. Soon his hands began to explore my body as he had never done before, but as I had dreamed of for weeks on end.

When his hand reached between my legs, my whole being shuddered, and I gladly welcomed him to explore further.

The rain had been pelting against the walls, but it suddenly stopped, and all I could hear was the sound of my own panting.

Mikhail's magic fingers were exploring further and had just reached inside me when the door opened with a gust of wind and rain.

Mikhail and I leaped up in a flash to see Mrs. Murray standing in the doorway. We scrambled for our clothes, but it was pointless trying to hide what we'd been up to.

"Oh, Lord!" exclaimed Mrs. Murray. "What's going on?!"

Mikhail and I mumbled apologies, and Mrs. Murray said that Mikhail had better leave. It was, without a doubt, the most embarrassing moment of my life.

Mrs. Murray excused herself and went into the washroom, clearly giving Mikhail and me a chance to say good-bye. We hurriedly got dressed.

"I'm so sorry, my sweet. I got carried away," Mikhail said in Ukrainian.

"Please, Mikhail. There's nothing to be sorry about."

"I'd better go," he said.

"Don't be silly," I said. "You can't go out in that downpour."

For better or worse, the rain seemed to further ease up at the moment, and Mikhail signalled with his eyes that that was a sign for him to leave.

He took me in his arms, gave me a quick kiss, looked me in the eyes, and said, "I love you, Sofiya."

"Oh, Mikhail, I love you so much."

And the next minute, he was gone.

Mrs. Murray must have heard the door shut because she came out.

"Lord have mercy, child! Do you have the devil in you? What do you think you're doing?"

I looked at her and burst into tears.

She came over to me quickly and hugged me, saying, "There, there, Sophie. I won't tell Miss Wilson. Your secret's safe with me."

I cried harder when she said that, not that I gave a fig about Miss Wilson, but because our lovemaking had been interrupted. And there was that familiar refrain about having the devil in me.

Then she gave me a lecture on watching out for "older" men and that I'd better be careful or I'd get pregnant and wreck my life.

"You need to have some control, lassie."

*   *   *

The next day, I headed over to the Downtown Café with Helen. There was debris everywhere in the streets from the storm.

When we got to the café, which was thankfully open again, we spotted Frank by himself.

"Mikhail told me to give you his regrets, but he can't make it today," Frank said.

"Why? What's he doing?" I asked.

"He said he had to see some of his family in the north end, that he'd been neglecting them, and it was time he saw them."

I knew that Mikhail had some cousins who lived in Winnipeg, although I had never met them. It didn't seem right that he wasn't there after what had happened the previous day, but I didn't want to make too big a scene with Frank.

We spent some of the afternoon at Victoria Park, but it wasn't the same without Mikhail. The storm had done a lot of damage to trees and some buildings throughout the city, and there was a much smaller crowd than usual. Somehow it was all a bit depressing, and Helen and I decided to go home early.

On Monday after work, I decided to stay home. I was annoyed at Mikhail for not showing up on Sunday, and I didn't want to look like I was too dependent on him. Perhaps Mrs. Murray's lecture about not getting pregnant and showing some control also had some impact on me.

Tuesday morning, we servants woke to sensational news. The North West Mounted Police had raided the homes of the strike leaders in the middle of the night, arrested ten of them, and locked them up in the Stony Mountain Penitentiary twenty miles north of Winnipeg.

"What!?" I said. "On what grounds are they arresting them?"

Before anyone could answer, the radio announcer said, "*It is believed that all ten men are being charged with sedition and, as such, could be subject to deportation without a trial.*"

"Serves them right," Miss Wilson said. "They need to learn what it means to live in a law-abiding country."

"You mean what it means to live in a country where the law protects the rich?!" I almost yelled.

"Now, you listen to me, young lady. One more word from you, and you're sacked!"

I was about to shoot back, but Anna and Polly both stood up, put their arms around me, and said, "You be quiet and come with us."

I tried to fight them off for a moment but thought better of it. Papa had always taught me to be calm and patient, and Mikhail was as well. But the strike, the injustice of it all, and my unfulfilled passion with Mikhail were raging through me, and I just wanted to scream at everyone.

As I cleaned the house later, I could hear Mrs. Reynolds on the phone celebrating the arrest of the strike leaders with one of her friends.

"They'd better get the message and get back to work," she said.

I felt like smashing the glass I was wiping but managed to control myself.

Since it was late June, there was light until almost ten o'clock in the evening, and people continued to converge on Victoria Park. After work, I hurried over to Helen's place. Mr. Andrews, the leader of the Committee of 1000 and the acknowledged leader of the anti-strike movement, had his home between our houses. I spat on his lawn as I passed it.

Helen and I made our way down to Victoria Park by our usual combination of streetcar and foot. We normally met Mikhail and Frank near the entrance because it would otherwise have been hard to find each other with the large crowds milling about. After a few minutes, I spotted Frank with someone I didn't recognize.

"Where's Mikhail?" I asked, without even asking how Frank was doing.

"Whoa, sister, I'm fine, thank you."

"Sorry about that, but you look fine to me."

"Yes, I know, you're wondering where Mikhail is. I'm sorry he won't be coming tonight, and he told me to give you this."

He handed me a folded piece of paper in a little envelope with my name on it.

I quickly opened it up, being careful not to tear the envelope or paper.

Dearest Sofiya,

    Forgive me for not coming out tonight, but I think it is best if we do not see each other for a little while. I am very sorry for what happened on Saturday night. I should show more restraint.

You are worthy of the greatest respect, and I am ashamed that I did not behave like a gentleman.

I am visiting my cousins in the north end for a few days. They are having some family problems and need some help. We will see each other soon.

Love and Solidarity,
Mikhail

*   *   *

The arrest of their leaders greatly shook the strikers' confidence. The business leaders, the city, and the federal government had all been adamant in their resistance to the strikers' demands, and it now appeared that the working class wouldn't prevail after all.

I didn't see Mikhail all that week. I was upset at him but was missing him badly. I knew he was right about Saturday night, but all I could think of was lying in his arms and consummating our love. Despite Mrs. Murray's lecture, I couldn't wait to be alone with Mikhail again.

Although the strikers seemed to be in disarray since their leaders were arrested, the returned soldiers were not. Apparently, they had a big meeting on Friday night and agreed to mount a "silent parade" on Saturday in protest of the arrest of the strikers.

Crowded around the breakfast table on the morning of Saturday June 21st, we heard the announcement that the soldiers were going ahead with their plan even though Mayor Gray had banned all parades. The Mayor was quoted as saying that "any women taking part in a parade do so at their own risk."

The radio announcer stated that the parade was slated to start at 2:30, and I immediately determined to be there to lend my support and, hopefully, to see Mikhail.

After finishing my chores and eating a hurried lunch, I rushed off to the Downtown Café, hoping to run into my men. I hadn't intended to take Helen because of the Mayor's warning, but she was in the street in front of her family's house, so she came along with me.

Although the Reynolds had a phone, Frank, Mikhail, and I had no way to get in contact with each other except by going to our favourite meeting places. We arrived at the café about 2:00 and hung around for about fifteen minutes before Frank showed up.

"Before you ask, I don't know where Mikhail is," Frank said. "I haven't seen him since Monday."

I was disappointed, but I still hoped to see him at the parade.

"The parade is supposed to start soon. Let's get over to Main Street."

We got into Main Street at William Avenue and walked a bit north to get to where the crowd was thinner. I noticed several other women and even some children out for the parade, but it was mainly men. Given the size of the crowd, it was pretty clear that the vast majority of people in the city supported the strike.

I sensed that the crowd was restless and angry, and people were randomly yelling out slogans. The strike was well into its sixth week, and there was no sign of any concession from the business leaders. I was sure that many of the strikers were going hungry and having problems feeding their children.

We were waiting for the soldiers to come marching down Main Street when a streetcar came from the north. The streetcar operators were on strike, but the Citizens' Committee had hired scabs to run the streetcars, which really provoked the strikers. A bunch of young men ran into the street, blocked its way, and, when it stopped, pushed it off its rails. The crowd yelled, booing the scabs and cheering on the young men.

The streetcar operators got out and, seeing the size of the crowd, wisely beat a retreat. The young men, encouraged by the crowd, pushed the streetcar over on its side to even louder cheers. A lot of people started pouring into the street.

14. Streetcar Tipped Over on Main Street
June 21, 1919

Right about this time, about fifty Mounties came riding up the street from the south. They rode straight into the mass of people, swinging their clubs, and managed to disperse the crowd from the middle of the street. I couldn't see exactly what was happening, but everyone started to yell at the Mounties, calling them all sorts of names and throwing stones and bricks at them after they passed by.

"You capitalist goons!" I shouted.

"Be careful," Helen said. "You might get arrested."

"I just wish I had a brick," I said, somewhat shocking myself.

The Mounties kept moving up the street and disappeared from view to the north. When they were gone, a couple of young men ran back to the street car and hopped inside. I couldn't see what they were doing, but a few minutes later, they exited, and smoke billowed out—they had set it on fire.

"Yeah!" the crowd screamed louder. All the pent-up frustration of the strike was coming to a head. The workers had gone without wages for more than a month, and their anger was boiling over.

The Mounties soon came riding back from the north and were pelted with sticks, stones, and whatever people could find. I was completely swept up in the moment, reached down, found a stone and threw it as they rode by. I had a weak arm, no aim, and no idea where my stone went, but I doubt it hit anything.

Everyone wondered where the soldiers were, and I had no idea what happened to them. All I know is that people kept pouring into the street, yelling and milling about. I suppose it could be called a riot, but no one started breaking storefront windows and looting or anything like that. The crowd's anger was clearly directed towards the

Mounties, who had arrested the strike leaders and who we guessed had broken up the silent parade.

About ten minutes later, the Mounties came charging back from the south again. There were fewer of them this time, but they seemed better organized. They thundered through in a tight group, and everyone scattered before again throwing rocks at them as they passed by. I think a couple of them were hit pretty hard, and at least one fell off his horse. Pandemonium ensued, and some protesters dragged a person off to the other side of the road.

Frank was screaming the whole time and looking for things to throw, while at the same time yelling at us, "Go home. It isn't safe for you here."

Helen grabbed me by the arm more than once. "Come on, Sophie, he's right. We should go."

But she didn't make a move to leave herself, and there was no way I was going to miss out on the excitement and action. Staying showed support for the strikers—leaving would be cowardly.

The whole thing unfolded like some surreal film, being run over and over again, with the Mounties making successive charges from one end and then the other along Main Street. They once again rode back through the crowd with their clubs, and this time it seemed that the crowd only hurled insults.

"Bastards!"

"Capitalist lackeys!"

"It's not fair! We just want a fair deal!

Someone next to me yelled, "What the hell do they think they're doing? We weren't doing anything except standing on the curb to watch a parade!"

After they passed, people again poured into the street, but Helen, Frank, and I at least retained enough sense to stand on the sidewalk as the Mounties regrouped for their next charge.

This time, they came holding their guns in their right hands and clubs in the left, and they charged right into the people on the street. I couldn't see how they held their reins, but I remember thinking they were darn good riders.

Suddenly, to our collective shock, they started firing their guns. Everyone started running, and women's screams joined the general cacophony.

"Someone's shot!"

"Don't worry. They're using blanks!"

My heart was hammering away, and Helen and I hugged each other. Frank was yelling obscenities and tried to drag us away.

"They wouldn't use live ammunition on us!"

"Don't be afraid. They're not real bullets!" another person yelled.

It's impossible to explain our actions. The whole crowd seemed to go into denial—no one believed there was any real danger.

The film played itself out again with a few minutes of calm as the Mounties passed off north and circled around, preparing to charge again. I looked up the street in the other direction and saw that a huge group of Specials had gathered in the street, carrying their "emblems of democracy."

People started yelling, "They're coming again. The bastards are coming back!"

The hoofbeats of the returning horses reverberated down Main, causing my heartbeat to accelerate. I looked across the street and saw Mikhail. I yelled his name as loud as I could—he turned, and our eyes locked for an instant. Even at that distance, his eyes shot lances into my soul.

And then an older man ran into the street in front of the on-charging Mounties. I saw him reach down for a brick and turn when he was shot at point-blank range in the chest. He flew back into the dust, and several people, including me, simultaneously screamed. The horses roared by, and then dozens of people ran into the street, totally obscuring my view.

Before I could catch my breath, the Specials had descended on the crowd, freely swinging their clubs. There were too many of them between Mikhail and me. Frank grabbed me by the arm and yelled, "Run!"

15. Specials Marching Down Mainstreet
with Clubs in Hand
June 1919

I tried to resist, but it was crazy. The Specials were hitting people indiscriminately, and to stand in their way would have been insane. We made it to William Street and ran away from the meleé. Looking back, I saw a Special raise a club and hit a defenseless man on the head and knock him to the ground—it looked as if the man had partially blocked the blow with his arm, but it was horrible, just horrible.

We ran for about two blocks before we stopped to catch our breath.

"I've got to go back to find Mikhail," I panted.

"No, Sophie, that would be madness," Helen said.

"Mikhail can take care of himself," Frank said. "He's strong, and he's fast. I'm sure he'll get out of there."

I argued for a couple of minutes before my energy seemed to seep away. As the adrenaline faded, I started to shake and sob.

"How can people be so awful to one another?" I cried.

Helen hugged me, and I cried like a little girl in her arms. The inhumanity of it all was more than I could comprehend.

Frank said, "Come on, I'll walk you both home, and tomorrow we'll meet Mikhail at the Café."

Chapter 17

CHASING A DREAM

I slept badly that night and woke up feeling like a wreck.

At breakfast, the radio trumpeted the news, the announcers glorying in the horrors of "Bloody Saturday."

Apparently, the Specials had beat up a lot of people, and the hospitals were full of folks with injuries. The elderly man I had seen shot had died on the spot, and another man was in critical condition in hospital, also after being shot by the Mounties.

"I was there. It was awful," I told Anna and Polly.

"I'm worried about Mikhail," I said after breakfast. "I'm going to see if I can find him."

"Is that the lad who was here with you the other day?" asked Mrs. Murray.

I nodded.

"You remember what I told you, now," she said.

I was angry at her and almost lashed out, but I knew she meant well.

"He's a good man, Mrs. Murray," I said.

I caught the streetcar and made my way downtown, not noticing what the day was like. I was sick with worry that the Specials had beaten up Mikhail, and he was lying somewhere in a hospital, or worse.

It was still early, so there was no point in going to the Café, and I headed straight for Mikhail and Frank's shack. When I got off, debris lay all over Main street, although a few cleaners were sweeping it up. The burnt trolley was still on its side in the middle of the road, and there were a number of Specials hanging around in little groups, clubs in hand.

As I walked past the Vulcan Ironworks, a shiver of foreboding ran up my spine—something didn't seem right. It was eerily quiet, even for a Sunday.

A few scruffy men were sitting outside their shacks, smoking and drinking tea out of ceramic cups. I scurried up the steps and, heart in my mouth, knocked on Mikhail and Frank's door.

"Mikhail, Frank," I called, "Are you in there?"

After a moment, Frank responded, "Just a moment, Sophie."

My palms were sweating and my heart was racing. Where was Mikhail?

Frank opened the door and, hardly giving him a glance, I pushed inside.

I looked around at the empty room and sagged.

"Where's Mikhail?"

"I'm fine, thanks, sister," he said.

"Sorry, Frank, but I can see that. Where's Mikhail?!" I demanded, my voice rising.

Actually, Frank looked like heck. He was unshaven, his hair was a mess, and the shack stunk.

"I don't know. I never saw him again after we split up."

"So he could be in a hospital?"

And an even worse thought, "Or in jail?"

Frank rubbed his head.

"Sorry, Sophie, I just don't know."

I looked around and spotted an empty whiskey bottle on their table.

He saw what I was looking at. "Yeah, everyone was feeling like crap last night. A lot of the men were beaten up by them Specials, and they were passing bottles around to ease the pain."

"So you just got drunk without knowing what happened to your best friend?"

"Hey Sophie, get off your high horse for a moment, will ya?! It was crazy last night. Besides, Mikhail might've gone off to his cousins. How the hell am I supposed to know?"

I realized that it wasn't helpful to blame Frank when we didn't even know where Mikhail was.

"Sorry, brother, I'm just really worried about him."

"Yeah, I can see that."

"Can we please ask some of the other men if anyone saw him?" I pleaded.

He scowled but nodded. "Can you just give me a few minutes?"

I stepped outside, smoothed my skirt, and sat down on the steps in front of their shack, like the other men. Frank came out after about ten minutes, looking not much better. He had probably relieved himself in his bedpan and splashed some water on his face, but he was still bleary-eyed.

"Alright," he said, and we started walking along the row of shacks.

Frank greeted each man in turn and exchanged a few words about how "shitty" things were.

About the third shack down from Frank's, we came across a man as he stepped out of his shack. He sported an ugly black eye that was completely shut and he limped badly for the two steps it took him to make it to the stairs. He awkwardly sat down, grabbed at his shoulder, and groaned in pain.

"Mornin' Stephen," Frank said. "Are you okay?"

Stephen swore and said, "I got beat up pretty bad. One of them Specials hit me with his club, and when I fell down, the others gave me a good kicking."

Tears came to my eyes. "Shouldn't you go to the hospital? I asked.

"Yeah, mebbe, but I don't wanna get 'rrested," he said.

"Arrested?" I asked.

"We heard that they were grabbing people outside the hospital and locking 'em up," Frank said.

"That's horrible." I said, putting my hand to my mouth.

Looking at Stephen, who was in obvious pain, I asked, "Would you like some water or something?"

"Yeah, I wouldn't mind a cuppa tea." And looking at Frank, he said, "Think you could roll me a smoke?"

Stephen told us to go inside his shack. I got a pitcher and went around the back to the pump to get some clean water while Frank got his tobacco and rolled him a cigarette.

I fetched him a cup of water and looked at his eye.

"I should wash that up," I said.

He grunted, which I took as a sign of agreement that I could clean his face. I went back into the shack, found a cloth that wasn't too dirty, put some water in a pan, and carried it outside.

Dried blood was crusted on his forehead, in his eyebrows, and around his eye where it had run down and congealed.

I gingerly dabbed at it while he winced. I could tell he was grateful to get a little attention, and I realized that these men probably never got any personal care.

"Do you know Mikhail?" I asked.

"Ow, that's sore," he cried as I wiped some blood off his closed eyelid. "Yeah, I know 'im," he added.

"Do you know where he is by any chance?"

"He was in that alley with me yesterday where we got cornered by them damn Specials."

"Yes?"

"Mikhail's a right good fighter, he is."

"What happened?"

"A bunch of us men ran into that alley to escape, but the Specials had closed off the other end, so we were trapped. They followed us in and started beating us with their clubs."

"And you were with Mikhail?"

"Yeah, he ducked one of their clubs and landed a good one on the bastard's face. Course, that brought a couple more of 'em on top of Mikhail, and me, since I was next to 'im."

My heart was racing, and I thought I was going to be sick.

"And then?"

"Mikhail managed to punch another one real good, but then they were all over us with their damn clubs. I couldn't see what happened, but I think they were beatin' hard on him. I was down on the ground trying to cover my head when I heard them yell to take this one away."

"What do you mean?"

"I think I saw a couple of them dragging Mikhail away. There was a lot of yelling about 'rresting the troublemakers, and I guess Mikhail was one of 'em."

"Ow, what the hell are ya doing?!" Stephen yelled.

I was so stressed that I had wiped too hard below his eye and had hurt him.

"Sorry, sorry," I said.

I forced myself to finish cleaning his face carefully.

"Do you know where they took him?" I asked.

"Who knows? Prison, I s'pose."

I was desperate. Frank came out of Stephen's shack, holding a cup of tea for him.

"Frank, what are we going to do?" I demanded.

He scratched his head, then said, "Let's ask some of the other men if they know anything."

"You take care," I said to Stephen.

"Thanks for your help, miss. Much appreciated."

Frank and I walked along the row of shacks, asking each of the men if they'd heard what happened to Mikhail. We didn't learn anything new, except that another man thought he had seen a couple of the Specials dragging him off.

"I heard they were taking some of the men to Stony before deportin' em," he said.

My chest clenched. *Oh no, please no.*

By "Stony," he meant the provincial penitentiary.

"Frank, what should we do?" I don't know how many times I asked him that that day.

He could see I was in distress. "Be calm, Sophie. We don't know he's in prison. Let's go to the hospital and see if he's there."

We headed back to Main Street and William Avenue, the same place we'd been the previous day when everything still seemed so hopeful.

A couple of Specials were hanging around the corner, and the thought occurred to me that they might know what had happened to the arrested men.

"Excuse me, sir," I said to one of them. "Can you tell me what they did with the men they arrested yesterday?"

"What's it to you, sweetie?" he sneered.

"I'm trying to find my brother," I lied, thinking that they would be more helpful for a brother.

"You're sure you're not looking for your boyfriend?"

The other one intervened. "Miss, anyone who was arrested was either taken to the hospital or the Vaughan Street Gaol."

"Do you know if any of them were taken to Stony?" Frank asked.

"Don't know 'bout that," the second one answered.

He looked at the first one, who shrugged and said, "I heard some of 'em were taken there last night."

"Thanks," Frank said. "Let's go, Sophie."

The first one stepped in front of me. "If your boyfriend's in the clink, mebbe it's time to look elsewhere."

I just gave him a baleful stare and bit my tongue. After all, they were still carrying their clubs. I managed a half-smile and stepped around him. He smirked and let me by.

Frank and I continued down William Avenue and headed to the Winnipeg General Hospital. It was already past mid-morning, and Frank was hungry. The hospital had a little canteen, so I gave Frank some money to buy a coffee and a fried egg with toast while I looked for Mikhail.

An admitting desk stood at the front where one could inquire about patients, with a young woman staffing the desk.

"I'm looking for a patient that I think was admitted yesterday evening by the name of Mikhail Shevchenko," I said.

She started looking through her list. "There were a lot of men admitted with injuries yesterday."

"Yes, I think he was one of them."

"I guess some of them strikers got what they deserved," she said and looked at me slyly.

"You think they deserved to get beaten up because they were peacefully protesting?" I gritted my teeth.

The woman put down her list, plainly stopping her search.

"I don't think there's anyone here by that name," she said.

I could see that she was playing with me and held all the cards.

"Please, could you have another look?" I asked. "He's my brother, and it's important to me and the family to know if he's alright."

"Hmmph, what kind of work did he do?"

I felt like screaming at her that it was none of her business, but I said, "He's an ironworker at Vulcan."

"Mmm, I've heard that's difficult work," she said and turned back to her list.

"I'm sorry," she said after a minute, "but there's really no one here by that name."

My stomach lurched again. I hadn't realized it, but I was hoping he was in the hospital—somehow, it would have been better to find him injured in a bed than locked up in prison.

I wanted to ask her to check again, but several people arrived behind me, asking about their loved ones. The clerk turned her attention to them, clearly indicating that she had done with me. I sighed and went to find Frank.

"He's not here," I told him. "Let's go to the gaol."

Frank likewise sighed, apparently resigned to following me around.

The Vaughan Street Gaol was Winnipeg's prison, and it was within walking distance, just south of the Fort Garry Hotel. We left the hospital, walked back up William Avenue, and turned south on Balmoral. After crossing Notre Dame, and ten minutes later, Portage Avenue, we soon came to the prison.

The building was an imposing stone structure, but there were no barbed wire fences around it or anything. If you looked at it from a distance, you might think it was an extremely rich person's home or perhaps a nice government office. Only when you looked at the windows and saw the iron bars could you tell it was a prison.

Frank hesitated. "I don't think I wanna go in there, Sophie."

"Why not? We haven't done anything wrong."

"You know that I'm technically an illegal alien. They might arrest me."

Frank had a point. The prison was located near the legislative grounds, which were just on the other side of Broadway.

"Why don't you go across to the legislature, and I'll meet you in the gardens once I find out about Mikhail?"

He agreed and sauntered off, while I turned and went up the stairs.

A burly guard intercepted me before I could open the door.

"Excuse me, miss, what business do you have here?"

"Uh, I believe my brother was arrested last night, and I just want to see him for a minute."

"It ain't visiting hours now."

"But can I just confirm that he's really here? Please?" I added.

He hesitated before saying, "Follow me."

He opened the heavy door onto a foyer. A man was seated behind glass to our right, and another guard stood in front of two more doors that were clearly the entrance to the prison. He guided me to the man behind the glass.

"This lassie thinks her brother might be locked up here," he said.

The man behind the glass was older, balding, and wore wire-rim glasses.

"Alright then, what's his name?"

"Mikhail Shevchenko."

"Ah, a Bohunk then?" he asked.

I just gritted my teeth, something I was getting used to. He flipped through some papers.

"Shevchenko, you said? Starts with 'she'?"

"Yes."

"Doesn't look like we've got anyone here by that name."

Where could Mikhail be?

"Are you sure?" I asked. "No Mikhail Shevchenko?"

I spoke loudly and looked at the guard blocking the entrance to the rest of the prison.

"Hey, boss," the man called. "I think we had a Bohunk by that name in here last night. He was a real troublemaker, and they shipped him out to Stony."

"Pardon me?" I asked.

"Yeah, there were a coupla bad 'uns that they decided to send on."

"What does that mean? What will they do with him there?"

"Beats me, but they might be getting ready to deport 'im. Probably serves 'im right too," he added.

I looked around at the faces of each of the men and found little sympathy there. I think a tear escaped one of my eyes.

"How can I be sure he's been sent to Stony Mountain?"

The balding man behind the glass said, "Not sure, but if you think he was arrested and he ain't here, then he's probably at Stony."

I wrung my hands, the seemingly endless chase getting to me.

"Sorry, lassie, but there's not much else I can tell ya," the balding one said.

I stumbled outside in a daze and went to find Frank.

When I found him sitting complacently on a bench, I sat down next to him and started weeping.

"He's not there, Frank," I moaned. "They say he's probably gone to Stony and will be deported."

Frank clearly didn't know what to do with my tears, but he put his arms around me and muttered an attempt at comfort. We sat like that for a few moments, the massive frontispiece of the legislature looming over us.

Presently I stopped crying and, having had my emotional release, jumped up and said, "We've got to go there now, Frank!"

He half protested, but I was soon dragging him towards the CPR station.

"Hang on, Sophie. Do you have enough money for tickets?"

That was a good question.

"And do you have enough money for some food? And what if you have to bribe a guard?" he asked.

I stopped in my tracks and looked in my purse. There was enough money for tickets and probably enough for a bit of food, but that was it.

"And what if we have to spend the night in Stony?" Frank asked. "Do you know if there's a return train today?"

I was so anxious to go to the train station. What if I went to the Reynolds to get some more money and we missed the train? We didn't know the schedule, so I fretted for a moment. Frank's point about money for a bribe worried me. Maybe he was right? But most of my money was in the bank, and the banks were closed on Sundays.

"We're not that far from your house, Sophie."

"Okay, okay! Let's go quickly!"

We half walked, half ran past the legislature, over the Osborne Street bridge, and headed to the Reynolds on foot. Although the day wasn't too hot, we were drenched in sweat by the time we got there.

"I'm starving," Frank said.

"You just ate at the hospital!"

My heart was pounding, and I couldn't stop imagining that we would miss the train, that Mikhail would be deported, and we'd miss seeing him. I forced myself to be calm and told myself that was nonsense. They couldn't possibly deport someone so quickly, could they?

When we arrived, no one was around, so I got Frank some bread and cheese out of the fridge in the servants' quarters. Then, I went to the washroom, dabbed myself with a washcloth, and quickly made up a small travelling bag in case we had to stay overnight in Stony Mountain.

Soon we were scrambling back up Wellington to get to the streetcar station. We were going full circle because the CPR station was pretty close to the Vulcan Ironworks and Frank and Mikhail's shack.

It seemed to take forever for the streetcar to arrive. I was going out of my mind imagining the worst and had to keep moving.

After an eternity, we descended from the street car on Main Street and Higgins, just in front of the magnificent CPR station. Not that I noticed that day, but it was a beautiful building constructed of red brick and Tyndall

Limestone. It was now a bright sunny day, but it was anything but cheerful for me.

At the ticket booth, we found out that a train had just arrived a little while ago from Stony Mountain and that one wouldn't be going back for a couple of hours yet. There would not be a return to Winnipeg that night. I bought the tickets, and then we wandered out into the station.

We heard some yelling coming from the direction of the platform and, wondering what was happening, drifted out in that direction. You could just go out on the platform whenever you wanted—you only showed your tickets when you were on the train.

"What's going on?" Frank asked a couple of men that we encountered.

"They just loaded a couple of men onto the train that's leaving for Toronto—they're being deported."

My heart sank through my feet. *No. Please, no.*

"We were just giving 'em a send-off," the other man grinned.

"What car did they get on?" Frank asked.

The man pointed to a car a bit down the track.

"When is this train leaving?" I demanded.

"Coupla minutes, I think," he said.

I grabbed Frank by the hand and ran down the platform. When I got to the car the man had pointed out, I quickly looked in the windows, but I couldn't see anything because the light was just reflected.

I ran to the entrance and jumped up the stairs, thinking to go into the car and see if I could find Mikhail.

A man in uniform met me at the door into the car and said, "You can't come in here, miss."

"Why not? Who's in there?"

"We have some illegal aliens that are being transported to Toronto for deportation. You have to leave."

"Please, can I just say good-bye to one of them? Please?"

"Sorry, miss, but I can't allow that."

"But, but…" I tried to push by him, but he was huge, and he grabbed me by both arms.

The train started to move, and he shoved me in the direction of the stairs.

"Mikhail, Mikhail," I screamed. "I'm here."

I felt sure he was in that car.

"You have to get off now."

"Please, no! Mikhail!" I screamed again.

I thought I heard Mikhail's voice calling my name, but the guard was pushing me off the train. Frank was at the bottom of the stairs on the platform.

"Sophie, you have to get off. You can't go to Toronto. They'll throw you off the train without a ticket."

I kept struggling, but I was no match for the guard, and he pushed me onto the platform, where I fell in an ignominious heap. Frank quickly helped me up.

"Is Mikhail on this train?" Frank asked frantically.

I looked at the guard again, but his bulk blocked any way back up the stairs—my eyes darted to the stairs at the next car, thinking I could climb on there, but Frank sensed what I was thinking.

"No, Sophie," he cried. "You can't get on that train!"

He grabbed me and held on tight as the train began slowly pulling away.

With a surprising burst of strength, I struggled free of his grip and ran to the next car, but there was another equally large guard blocking my way. He was on the bottom step, and there was no way I could get on with him standing there.

I turned and ran alongside the train, banging on the side of the car where I thought Mikhail was, but I couldn't see inside. Soon the train picked up speed and, although I ran as long as I could, I had to give up when the platform ended.

Frank ran up beside me. I was shaking and sobbing uncontrollably.

He took me in his arms and said, "Sophie, we don't know that Mikhail was on that train."

But his words meant nothing, nothing at all. I knew in my bones that Mikhail was there. I could sense it, and I could feel him moving away from me as if I could see him with my own eyes.

* * *

I won't torture you with the rest of this part of my tale. Since we had the tickets, we waited at the station and went to Stony Mountain later that afternoon. After using ten dollars of my money, a guard told me that, in fact, one Mikhail Shevchenko had spent the night in the penitentiary and then was returned to Winnipeg by train for immediate deportation.

I never saw him again.

BOOK THREE

MOVING ON

Chapter 18

LIFE CONTINUES

The Monday after Bloody Saturday and the day after Mikhail was deported, the Strike Committee called an end to their work stoppage. They managed to squeeze some minor concessions out of the big companies, so they could claim that it was time to return to work. But the reality was that the state had beaten down the strikers, and the violence of that horrible Saturday had crushed any remaining spirit of the workers to keep up their resistance.

I didn't make it back to Winnipeg and the Reynolds' until later on Monday. When I straggled in, I expected Miss Wilson to unleash on me, but she just gave me a quizzical look.

"I'm sorry," I said. "Something happened yesterday, and I had to leave town in a hurry. There was no train until this morning, and I didn't have access to a phone."

Not showing up for work was potential grounds for dismissal, but all she said was, "Alright then. You better get changed and go help Anna. She's had a load to carry."

Mr. Reynolds was out, but when I passed within earshot I heard Mrs. Reynolds talking on the phone to one of her hoity-toity friends.

"Thank God those strikers have finally come to their senses, Martha. Maybe they'll understand what's good for them from now on."

I sighed, having no fight left in me, but I knew then that I couldn't continue working in that household for much longer.

*   *   *

The papers on Monday were full of sensational pictures and reports about Bloody Saturday. There was nothing about arrests and deportations, but a few lines in Tuesday's *Free Press* confirmed that a handful of men had been deported. Mikhail's name was among them, removing any remaining doubt that he was gone.

I sunk into a deep depression and wallowed in misery for the next couple of months, hoping in vain for news about Mikhail. I imagine I was a royal pain to everyone around me.

A letter finally arrived in late August. I was in the servants' quarters and wanted to rip it open, but I couldn't read it in front of the other women. I took a small knife with me and walked down to my favourite little park by the river, where, with trembling hands, I cut the envelope and let the letter spill out.

My dearest Sofiya,

I am so sorry that we were separated in such an abrupt and brutal manner. But I want you to know that I am okay. I am here in Vienna and it is a very exciting time.

The Bolshevik revolution is sweeping across Russia and we are on the dawn of a new age of equality for all. But the remnants of the old monarchists are fighting on, under the banner of the White Army.

You know I am not a violent man, but I believe it is my duty to go back to my homeland and do what I can to defeat the monarchists and help build a new society. I will be leaving tomorrow and do not know when I will be able to write again.

You are the most intelligent and beautiful woman I have known, and I am sure we could have built a good life together. But our love is a small thing on the grand stage of events now sweeping the world. We cannot put ourselves above the greatest undertaking in the history of the world—to remake humanity into equals!

Although it pains me to say it, I think it is best if you go forward with your life and forget about me. Perhaps it will be possible for me to return one day, but as long as the monarchists rule in Canada, it will be impossible.

> *Please give Frank a hearty embrace for me, and tell him that I expect him to carry on the good fight for the common man in whatever way he can.*
>
> *I will always carry your memory in my heart.*
>
> *Love and solidarity forever,*
> *Mikhail*

I sobbed and sobbed as I read the letter again and again, waves of alternating emotions washing over me.

"*You are the most intelligent and beautiful woman I have known*" was thrilling, but "*our love is but a small thing*" was a dagger to my heart.

I sunk even deeper into my depression after the letter. Everyone was supportive, and Anna, in particular, was a rock for me. She listened to my 'woe is me' story endlessly until one day in mid-September, she walked to the park with me, sat me down, and told me to grow up and get on with my life.

My reaction was, not surprisingly, to get angry with her. I said stupid things like she had never known a love like mine, so how could she know what she was talking about? But I knew in my heart that she meant well and that there was no other option.

Fortunately, something happened soon after, which, in retrospect, was the best thing for me at the time.

One fine Sunday, I had joined Frank for lunch at the Downtown Café. I was being my usual miserable self, and Frank wasn't much better.

"I s'pose I'm lucky to have work again," Frank said, "but they're treating us as bad as ever at the works."

Frank had been rehired at the Vulcan Ironworks and was still living in the shack behind the plant.

"I guess there are still a lot of unemployed men, so they have their pick, and if you don't do what they say, they just show you the door?"

"Yep, that's pretty much it. The other day, a fella by the name of Walter broke his arm badly when an iron rod swung into it. They just gave him a day's pay and sent him on his way. The next day there was a new guy in his place alright."

Like the rest of the country, Winnipeg had sunk into a serious recession after the war. Orders for the factories that were supplying the war effort had dried up, and with all of the returned men around, there was a surplus of workers.

Rose, however, was her usual cheery self.

"What'll it be, you two? We've got some great beef and cabbage soup on the boil today!"

"Sounds wonderful, Rose," I said.

"Sure, we'll both take the soup with about half a loaf of that bread of yours," Frank added.

"Coming right up," Rose answered and headed off to the kitchen.

"Things aren't great at the Reynolds either," I said. "The eldest daughter headed off to Toronto for university at the start of September, and with poor Sally gone, there are two fewer people in the household. Although Mr. Reynolds' business has picked up a bit since the strike ended, it's not going as well as it was during the war, so they'll probably have to let one of us go."

Rose returned with the bread and soup, which was steaming heartily. She seemed to be having some difficulty carrying the tray.

"Do you need any help with that?" I jumped up and asked.

"No thanks, I can still manage, although I don't know how much longer I'll be able to keep it up." She smiled.

Rose was pregnant and getting bigger by the day.

"Say, did I hear that you might be losing your job, Sophie?"

"Yeah, there isn't as much work to do in our household, and I was the last one to be hired, so I suspect I'll be the first one to go."

"Hmm, don't suppose you'd be interested in working here, at least for a while?" she asked.

"Wow! Really?"

"I'll have to talk to Joe, of course," she continued. "But it's a sure bet that I won't be able to keep doing this for much longer when the baby comes."

My brain was clicking away. It would be great to get away from the Reynolds' and do something different. I loved Anna and Polly, but I needed a change. Of course, there were practical matters to think about as well—like where would I live?

To make a long story short, early the next month, Rose and her husband Joe made a formal offer to me to start working at the café at the beginning of November, which would be a few weeks ahead of Rose's due date.

I recall that it was just after Thanksgiving weekend when I announced that I would be leaving the Reynolds. After breakfast in our quarters, when Mrs. Murray, Polly, and Miss Wilson had gone to the big house, I spoke with Anna.

"Anna, I have news. I've just accepted a job in the Downtown Café. I'll be giving my notice to Miss Wilson right away."

"Oh Sophie, I'm happy for you!" she said. "But I'm going to miss you so much."

She stepped forward and hugged me for a good minute while we both shed tears of joy and sadness.

Later that morning, during a short break around 10:00, I asked to speak with Miss Wilson alone for a moment.

We went into the dining room, where I told her that I had accepted another job and was giving my notice to leave at the end of October.

She stiffened and said, "We'll all be sorry to see you go, Sophie, but it's probably for the best. Mrs. Reynolds has been telling me that we'd probably have to let someone go soon anyway. This makes it easier all around."

I nodded. "I'm glad that it won't cause you any difficulties."

She cleared her throat, managed to step forward, and held out her hand. "You've always been a good worker, Sophie, and I wish you all the best."

It seemed difficult for her to get those words out, but at least she did, and that was a minor miracle in itself. I shook her hand, and I must say, it felt good to be leaving without any serious hard feelings between us.

The next day at lunch, we were all gathered in the kitchen for a moment when Iain announced that he was being laid off at the end of the month.

"Oh no, where will you go!?" I asked.

"Ah, don't ye worry about me, lassie," he responded with a brave smile.

In them days there were no old-age pensions, no welfare, no nothing, and many elderly people lived in fear of losing their livelihood. The harsh reality was that loss of work often meant a quick descent into poverty, with death often not far behind. Older people usually had to rely on family members to take care of them.

Not surprisingly, Iain said, "I can go stay with my sister. She has a little spare room that I can bunk down in."

Anna, who was warmer and more spontaneous than me, ran up to him and gave him a big hug.

She wiped tears from her cheeks and said, "We're going to miss you, Iain. You're a good man."

Polly and I hugged him in turn, and there were tears all around.

Poor Iain was another victim of the changing times. His lifetime of training with horses and carts wasn't very useful in the new world of automobiles.

"Mrs. Reynolds did say she expected that they would need me for next summer's gardening work," Iain added.

That would be a very good thing, I thought. It would keep him working for a while longer, get him outside, and provide him with some purpose.

Later that afternoon, I ran into Mrs. Reynolds in the library.

"I hear you'll be leaving us, Sophie," she said.

"Yes, ma'am," I gave her my habitual curtsey.

"I would like to say that we've appreciated you very much in the time you've been here. We'll always remember how important you were to Sally."

"Thank you, ma'am."

She managed to smile, shake my hand, and wish me good luck.

"And if you ever need a reference, you can count on me," she added.

This was quite gracious of her because the references would normally only come from Miss Wilson. I must admit that it gave me some not little satisfaction—after one has spent so much time at a place, it feels good to know that you were appreciated and made a positive difference.

On our last day of work, the group hosted a special lunch for Iain and me. With Miss Wilson's permission, Mrs. Murray managed to bake a ham with roast potatoes and a variety of veggies. It was a right little feast and provided a memorable send-off for us.

We were looking at life from different ends of the road—me, still young with many unforeseen miles to travel—Iain, looking back at the road he had travelled, wondering if there was much left on his journey. Both of us had tears in our eyes as we said our good-byes, but I expect his would have tasted more bittersweet than mine.

*   *   *

I was worried about finding new living arrangements, but fortunately Bea had been able to help me out. She had a friend who had been a servant at her house but who had landed a job at Ashdown's, the biggest department store in Winnipeg at the time. Her name was Oksana, and she also had to find a place to live.

Beatrice had arranged for us to have tea with Oxie, as she liked to be called, and she and I hit it off reasonably well. Oxie had some time off, and she had found a little apartment on Hargrave Street, between Graham and St. Mary's Avenue. It was a bit of a walk from there to the Downtown Café and Ashdown's, but beggars can't be choosers.

It was a small one-bedroom apartment, semi-furnished with two little cots in the bedroom, a table and chairs in the kitchen, and a couch in the sitting room. We didn't need much more, so we were quite happy with the arrangement. Oxie was about a year older than me, and the apartment was the first place where either of us ever lived independently.

When I packed my things on October 31 and gave my last good-byes to the people with whom I had lived ever since I came to the city, it felt as if I was more than turning the page on a chapter in my life—it was as if I were closing the cover on an entire book.

Chapter 19

THE NOT-SO-ROARING
TWENTIES

As Winnipeg moved into the 1920s, it seemed to me that the ravages of the war, the senselessness of the Spanish Flu, and the strife of the general strike had exhausted everyone and had a combined softening effect on the divisions in the city.

Although the strike hadn't achieved any of its immediate goals, there were a number of knock-on effects in the ensuing years. In the next Winnipeg civic election, pro-labour candidates won half the seats on city council. In the 1920 provincial election, the new Manitoba Independent Labour Party won eleven seats even though three of its winning candidates were former strike leaders who were still prisoners in Stony Mountain!

These political inroads didn't result in immediate changes to legislation, but they definitely impacted the whole tone of discourse in the city. Public discussion of ideas such as unemployment insurance, disability insurance, and other worker protection measures became less charged, and there were much more balanced editorials in the papers than there had been during the strike. Thankfully, as the war receded, animosity towards people of Eastern European origin also slowly waned.

While things may have been roaring everywhere else during the '20s, it was not so in our city. By the end of the war, Winnipeg was the third-largest city in Canada, and it was the supply hub for Western Canada to the Rockies. However, in the ensuing years, production of many goods shifted to cities like Edmonton, Calgary, and Regina, which, after all, were much closer to their populations, and the economy somewhat stagnated in Winnipeg.

Fortunately, people always have to eat, the Downtown Café was well situated, and the prices were reasonable. We seemed to have a bit of a reputation with downtown dwellers and workers as a good place for cheap eats and were always busy, especially at lunchtime on weekdays.

I was naturally outgoing and energetic, so I suppose I was good for Joe and Rose's business. At first, I mainly waited on tables and cleaned up, but as it was a small family operation, I was soon involved in cooking and doing whatever was necessary to keep things running.

We had a number of male customers, and several of them would flirt with me when I'd take their orders or when they paid up. But I was still pining for Mikhail. He was the perfect man in my mind, and none of the "boys" who asked me out measured up to my expectations.

Still, life has a way of continuing despite our personal dramas.

There was a young man who came in occasionally at lunch who, I must admit, wasn't much to look at. He was on the thin side, with wispy hair and rather undefined facial features. He was just one of many customers, and I never paid him much mind, although I did notice that he always tried to be friendly with me.

One day in late September 1924, he came into the restaurant about 3:00 in the afternoon, a time when we were mostly empty. I was sitting behind the cash register, reading *Silas Marner* by George Eliot.

"Hello," he said with a shy smile. He glanced down and saw what I had in my hand.

"Oh, you like to read, do you?" he asked.

"Yes, I suppose it's my main hobby," I responded. "Would you like tea or coffee?" I continued, not wanting to encourage him too much.

"A tea and a scone with jam, please."

"Coming right up," I said as I walked to the kitchen.

When I brought the tea and scone to the table, he smiled and thanked me.

With what seemed to be some difficulty, he asked, "Do you know who George Eliot really was?"

"Of course! She was Mary Ann Evans. It's one of the reasons that I'm reading her novels."

"I'm sorry," he said as he looked down. "I didn't mean to suggest that you wouldn't know."

I think I felt a bit sorry for him at this point, so I said, "That's okay. I wouldn't have known about her if the librarian hadn't told me."

He brightened up. "So, do you read other English novels?"

"Yes, I've been working my way through most of the famous English novelists for several years now."

"You know I teach English literature at Wesley College!" he blurted out.

At that moment, two other customers came in, so I excused myself to greet them. I left my little professor sitting by himself and went back behind the cash register after taking care of the recent arrivals.

I could see that he was trying to make eye contact with me, but I put my head down and went back to my reading.

When he came to pay, he said, "Uh, uh, I know your name is Sophie because I've heard some of the customers call you that. My name is Edward."

I might have held out my hand, but the cash register was sitting between us.

"I'm giving a talk next Wednesday evening at Wesley College on Dickens and Social Awareness. Perhaps you'd like to come?" he asked me.

I must admit that that piqued my interest, but I hesitated.

"Uh, I just thought that if you enjoy English literature, you might be interested."

"If I'm not working, I might be able to make it," I said.

He smiled wide, revealing a mouth congested with none-too-white teeth.

*   *   *

Edward came in for lunch the next day and left a little one-page flyer advertising his talk. He reiterated his invitation, and I assured him that I would go.

Wesley College was the forerunner of the University of Winnipeg, and it dated back to the 1880s. It was, and still is, a beautiful four-story stone building, built in the style of the famous old English colleges.

I have to admit that I was rather intimidated as the day approached. I imagined that everyone there would either be a professor, in college or a local hoity-toity, and that I would be the only uneducated person there. I dressed modestly but carefully, essentially putting on my Sunday best clothes. Although I still sent most of my surplus earnings to my parents, I had managed to buy myself a couple of decent dresses and pairs of shoes.

When I rather timidly entered the building, I was pleased to be greeted by a young woman who asked if I was there for the Dickens lecture. She directed me to the lecture hall, which was mainly empty when I arrived. I took a seat on the side, near the exit, about two-thirds back.

After a few minutes, Edward appeared at the front of the room. He craned his neck, quickly spotted me, and came over to say hello.

"I'm so glad you came," he said. "Please come sit a little closer to the front."

At his insistence, I moved up but stayed near the side.

He stood nervously making small talk for a moment before saying he had to go and get ready for his presentation.

About twenty-five to thirty people eventually sauntered in, with about half of them being young women.

One of them sat down close to me, looked over, and, giving me a slight smile, said, "Hello, I don't believe we've met? Are you in one of Professor Thompson's classes?"

"No, I'm just a member of the public who's interested in the topic."

"Oh, I see," she responded and glanced away, not deigning to look in my direction again.

As it turned out, Professor Thompson, as I now knew him to be, gave what I found to be a very inspiring talk. It ran something as follows:

"Dickens was clearly getting the word out to the masses that their lot was not what God intended for mankind. He was undoubtedly a genius of the highest order and was able to widely spread ideas about the unfairness of the lot of the common man without invoking the ire of the authorities.

"Dickens got his message across by telling stories that touched the hearts of every man and woman of sensibility but particularly of the poorer classes that could relate to the conditions of his heroes and heroines.

"While Dickens communicated many good socialist ideals, he himself profited enormously from the sales of his books."

Edward quoted extensively from Dickens' works to make his points. As he spoke, I couldn't help constructing parallels in my mind with Mikhail. He was clearly passionate about equality for all, but unlike Mikhail, he sprinkled his talk with frequent references to Jesus's teachings.

I later found out that the Methodists founded Wesley College, and one of its principal aims was to train men for the clergy, so the references to Jesus were hardly surprising.

When he finished his talk, there was polite applause, and the man who had introduced him invited all to a salon next door for some refreshments. A few of the young women rushed to the front of the room and surrounded

Edward, so I used the opportunity to quickly slip out the side door as I doubted that I would fit into the society in the "salon."

The next day, Edward showed up at the restaurant again in mid-afternoon and eagerly asked me how I liked the talk. It was clear that he was interested in me, but I was still not particularly interested in a relationship with a man.

"I enjoyed it very much," I replied.

"We have a series of fall lectures, you know. I hope you can attend some more of them."

"Yes, I suppose I might come on occasion."

I wasn't that keen on going down this path, but Anna and Oxie both encouraged me to get out. Although Winnipeg's economy wasn't booming, it was still affected by the mood of the Roaring Twenties. It was a time when a lot of young women were celebrating new attitudes by smoking and going out to bars, dancing regularly, and drinking.

"Sophie, you should be out having a good time!" Anna said. "English literature lectures sound like Dullsville. Sure you don't want to go dancing?"

Anna was going out with a returned soldier who, apparently, was a lot of fun and with whom she would regularly go dancing.

"Jack has lots of good-looking friends. C'mon, you should join us!" she would say.

Oxie would also regularly ask me to go out, and I always declined. But with all the pressure on me to "have some fun," it seemed that the least I could do was go to the English lectures.

Edward soon became a regular at the café, and I did indeed attend several of the fall lectures. He eventually got up the nerve to invite me to a play, which I half-reluctantly accepted.

*   *   *

One freezing dark Sunday in December, I was sitting in a café with Bea and Helen, discussing our lives. Bea was still working as a servant but had risen to be the head housekeeper—although like most other English homes, the number of servants had been cut back, so her position was not that exalted.

Helen had, oddly enough, followed in my footsteps and was working at another restaurant close to the CP train station on Main Street, and that's where we were having lunch.

"So tell us more about your professor fellow," Bea said over a bowl of borscht.

"He's not 'my' fellow," I replied.

"But he's repeatedly asked you to his lectures, and now he's invited you out to a play, on a Saturday night no less!"

"That's got to mean something," Helen chimed in.

"I suppose he is interested in me," I admitted.

After all, it was pretty obvious. He surely wasn't inviting me along just for intellectual debates.

"How exciting!" Helen said. "And a real English gentleman as well."

This comment represented the common and widespread desire of the average daughter of Ukrainian immigrants. They wanted to marry Englishmen.

Marrying an Englishman was seen to be a sign of marrying up and improving one's social status, and it seemed to be the goal of all the Ukrainian and Polish girls I knew.

"So what?" I said. "It's not important."

"Isn't it?" Helen asked. "We all know they're superior."

"They're not superior!" I almost shouted. "They're just humans like the rest of us."

"You can't deny that they have an empire, dearie," Bea said.

"Look what John did," Helen said.

Our younger brother had moved to the city and told everyone his name was John Rose. We doubted that he was fooling too many people, but it certainly demonstrated that the desire to be like the "English" was pretty ubiquitous.

"You're both devout Catholics, aren't you?" I asked. "Doesn't Jesus teach that we're all equal?"

They were silent for a minute before Helen said, "I don't remember hearing that in the gospels."

"Well, then, you should come and hear Edward talk sometime," I said.

"Aha," Bea said. "You're really taken by him, aren't you?"

I seethed because I didn't think I was at all "taken" by Edward. "I just think he has some very good ideas, that's all."

Anyway, to get to the gist of the matter, Edward patiently courted me for more than two years. I regularly attended lectures at Wesley College and started attending readings by various local authors at the Winnipeg Public Library.

If there was any path to my heart at that time, Edward managed to find it. Looking back, I have to admire him because I gave him very little encouragement, and he had to persist.

In the end, I slowly felt him becoming a part of my life, and eventually, I couldn't imagine life without him. He encouraged my love of literature and helped guide me so that I was able to increasingly appreciate the novels I read. In time, we even began to have heated debates as I expressed my own views, which were often contrary to his, especially when the issues involved women.

Edward was a devout Methodist, and one potential stumbling block in our relationship revolved around his religious views. But, unlike the Catholicism I had been exposed to, Edward's brand of religion was much more focussed on taking action on social justice issues.

"Belief in Jesus means nothing if one doesn't take action to improve the lot of the underprivileged," he would say.

Edward contributed a significant portion of his earnings towards various charities and moved in a circle of people who wanted to build a more equal society. As I spent more and more time with him and, eventually, some of his colleagues, my respect and admiration for him slowly grew.

"Edward, I respect and agree with most of your ideas, but you know that I don't believe in God like you do," I told him.

"That's okay, Sophie. I think it's more important to agree on how one should live one's life rather than on one's exact theological beliefs."

He was telling me that we didn't have to agree on everything and, in effect, that I could be my own woman. Edward was also very supportive of expanding women's rights, and that was probably a clincher to winning my affections.

I always remembered Helen's comment when she said, "We don't count," and that we should defer to the men's wishes. Her comment threw a bright light on my own desire "to count." With my background on the farm, I never received the necessary stimulation to aspire to a higher profession. But I did know that I wanted my views to matter, and I felt that with Edward, they always would.

"I do believe that we have a soul, you know," I told Edward.

"That's good enough for me." He smiled.

Speaking of souls, I kept my promise to Sally and would pray for her soul every year. I always made a special point of praying for her on Remembrance Day because she had died just after the war had ended.

I didn't have to be prompted to remember my sister Annie and my little brothers Nicholas and Paulie. I continued to make a point of praying for them every Sunday. It was sometimes difficult because I didn't believe that there was a god taking care of them, but I learned to pray directly to them. Whether or not my prayers made a difference to their souls, I'll never know, but I do know that they brought solace to my own soul.

*   *   *

All in all, the 1920s in Winnipeg were good years, even if they weren't boom years. The strife and conflict of the war years and the strike continued to subside as the decade progressed. Further, the divide between the English and the Ukrainians continually shrank, as we were all becoming Canadians.

Bea found an English man to be her beau, and they were married in early 1926. Helen also found an English beau, or I suppose what was to us the same thing, a fellow of Scottish heritage. It was an odd thing, but there were lots of "English" men who married Ukrainian and Polish girls, but there were very few English girls who married Ukrainian men. There was undoubtedly some lingering racism, and the English girls' parents probably wouldn't have approved of them dating a Bohunk.

Edward eventually proposed to me and, after some deliberation, I accepted. Bea and Helen said I'd be crazy not to marry him. After all, he was English, he had a good job, and everyone agreed that he was nice. Helen did remark that he wasn't as handsome as her man, Dan, or Bea's beau, Arthur. While it might not have been kind of her to say that, it was the plain truth.

Dan was tall with a high intelligent brow and sparkling eyes. Arthur wasn't as tall, but he was a strong, burly man with the ability to make everyone laugh. In comparison, Edward presented himself as what he was— shy and bookish.

Edward never pressured me to have sexual relations with him before we married, and I was glad of that.

16. Helen Lesko
circa 1927

We were married in late August 1926, shortly before the fall semester was due to start and ten years to the day after I had first arrived in the city. It was a modest affair, but I was very happy to have my brothers and sisters all attend, including Mama and Papa. It was a big event for them, as they rarely left the farm, and a trip to the city was a huge occasion.

Mama had continued to produce babies until she was forty, and by the time I was married, I had another younger brother, Alfie, who was six, and a younger sister, Jessie, who was three.

Edward and I had a brief honeymoon at Minaki in Lake of the Woods, across the border in Ontario. It was a lovely spot, and it went as well as it could have.

Edward was clearly a virgin, and our attempts at lovemaking were extremely awkward. The sad truth is that I closed my eyes and imagined that I was with Mikhail.

I did my best to be a good wife to Edward, and I think I succeeded. He always seemed happy with me, and I slowly learned to love him.

At times, I felt like a bit of a phony and undeserving of his love because I couldn't shake my memories of Mikhail. I suppose reality can never match the promise of our unfulfilled dreams, and so it was for me. No man could ever match what I imagined I would have had with Mikhail, and for many years, I lived haunted by regret, no matter how foolish that may be.

One thing that was crystal clear was my fate was much better than my sisters'. Both Arthur and Dan turned out to be drinkers and slowly descended into alcoholism as they got older. I saw a lot more of Helen and Dan and observed him when he drank—a small mercy perhaps, but he was what we used to call a "happy drunk." He would become silly, then start singing songs and nod off.

Both Dan and Arthur had served in the war and had spent time at the front in the trenches. One can only imagine the horrors they witnessed and what they had needed to do to survive the human slaughter around them. While I think that Bea and Helen's love for their husbands slowly dissolved into resentment and possibly even hate with the passage of the years, I can only say that it is not my place to judge. I believe I was fortunate that my own Edward was a little younger than them and had mercifully escaped being sent overseas. Who knows how it would have affected him, particularly with his sensitive nature?

In the end, out of we three girls, I was the one who made the lucky match. And I do think it was mainly luck, although I can honestly say that I didn't marry Edward in a befuddled state of infatuation. And perhaps there's a lesson for all of us in that.

Chapter 20

EVERYTHING, INCLUDING
THE PUMP HANDLE

When did "Them Days" end?

That's a very good question to which there may be no clear answer.

When Helen refers to Them Days, I know she is mainly referring to our childhood growing up on the homestead, our early years as servants, and possibly the days when we were still single young women in the 1920s. I think, for me, when the three of us got married, it marked the end of Them Days.

Still, Them Days are associated in the collective memory of my family with the hard times of our youth, and, sad to say, the 1930s brought more hard times for almost everyone. Besides, our youngest siblings were still growing up on the homestead at that time, and in their minds, Them Days would definitely include the dirty days of the depression.

One thing that is clear is that Them Days ended with the advent of WWII. The second great war stands out as a separate time period in all of our minds, and for us old folks, anything after that war was modern times. So, if we can agree that Them Days extended into the '30s, I will conclude with one last story.

Mama had really started to put on weight after the birth of her last child, Jessie, and I think that all that extra weight was hard on her heart. Whatever the cause, one day in early June 1934, Papa found her lying dead on the kitchen floor. Although they never did autopsies in them days for such cases, it was presumed she had had a heart attack.

She had given birth to twelve children in her lifetime, and seven of them survived to adulthood. After the voyage from the old country, her life had been a non-stop carousel of cleaning, cooking, garden work, and taking care of children. The three or four trips she made to Winnipeg were the highlights of her adult life, and I'm not sure she particularly enjoyed them. She never learned to speak more than a smattering of English and only felt comfortable on the homestead.

At the time of her death, five of us, Bea, myself, Helen, Mike, and John, were living in Winnipeg. Alfie was only fourteen, and Jessie was just on the verge of her eleventh birthday. Frank had moved to Calgary in the early 1920s, as Winnipeg's economy sputtered and the west boomed. He had stopped in Calgary for a while after his time with CP rail ended, and he liked it there.

Dear Papa had been developing arthritis in many of his joints, and it was increasingly difficult for him to maintain the farm. However, since Alfie was essentially a young man and Jessie was on the cusp of womanhood, it was decided that the three of them would continue living on the homestead. As the only female in the house,

Jessie would do most of the cooking and tend the garden while Alfie would do much of the work caring for the few remaining cows, pigs, and chickens.

Maintenance of the farm had boiled down to subsistence living as it still provided milk, cheese, eggs, veggies, and some meat from the pigs and chickens, but without producing much surplus to sell. The reality was that for many years Mama and Papa were mainly getting by on the money that Bea, Helen, and I remitted to them. Mike and John had moved to the city and were working, but somehow there wasn't the same expectation on them to send money home.

At least the farm wasn't suffering the effects of the Dust Bowl that had engulfed much of the prairies. After the first war, a large contingent of Ukrainians had left the Gimli area and migrated to southern Saskatchewan, where they obtained large tracts of land. Letters from cousins had indicated that they had done well at first, but in the mid-thirties, their lands had dried out, and cattle were starving to death. But the farms around Gimli were essentially built on swampland, so they still had water, and the farmers were able to plod on much as they had done since they had arrived.

Mama's funeral was a sad affair as it somehow signaled a turning point in our family's history. She and Papa had come from the old country, settled on this land, and had forged a life for us on the homestead. And now it was clear it was coming to an end. There was little hope that one of the boys would take on the farm and keep it running. Mike and John liked the life in the city, and although Alfie could conceivably stay on and take it over, it seemed rather pointless as it had never been profitable. Although Papa was stoic, I sensed a deep sadness creep over him.

* * *

Edward and I were fortunate to make it through the depression years relatively unscathed. He managed to hang onto his job as a professor at the college and, although he didn't make that much, prices were also depressed in them days so it was enough to get by on.

Edward and I had three lovely children together, Elizabeth, Mike, and Josie. Elizabeth and Mike were born in 1928 and 1930 and were quite close to each other. I had a miscarriage about two years later, so there was a four-year gap between Mike and Josie. Happily, all three were healthy, and we had no special problems with them—I remember the thirties as a difficult but happy time being a mother to our little brood.

On a personal level, papa's lessons about patience finally began to sink in, and I gradually became a calmer and more patient person.

Helen's husband Dan had a good job with the railroad, but he was constantly in danger of being dismissed for drunkenness. Helen had to often go to his boss and beg him not to fire Dan. Somehow, she repeatedly convinced them to keep him on, and Dan would promise to mend his ways—which he would for a while before inevitably relapsing. They only had one daughter, Irene, and Helen had to stay home with her until she was in school, after which she went back to working in a restaurant to help them get by.

Bea's husband Arthur managed to find enough work to get them through those dark days, but most of it was temporary. I asked Bea a few times whether they had enough to get by, and she always told me they were alright. I think it was a very difficult time for her, though.

Many decades later, we heard about Stalin's forced starvation of millions of Ukrainians in the early '30s, the Holodomor. It was hard to believe that such cruelty could be perpetrated on people who had been neighbours for centuries and essentially spoke the same language. Although very small comfort, the events that had taken over the Ukraine did in some way justify Papa's decision to move the family to Canada. By the time we found out about the Holodomor horror, we were living comfortably in the prosperity and security of modern-day Canada, while the Ukraine was still under Communist oppression.

I had long ago given up on Mikhail. It was easiest to assume that he had been killed when he returned to the Ukraine in 1919 to fight alongside the Bolsheviks. But who knows what happened to him? Perhaps he survived that war only to die in the mass starvation and pandemic that followed in the early 20s. If he got through that, perhaps the Holodomor did him in. And if by some miracle he survived all of those calamities, he likely finally met his end in WWII.

In any event, once Edward and I had children, Mikhail's memory started to fade, and the days of my infatuation seemed more and more infantile. I had three beautiful children to raise, and I was thankful for my family.

*   *   *

Two years after Mama died, it had become apparent that Papa, Alfie, and Jessie could no longer continue on the farm. It was no life for Alfie as a young man stranded on an unproductive piece of land in the middle of nowhere, and he wanted to move to the city. Unfortunately, Papa's arthritis had gotten progressively worse, so he couldn't help much at all, and it was an unfair burden on thirteen-year-old Jessie to continue doing so much yard and housework, taking care of the two men.

One day in late May, John and I went back to the homestead for a visit. Fortunately, Edward had an older sister who had a couple of children about the same ages as our children, and the cousins got along well. Edward didn't mind spending a weekend with them, and the children were ecstatic.

It was still a long trip because I didn't have access to a car, and the road to the farm was in poor shape. Edward had bought a car for city use, but he didn't trust it for a drive out to the homestead. We arranged for Alfie to pick us up with the buggy.

"Papa, it's so great to see you!" I said when we arrived.

He had been sitting outside in a chair against the wall of the house facing the sun when we rode in, and it was obvious that it had been an effort for him to stand up.

"Malenka kit, how wonderful to see you," he said as we hugged tightly.

"So good to see the strong young woman you've become," he continued.

We went inside for some tea, after which John and I took a short walk around the grounds with Alfie.

17. Hilko Lesko ("Papa") and grand-daughter Irene Gillis
circa 1937

The paint was peeling badly off the barn, the pigsty, the chicken coop, and the outhouse. They were all in a dilapidated state.

"What's the matter with you, Alf?!" John said. "Why aren't you taking care of the out-buildings?"

"Don't be so hard on him," I said. "It must be tough being on his own out here."

Alfie just nodded.

"Papa doesn't look too good," I said.

"No, he isn't," Alfie answered. "He really has trouble getting around now, and the arthritis is bad in his hands.

He has trouble holding things—even like a knife and fork."

Tears welled in my eyes.

"Doesn't look like there's too much of value here," John said.

"What do you mean?"

"Look at the harnesses and rigging. They're all old. No one would pay much for them."

"What are you talking about?! Aren't you concerned about Papa?"

"Yes, yes, of course," he answered quickly. "I was just thinking that if he and Jessie have to move away, there isn't too much of value left here."

I was angry and about to tear a strip off him when Jessie appeared.

"Hi, big sister," she said with a smile. "Can I show you the garden?"

"Of course!"

Jessie and I wandered off to the garden, which was doing amazingly well. Although it was early in the season, peas were climbing up their runners, beans were sprouting, tomato plants were standing tall, and the cabbages were well on their way.

"You obviously have a nose for the earth," I said. "It's beautiful."

Despite the bounty of the garden, it was only too clear that the farm was in a general state of disrepair, and it was time for Papa to move somewhere else. John and I had a short talk after Jessie showed me the garden, and we agreed that there was no other choice.

Papa was back sitting outside in the chair, enjoying the late-spring sunshine. I found a chair and sat down next to him, preparing myself for one of the hardest conversations of my life.

"Papa, you know that you and Mama did a wonderful job raising all us kids and setting us off on our lives."

He just reached across and patted my hand.

"Times are hard in the city, but we're all getting by, and I think things are going to start to improve."

He just nodded, and I sensed that he knew where I was headed.

"Alfie is becoming a young man, and he's ready to head off and make his way."

I looked across at him and saw a tear escape the corner of his eye.

"Yes, I know," he whispered.

There was no need for any further discussion. I reached across and gave him the biggest hug I could without hurting his frail bones.

It was soon arranged that Papa and Jessie would move in with Papa's cousins who lived on a nearby farm. Jessie could come to our homestead and tend the garden so that they would still contribute food to the family, and in the fall, she could go back to school for one more year. Alfie would move to the city and stay with one of us until he could sustain himself.

John was mainly out of work, only picking up odd jobs, so he volunteered to come and arrange the physical aspects of the move, including moving the livestock and chickens. The plan was for Bea, Helen, and me to come up, pack up the house and provide some moral support to Papa and Jessie.

Not long after we agreed to the moving arrangements, I had an appendicitis attack and operation. Somehow, I developed a post-op infection and was laid low for a month. I was never very big, and I lost so much weight after the operation that I was nothing but skin and bones for a while. Fortunately, I was in the city and had good health care. People in the rural areas still died from appendicitis attacks and infections in them days.

Unfortunately, I wasn't available to help out when the actual move took place. I kept asking Bea and Helen how the move went, but they were evasive, simply saying, "Papa's safe at cousin Schnerch's house."

As soon as I was well enough, I insisted on traveling out to the homestead and the cousin's place to see how Papa was doing. Everyone tried to dissuade me but to no avail. Finally, Bea agreed to accompany me one weekend.

Riding back to the farm with Bea, I had a strange feeling of reverse déjà vu. I recalled that first trip the two of us had taken to the big city. It all seemed so long ago, and now, to some extent, our roles were reversed. It wasn't as if I were her big sister now, but there was no doubt that I was the assertive one amongst the three girls and naturally took the lead.

One of the cousins, a young man by the name of Adam, had come out to the Gimli station to fetch us when we arrived on the morning train. He was good-natured, good-looking, and strong.

It was a hot July day, and, as it had been dry, we choked on the dusk thrown up by the horses' hooves. As we approached the old homestead, Bea patted my hand and told me not to be too upset by what we saw.

When we rolled into the yard, the first thing that struck me was the immediate sense of abandonment, of desolation. There was no sound of chickens clucking, no dog to greet us, no cows lowing in the fields—nothing.

Adam headed to unlock the door to the house, but I said I'd like to walk around the yard first.

I strolled over to the barn and forced the doors open with great difficulty—the hinges were rusting. The familiar smell of hay and livestock still hung over the place, but only empty stalls stared back at me. In fact, there was nothing on the floor and nothing hanging from the rafters—no harnesses, no tools, no buckets—nothing.

I bit my lip and noticed a quick scurrying in a corner, probably a rat.

Next, I duly inspected the pigsty, the chicken coop, and the vegetable storage cellar – all were completely empty.

"Where is everything, Bea?" I asked. "I don't see a single tool. It's like no one ever lived and worked here."

"Uh, John took a lot of it to the cousins'."

I noticed that Adam lifted his eyebrows at this but didn't say anything.

We wandered over to the garden, and, to my dismay, I saw that it was overgrown with weeds.

"Jessie hasn't had the time to come and take care of the garden," Adam said. "It's a lot of work to come here constantly, and she's been very busy back at our place."

We finally headed to the house, where Adam unlocked the door and stepped aside to let me in.

It took a second for my eyes to adjust to the darkness, but I immediately perceived that the kitchen was bare. Like the barn, there were no implements on the walls, nothing on the counter, and nothing on the floors. Even the table and the benches were gone—the room was completely empty.

I was thirsty after the long ride and moved to the pump to get a little water when I saw that there was no handle to the pump.

Bea had come in behind me.

"I'm sorry, dear, but John sold everything, even the pump handle."

*   *   *

Afterwards, when we visited Papa and Jessie at cousin Schnerch's, I calmed down a bit. Papa was well cared for and it was obvious that the Schnerchs were a loving family that enjoyed having them there. And I'm sure that Jessie did more than her share of work.

As things turned out, Adam and Jessie were married in early 1940, shortly after the outbreak of the war and when she was still only sixteen. Needless to say, I wasn't too happy about that, but as I lived in the city and Jessie lived on the farm, there was little that I could do or say that would change her mind.

After Papa and Jessie had moved away and John had sold everything on the farm, I had a meeting with Mike and John in the city. I was furious at what John had done and insisted that he at least pay the annual taxes, which weren't much. He agreed, and I thought that was that.

The following year, Edward and I rented a cottage for the entire summer on Bayview Road at Victoria Beach, a wonderful lake resort on the east side of Lake Winnipeg. It was a paradise for the children.

I wasn't aware of it, but John had not paid the taxes on the farm as he had promised. The farm went into receivership and was put up for sale by the bank. Incredibly, Helen went out to Gimli, paid the taxes, and took over ownership!

When I found out about this in the fall, I went to see her and gave her a giant hug.

"Helen, how could you afford to buy the farm?" I asked.

"I always put a little aside from my job, and I set up a separate account for myself a couple of years ago with a helpful young man at the bank," she said.

"You're amazing!" I said. "Can I give you some money, so we at least share the cost?"

"No, it's alright," she said. "Dan has been off the bottle for a while, bringing in steady money, and things have been going well at the restaurant."

"But what are you going to do with the farm?"

"I plan to give it to Adam and Jessie. Adam is going to take over their farm from his father and, with some more modern equipment, he should be able to take care of both places."

And so it came to pass. Adam was sent overseas in early 1943, and shortly after he left, Jessie discovered that she was pregnant. He was not around for the birth of his first child, Eleanor, and unfortunately, he never really developed a close relationship with her.

I'm not sure, but I think he may have suspected that Eleanor might not be his child, which was absolutely ridiculous. Jessie was the most steadfast person in our entire family, and I know with one-hundred percent certainty that she would never have cheated on him. Besides, the arithmetic didn't add up—Eleanor was born seven months after Adam left.

But there is no telling what impact war has on the minds of men. Although Adam was fortunate that he never had to fight on the front lines, the man that came back wasn't the same happy, carefree man Jessie had married.

Still, while the land on the old homestead was marginal at best, Adam has kept cows on the pasture and planted hay every year until the present day. We have all been glad that the farm stayed in the family and that we have been able to visit it from time to time through the years.

EPILOGUE

Chapter 21

When I look around the room where my siblings are waxing maudlin under the influence of time and a little wine, I can't help but think of how our family has grown.

If you can believe it, Mike had seventeen children, nine with his first wife and eight with his second. Bea and I each had three children, both of us having two girls and one boy. Helen only had one child, Irene.

John, the old scalawag, ended up having eight children with three different women, two of whom he married. While I have recounted some of John's youthful transgressions, I am pleased to say that he mellowed and matured, and as I write this, we have established an amicable relationship.

Alfie only had one daughter, and unfortunately, his wife absconded with her and disappeared somewhere in the US, so he never really knew her well. And lastly, Jessie had one more child, David, who was born after Adam returned from the war. In all, Papa and Mama had produced thirty-five grandchildren.

Papa ended up living until the autumn of 1943 when he passed away peacefully after a sudden and massive stroke. I think he took comfort in the last years of his life, knowing that he and Mama had left a large and growing legacy behind them.

All of the grandchildren have survived until today, with the exception of two. John's youngest child, a girl, died of leukemia when she was sixteen years old. Sadly, Helen's only daughter Irene died when she was thirty-six years old, leaving behind two young boys.

A few years ago, Edward was doing some historical research, and he came across the Manitoba census results from 1921. It showed that something like ninety percent of the population was English at the time! I had a good laugh at that.

The reality is that in 1921 very few Ukrainians or other Eastern Europeans would have admitted to their heritage. After all, the memory of the Internment and the Illegal Aliens Act was still fresh. Who in their right mind would say, "I'm Ukrainian" when asked by the census taker if you could say "English" and get away with it?

I eventually learned that about 100,000 Ukrainians and other Eastern Europeans came to Manitoba between 1896 and 1905. Assuming that they were comprised mainly of couples, that would have meant that about 50,000 couples had immigrated to the province. If they all had a dozen children like Mama and Papa (and that was the norm on the homesteads), but assuming only half of them survived to adulthood, that would mean that there would have been six children per couple or about 300,000 Eastern Europeans in the province by 1921.

The 1921 census said there were just over 600,000 people in the province at that time, and "officially" very few of them were Ukrainian. Ha! Even if there were only half as many as I estimated above, that would still mean that one-quarter of Manitobans were of Ukrainian heritage at the time. I don't really know the numbers, but I think that's a lot closer to the truth.

Of course, these days, no one much cares about that ancient history, and those feelings of being inferior because we were Ukrainian are long gone. And it's really wonderful that those old divisions have been forgotten.

Still, now that more immigrants are coming to Canada, I wonder how they feel in their first years in our country. Do they feel like second-class citizens compared to us established Canadians? I imagine so and can only hope that the troubles they endure are short-lived before they too become full-fledged citizens of this great country.

As a final thought, I can only say that Them Days were hard, much harder than young people today can imagine. But at the same time, it was all that we knew, and for us, it was just life—and after all, it's been a wonderful life.

Author's Notes

Them Days is a work of fiction and, as such, does not purport to present any particular scene in the novel as a historical fact. Nonetheless, I have done my best to check the historical record to ensure that the contextual facts are correct.

The early chapters of this novel are directly based on stories that my grandmother, Helen Gillis (neé Helen Lyszko), repeatedly told me when I was young. As such, I believe them to be "true" events, although filtered through my grandmother's memory and my memory of what she told me. I have no doubt that some of the larger events, such as the burning down of the original household, are factual. Of course, the precise details recounted in the novel are invented.

Helen was born on a farmstead near Berlo, Manitoba in 1905, the fifth consecutive daughter born to Hilko and Maria Lyszko, who had immigrated from the Ukraine in 1902. As was common in "them days," two of the girls died before their first birthday, so my grandmother was the third surviving daughter after Polly and Beatrice. My grandmother often told me the story of Beatrice and her riding the train to Winnipeg, where they worked as servants in an English home.

The family name of Lyszko was Anglicized to Lesko at some point, and other members of the Lesko household included Mike and John, Annie, Paul, Nicholas, Alf, and Jessie, all of whom are mentioned in the novel. While the exact details of their passing are unclear, Annie, Paul, and Nicholas all died young. I have recounted their deaths based on admittedly sketchy memories from my grandmother's stories.

Sofiya is an invented character, as is her personality. Although they were incredibly resilient women, neither my grandmother nor her sisters had the self-confidence that Sofiya exhibits—unfortunately, they believed to greater or lesser degrees that they were inherently inferior because they were Ukrainians and they were women. Once Sofiya moves to the city, almost all her experiences are fictional, although recounted against the background of events that my grandmother and her siblings lived through. For example, my grandmother did tell me about being in the streets on that fateful day when the NWMP and the "Specials" wreaked havoc on the working class of Winnipeg.

Frank, Sofiya's half-brother, is also an invented character. To my knowledge, no members of the immediate Lesko family were interned during WWI, but it remains a sad fact that over 5,000 young Ukrainian Canadian men were interned in twenty-four camps across Canada during the war.

I was very fortunate to find a wealth of historical material upon which to draw in constructing the novel. *Spruce, Swamp and Stone: A History of the Pioneer Settlements in the Gimli Area* by Michael Ewanchuk was an incredible find. In his 1979 publication, Mr. Ewanchuk carefully explores the histories of specific families on

318

their homesteads and delves into great detail about the development of schools and churches in the area, as well as covering other subjects such as the relationships with the earlier Icelandic settlers.

The Gimli Heritage Advisory Committee has also published a very informative booklet on the hamlet of Berlo, entitled *"Berlo: A Gimli Heritage Community"*, edited by Wally Johannson. I couldn't believe my good fortune in finding so much historic detail available on such a tiny place. I feel a debt of gratitude to people like Mr. Ewanchuk and Mr. Johannson, who take the time to bring the details of our collective history to light.

There are numerous academic studies on the Winnipeg General Strike, but a couple of more popular treatments that I relied on for the more colourful aspects of the Strike include *Winnipeg 1919—The Strikers' Own History of the Winnipeg General Strike* with an introduction by Norman Penner, and *The Winnipeg General Strike of 1919: An Illustrated History* by J. M. Bumsted.

Two sources upon which I relied for information on the internment during WWI included *Park Prisoners: The Untold Story of Western Canada's National Parks, 1915-1946* by Bill Waiser; and *The Stories Were Not Told: Canada's First World War Internment* Camps by Sandra Semchuk.

The Manitoba Historical Society was a great source of information on a host of events in early Manitoba, but most particularly concerning the internment. Briefing #56, by George Buri, Department of History, University of Brandon, entitled *Enemies Within Our Gates: Brandon's Alien Detention Centre During the Great War,* provided important detail for the chapter on Frank's internment at that camp, as well as mentioning the Ukrainians' march from Winnipeg to Emerson.

The 2017 film *That Never Happened: Canada's First National Internment Operations,* created and directed by Ryan Boyko, was also a great source of inspiration.

Jim Blanchard's book, *Winnipeg's Great War: A City Comes of Age,* provided useful background on the social context in Winnipeg at the time.

Beyond these official sources of information, family members were helpful in corroborating our family background. Lisa Munro, granddaughter of Sofiya's brother John in the novel, provided really helpful research on the family tree, including the records of their crossing of the Atlantic. Frances Allary, John's eldest daughter, corroborated some of the family stories, and Dorothy Carswell, Beatrice's eldest daughter, did likewise with respect to her mother's life.

My thanks to Dorothy, Sylvia Comm (John's youngest surviving daughter), my good friend Rita Murray of Edmonton, May Cummings and my wife Elisabeth, who read early drafts of the novel and provided useful and encouraging feedback.

Lastly, I'd like to thank my editor at TellWell, Melanie Cossey, for her very helpful plot/exposition suggestions and her thorough copy editing, all of which enhanced the story.

To the extent that there are any errors of fact regarding the context in Winnipeg over the time covered by the novel, they are, of course, my responsibility.

As this book is being prepared for publication, Russia has launched its horrific invasion of the Ukraine. Given that this novel is based on events that took place in the last century, I have not made any last minute changes that might have been suggested by this brutal attack. However, in listening to the many stories that are emerging about Ukrainians, it was wonderful to hear about positive interactions between some First Nations and early Ukrainian settlers, as evidenced by the 'Kokum" scarves worn by women in the Siksika Nation, which are based on the babushkas worn by Ukrainian women (CBC news).

As my grandmother sadly did not have any memories about such positive interactions, I decided to leave the story as is, although my heart was gladdened to hear of these stories.

As the war in Ukraine rages, I hope and pray (as Sofiya would) that the Ukrainian people can continue to display the courage and resilience that they have shown throughout their history, and that the Ukraine will emerge from this conflict with its cultural and territorial heritage intact.

List of Interior Photos

#1.   Early Ukrainian homestead near Gimli Manitoba, built by Wasyl Ewanchuk, 1904
      Source: *Spruce, Swamp and Stone, A History of the Pioneer Ukrainian Settlements in the Gimli Area,* by Michael Ewanchuk, 1977

#2.   Saints Peter and Paul Roman Catholic Church, Berlo Manitoba, circa 1915
      Source: "*Berlo: A Gimli Heritage Community*", edited by Wally Johannson, from a booklet produced by the Gimli Heritage Advisory Committee

#3.   Bismarck/Berlo school, circa 1915.
      Source: "*Berlo: A Gimli Heritage Community*", edited by Wally Johannson, from a booklet produced by the Gimli Heritage Advisory Committee

#4.   CPR Station, Winnipeg at Higgins and Main Street, 1912
      Source: Manitoba Historical Society, Historical Sites of Manitoba
      Photo by Rob McInnes, WP1339

#5.   Typical Winnipeg Wealthy Person's Home, circa 1915
      Source: Manitoba Archives

#6.   Armistice Day Parade, November 1918
      Manitoba Archives, photograph by L.B. Foote

#7.   Brandon WW1 "Alien" Internment Building, circa
      1912
      Manitoba Historical Society
      *"Enemies Within Our Gates: Brandon's Alien
      Detention Centre During the Great War"* by George
      Buri, Department of History, Brandon University.
      #56, October 2007

#8.   Brandon Internees' English Class
      Manitoba Historical Society
      *"Enemies Within Our Gates: Brandon's Alien
      Detention Centre During the Great War"* by George
      Buri, Department of History, Brandon University.
      #56, October 2007

#9.   Internees Leaving Castle Mountain Internment
      Camp, 1915
      Glenbow Archives, Caruthers Collection, NA-3959-2

#10. Ice Palace built by Banff Internment Camp
      Internees, January 1917
      Provincial Archives of Alberta, A4837

#11. Newspaper Carriers for the Manitoba Free Press, 1918
      Winnipeg Free Press Archives, Photo by L.B. Foote

#12   Typical North Winnipeg Home, circa 1915
      Manitoba Archives, Photo by L.B. Foote